THE GOLDEN MAIDEN
The flames died suddenly away, and out of the vessel there
sprang a wonderful image—the image of a beautiful maiden.
(See page 163)

NORDIC
HERO TALES
FROM THE KALEVALA

JAMES BALDWIN

ILLUSTRATED BY
N. C. WYETH

DOVER PUBLICATIONS, INC.
MINEOLA, NEW YORK

Bibliographical Note

This Dover edition, first published in 2006, is a newly reset, unabridged republication of the work originally published by Charles Scribner's Sons, New York, in 1912 under the title *The Sampo: Hero Adventures from the Finnish Kalevala*. The four original color plates by N. C. Wyeth have been reproduced on the front, back, and inside covers. These plates also appear in black and white in their original positions in the book.

Library of Congress Cataloging-in-Publication Data

Baldwin, James, 1841–1925.
    Nordic hero tales from the Kalevala / James Baldwin ; illustrated by N. C. Wyeth.
    p. cm.
    Summary: An illustrated retelling, drawn from professional minstrels and from an epic poem called Kalevala, of the adventures of three Finnish heroes who are rivals for the hand of the Maiden of Pohja.
    ISBN 0-486-44748-0 (pbk.)
    1. Tales—Finland. [1. Folklore—Finland.] I. Wyeth, N. C. (Newell Convers), 1882–1945, ill. II. Kalevala. III. Title.

PZ8.1.B193Nor 2006
[398.2]—dc22

2005053731

Manufactured in the United States of America
Dover Publications, Inc., 31 East 2nd Street, Mineola, N.Y. 11501

PROEM

This is a tale which the *runolainen* of the far North used to sing in hovel and hall, and which the heroes of primeval times learned by heart and taught to their children. In its original form it was related, not in plain, unvarnished prose, as you shall find it here, but in endless monotonous measures, tuned to the music of the *kantele*.[1] It was made up of numerous stories, songs, folk-melodies, and incantations, with which were interwoven many independent episodes that are neither interesting nor necessary to its completeness. The weaver of tales, who now relates these adventures to modern readers, has chosen to deviate widely from the methods of the ancient story-tellers. He has combined various parts, as pleased his fancy, into one complete harmonious fabric, and, while he has retained much of the original warp and woof, he has added various and many colorings and connecting threads of his own invention. In doing this he has merely exercised the time-honored right of poets and story-tellers—the right to make new cloth out of old.

---

[1] See Note A, at the end of this volume.

Contents

Illustrations

I. MISTRESS AND MINSTREL

"You must rise early in the morning," said Dame Louhi, the Wise Woman of the North. She stood at the door of her chamber and looked back into the low-raftered hall where her daughter was spinning. Her face was wrinkled and grim, her thin lips were puckered over her toothless mouth, her gray-green eyes sparkled beneath her shaggy eyebrows.

She paused and listened. No answer came from her busy daughter. The day was almost ended. Already the swallows were asleep under the eaves, the reindeer were lying down in their paddock, all the underlings of Dame Louhi's household had retired to rest. So near was her dwelling to the sea that she could hear the waves lapping on the beach and the ice-floes crunching and grinding and pounding against the shore. But other sounds there were none.

The Mistress, Dame Louhi, grew impatient. She stamped her foot angrily, and loudly repeated her command: "You must rise early in the morning, my daughter."

This time the maiden heard her. She ceased twirling her spindle, and sweetly answered, "Yes, mother, for there is a great deal to be done to-morrow."

The Mistress was satisfied; and as she turned to enter her chamber you should have seen how unlike the mother was the fair daughter whom men called the Maid of Beauty. Nature had given to the maiden all the loveliness that had been denied to the dame. And she was not only surpassingly beautiful, but she was wise and skilful and very industrious. The housekeeping in

1

the roomy dwelling beside the sea would have been shabbily attended to had it not been for her daily care; and the sun would have shone but seldom in the Frozen Land[1] had not the Maid of Beauty encouraged it with her smiles.

So, on the morrow, long before any one else had risen, she was up and bustling hither and thither, attending to this thing and that and putting the house in order. She went out to the sheepfold and sheared six fat lambs. She spun their six white fleeces into snowy yarn, and of the yarn she wove enough cloth for six warm garments.

Then she went into the kitchen and rekindled the fire upon the hearth. She swept the floor and dusted the long benches. She scrubbed the birchwood tables till they were as white and glistening as the frost-covered meadows. She made the rooms neat and tidy and set the breakfast things to cooking. By this time the day was dawning; the sky in the east was becoming flecked with yellow and red; the cock was crowing, wild ducks were quacking by the shore, sparrows were chirping under the eaves.

The maiden paused and listened—listened long and intently. She heard the joyful sounds of the morning; she heard the cold waves lapping and splashing upon the shore. She looked out of the door and saw the first rays of the sun dancing and glancing upon the uneasy surface of the sea. Away from the shore, she saw the broad meadows lying lonely and still under the lonely sky and beyond them the dark line which marked the beginning of the forest and the rugged land of mountains.

Suddenly, as she looked and listened, she heard a wailing which was not the wailing of the sea. She held her breath and listened again. She heard a cry which was not the cry of a sea-bird.

"Oh, mother," she called, "what is that strange sound? The wild geese never call so hoarsely; the waves never make such moaning. Listen, mother! What can it be?"

Wise old Louhi, grim and toothless, rose quickly and hastened to the door, chattering and mumbling and grumbling. She paused and listened, but the sound seemed very faint. She ran

---

[1] See Note B, at the end of this volume.

down to the landing-place before the house, and there she listened again. Soon the sound came to her ears, louder and more distinct, and yet hard to make out. Once, twice, thrice she heard the call; and then she knew what it meant.

"It is a man's voice," she said. "Some hero has been shipwrecked near our shore. He is in distress; he calls for help."

She leaped nimbly into her boat. She pushed it from the shore and rowed with speed out of the little inlet and around the rocky point which jutted far into the sea. The cries grew louder, the calls were more frequent as she urged her boat forward over the sullen, icy-cold waves.

Soon she saw the shipwrecked man. He was not fighting the waves as she had supposed, but was clinging to the branches of a tree that had been uprooted and carried to sea. Ah, the sad plight of the poor man! He seemed wounded and helpless; his face was gaunt and pale; his eyes were filled with sadness and salt-water; he was shivering with cold and deep despair.

Shouting words of cheer, the Mistress hurried to him. She lifted him from the place of danger and seated him in her boat. Then with steady arms and mighty strokes she rowed homeward, nor did she pause until the boat's keel grated on the beach before her door.

She carried the stranger into the house; she placed him by the warm fire; she bathed his limbs, his face, his head in tepid water and wrapped him up in soft skins of the reindeer. For three long days—yes, for four summer days—she tended him as though he were her son, and no questions did she ask. Then, to her great joy, he sat up and soon grew well and strong.

"Now, friend and fellow of the sea," said the gray woman, "tell me your name. Tell me why and how you have come to our lovely land and to Pohyola, the sweetest of homes."

The stranger, who also was old and gray, answered, "My name is Wainamoinen, and all the world knows me; for I am the first of minstrels, the prince of wizards, the man whom other men delight to honor. Luckless was the hour when I embarked on a ship to go fishing; still more luckless was it when a storm overturned the vessel. Nine days did the sea toss me—yes, ten days did the waves buffet me—ere I was cast upon these shores."

"I welcome you, Wainamoinen! cried the grim Mistress. "Welcome, welcome to this northern land! Your name is well known to me, and long have I honored it. Men call you the sweet singer of Hero Land, and they say that no other songs cheer the dreary hours of winter as yours do. You shall stay here in Pohyola and sing to me and my people. My house shall be your home and this delightful land shall be your country."

The gray-bearded Minstrel shook his head and sighed. He looked out and saw the lonely meadows and the snowy mountains and the cold gray sea. Then his eyes filled with tears and he wept.

"O singer of Hero Land, why are you so sad?" asked the woman. "Have I not been kind to you? Why, then, do you weep and gaze towards the sea?"

"I weep for my own dear country; I am sick for my home," answered the Minstrel. "I do not wish to remain in this Frozen Land. I am lonely and heart-broken."

"Cheer up, cheer up!" said Dame Louhi, trying to look pleasant. "Beautiful Pohyola shall be your country. This comfortable house shall be your home. My fireside shall be your fireside, and my friends shall be your friends."

But the Minstrel still wept.

"Stay here and be our honored guest," continued the Mistress. "You shall sleep in the warmest corner, you shall sit at the head of our table. Good food we will give you—choice bacon, fresh salmon from the sea, white cakes of barley, hot from the oven. Stay with us and cheer us with your sweet songs."

"Nay, nay!" moaned the sad Minstrel. "How can I sing in a strange land? My own country is the fairest; my own home is the dearest; my own table is the sweetest. All that I can ever do in this Frozen Land is to sigh and weep; and I shall sigh and weep till my eyes are out and my voice is gone forever."

"You are foolish," then said the unlovely Mistress. "Pohyola is the fairest place in all the world, and you must learn to love it."

The Minstrel still shook his head and sighed. All his thoughts were with his home land.

The summer passed swiftly, but to Wainamoinen the days were full of loneliness. He wandered over the silent meadows, he went out with the fishermen to catch salmon in the sea, he visited one place and another in the vast Frozen Land, vainly trying to forget his grief. And not once did he open his lips in song, for there was no music in his heart; and how shall a minstrel sing if his heart is empty?

At length Dame Louhi relented.

"How much will you give me if I send you back to your own country?" she asked. "Come, let us make a bargain."

"How much will I give?" answered he. "I have nothing here that is my own, but I promise to send you many rich treasures. I will send you gold, I will send you silver."

"But you claim to be a mighty wizard," said Dame Louhi. "Show us some of your work in magic."

"Never was there a greater magician than I," returned the Minstrel boastfully. "You have but to name some wonderful act and forthwith I will perform it. But first, I must have your promise to send me home. My heart is so full of the thought."

"Very well, then," answered the gray woman. "If you will make the magic Sampo for me, I promise to send you home at once. It must be the real, the wonderful Sampo; I will have nothing else."

"The Sampo! What is that?"

"Do you ask me what is the Sampo? Minstrels from the earliest times have sung of its power, and all the wizards of the North have tried their spells, hoping to make something equally precious and potent. And do you, a minstrel and a wizard, ask what it is?"

The Minstrel was cunning, and he answered: "In my own country we call it by another name. If you will describe it I will tell you what that name is and also some strange things which no other minstrel knows."

The Mistress was off her guard. "The Sampo," she said, "is the mill of fortune which wise men, since the beginning of things, have sought to invent. It is the magic mill which grinds out all sorts of treasures and gives wealth and power to its possessor. One has only to whisper his wishes to it and they will all come true."[2]

"Ah!" answered the Minstrel. "In our country we call it the Stone of the Wise Men."

"That is a good name. And now, if I promise to send you safe

---

[2] See Note C, at the end of this volume.

home, will you try your magic power and forge me such a mill? Have you the skill to fit it with wheels and levers? Can you hammer into shape a becoming lid for it—a lid of rainbow colors?"

Wainamoinen sat silent for a long time, shaking his head and thinking. Then he said:

"It is a thing so strange and so difficult that I must have time to consider my strength. In three days you shall have my answer."

He went out alone, and for many tedious hours he walked up and down by the seashore pondering upon the subject. He repeated all the magic runes that he remembered, and recited spells to the winds and the waves and the gray-blue sky, he recalled all the words of power that he had learned from the sages of old. Then, at length, on the third day, he went back to the house where Dame Louhi was still sitting by her fireside.

"I cannot make the Sampo for you," he said. "My magic is not strong enough; my skill is not of the kind that forges mills of fortune. But I have a friend who can do wonderful things. It was he who shaped the sky that bends above our country; and, surely, to forge the Sampo is no more difficult than that."

"Ah, that is the man whom I am looking for," cried the woman eagerly. "What is his name? Will you send him to me?"

"His name is Ilmarinen, and he is dear to me as a brother," answered the Minstrel. "He is the prince of all smiths, and there is nothing in magic or in smithing that he cannot do. If you will permit me to return to my dear home land, to the Land of Heroes, I will send him to you without delay."

"But suppose he doesn't wish to come?"

"Then I will send him against his will. My magic is strong enough to command him."

"Can I trust you? Do you promise?"

"You have my word, and I will perform," answered the Minstrel. "Never yet have I failed to do that which I have agreed to do."

"You shall go home, then, quickly," said the gray woman. "You may promise the skilful smith a rare reward if he will forge the Sampo for me. I will even give him, if he so desire, my daughter for his wife—this I promise."

Forthwith she hurried to the paddock. She chose the fleetest

reindeer and harnessed it to her birchwood sledge. She brought
warm furs for the Minstrel to wrap around him. She put the
whip and the long reins in his hands.

"Now fare you well, and speed you to your home land!" she
said. "Drive swiftly while the sun shines, but remember to keep
your eyes upon your pathway, and do not look upward. If you
should gaze towards the mountain top or the sky, sad misfortune
will befall you. Fare you well, first of minstrels! Send me the
wizard, the prince of smiths, and fail not, lest my curses follow
you and blight your life."

The Minstrel cracked his whip joyfully, the reindeer sprang
forward, the journey homeward was begun. Merrily did the
birchwood runners whistle as they glided over the half-frozen
earth. With a glad heart did Wainamoinen speed across the
brown meadows and into the silent forest; his face beamed like
the sunlight, his eyes glowed like twin stars, and a song was
ready to burst from his lips.

II. THE MAID OF BEAUTY

Swiftly as a shooting star did the reindeer rush through the forest ways. In his sledge, the Minstrel sat upright and deftly handled the whip and the reins. His eyes were upon the road before him, and all his thoughts were about his home land and his own pleasant fireside so far, far away.

Now he was among the snowy mountains; and now his sledge was skimming along untravelled paths in the deep and shadowy valleys. Suddenly his thoughts were disturbed by a strange sound in the air above him. Was it the song of a bird? Was it the sighing of the wind? Was it the humming of wild bees? Or was it the sound of some distant waterfall?

He listened. Could it be the buzzing of a weaver's shuttle shooting through some loom on the craggy heights above him? It certainly sounded so; and yet it was so loud, so musical. Forgotten, then, was Dame Louhi's latest caution. Quickly the Minstrel checked his reindeer steed; quickly, and in wonder, he lifted his eyes and looked aloft. High in the sky he saw a rainbow, and on it sat the Maid of Beauty, busily weaving with a golden shuttle. Swiftly, to and fro, she drove the shuttle, and the fabric which she wove was wondrously fine. Threads of silver, threads of gold, threads of every brilliant color were mingled in that web of magic. But fairer than that fairy fabric, fairer than all else in that radiant vision was the maiden's radiant face.

Wainamoinen pulled upon the reins with all his might; his steed stopped short upon a hillside. Then he called loudly to the maiden on the rainbow.

8

THE MAGICIAN AND THE MAID OF BEAUTY
High in the sky he saw a rainbow, and on it the Maid of Beauty.

"Come hither, come hither, most beautiful one," he said. "Come down and sit in this sledge by my side."

Faster and faster flew the magic shuttle, and the buzzing sounded louder; but the maiden had heard the Minstrel's call. She turned her face towards him and spoke disdainfully.

"Who are you?" she asked. "And why should I sit in your sledge?"

"I am Wainamoinen, chief of singers, master of wizards," answered the hero. "I am now on my way to my sweet home country, the Land of Heroes. I know you would love that land, and I would rejoice to take you thither with me. You shall be the queen of my house. You shall bake my honey cakes, fill my cups with barley-water, sing at my table. All my people will honor you."

The Maid of Beauty looked down from her rainbow seat and laughed.

"You are a foolish old man," she said, "to think that I care for you or for all that you promise. Let me tell you a story."

"Certainly," said the Minstrel.

"Well, yesterday I was walking in the meadows of the West. I was picking flowers and making this wreath which you see on my head. Suddenly I heard a thrush singing sweetly to his mate and nestlings. I stopped and listened to the little songster, and this is what I heard him sing:

> "Summer days are warm and bright;
> A maiden's heart is always light.
> Winter days are bitter cold;
> Beware, beware of the suitor bold—
> Beware the more if he is old."

"That was a very silly bird," said Wainamoinen, "and I wonder that his mate listened to such foolish chatter."

"But his song was very pretty," laughed the maiden.

"I too can sing," said Wainamoinen. "I am the sweet singer of Hero Land. I am a great wizard. I am a hero. Come with me to my dear home land and be my queen."

The Maid of Beauty looked down from her rainbow throne, and the mountains echoed with her laughter.

"If you are indeed a wizard," she said, "show me some of your magic arts. Can you split a hair with a knife which has no edge? Can you snare a bird's egg with a thread too small to be seen?"

"Nothing is easier to one skilled in magic," answered the hero. And thereupon he picked up a golden hair which the maiden had let fall, and with a blunted knife he split it into halves and quarters. Then from a bird's nest on the side of the cliff he drew up an egg with a snare too fine for eyes to see.

"Now I have done what you wished," he said. "Come and sit in my birchwood sledge. Swiftly will we speed to Hero Land, and great honor shall be yours, for you shall be a minstrel's queen."

"Not yet, not yet, O matchless hero," she answered, still laughing. "Let me see some more of your wonderful magic. Split this cliff of sandstone with your bare fingers. Then cut a whipstock from the ice in the gorge below you and leave no splinter."

"Nothing is easier to one skilled in magic," answered the hero. Then he climbed the tall cliff and split the sandstone with his fingers; and next he leaped upon the river of ice beneath him and cut therefrom a slender whipstock, losing not the smallest fragment.

"You have done well," said the Maid of Beauty, and she smiled from her rainbow throne. "But I will give you another task. Here is my spindle and here is my shuttle. See, I break them into splinters and I throw the fragments at your feet. If you wish me to go home with you, you must pick up these fragments and build a boat from them. Then you must launch the boat, using neither arm nor foot to set it floating. Is your magic equal to that?"

Wainamoinen stroked his gray beard, for he was puzzled. "Your task is very hard," he said, "and I am the only person under the sun who can perform it. But perform it I will, and you shall see what a master of magic I am."

Then he picked up the fragments of the spindle, he took the

splinters of the shuttle in his hands, and began to build the fairy boat. But such a task could not be done in a moment. It required time. One whole day he swung his hammer; two whole days he plied his hatchet; three days and more he worked to join the many pieces together.

At length the boat was almost finished. Proudly the Minstrel looked upon it. He hewed it on this side, he shaped it on that, he smoothed it fore and aft; and the Maid of Beauty looked on and smiled. Suddenly the hero's sharp-edged hatchet of iron flew from his grasp. It broke the fairy boat in pieces, undoing the work of many days. It struck the Minstrel's knee, cutting a red gash that was both wide and deep.

A stream of blood gushed forth; it flowed like a crimson torrent down the mountain side; it stained the snow in the forest and the brown grass in the meadows. Great pain fell upon the Minstrel, and yet he was fearless and undaunted. He quickly gathered lichens and mosses from the tree trunks and the rocks, and these he bound upon the wound to stanch the bleeding.

"O cruel hatchet," he cried, "why were you so disobedient, so ungrateful? You may cut the pine tree and the willow; you may cut the birch tree and the cedar; but turn not your edge against your master."

He looked upward. The rainbow had vanished and the Maid of Beauty had fled. Then, too late, he remembered Dame Louhi's caution: "Keep your eyes upon your pathway. If you should gaze towards sky or mountain top, sad misfortune will befall you."

His wound was very painful, so painful that he groaned with anguish. He felt that he must find help, and find it quickly. He looked about for the reindeer which the Mistress had lent him and which had wandered into the woods while he was working magic. When he had found the beast he harnessed it to the sledge again. Then he climbed in carefully, painfully, and sat down on the soft furs. He cracked his whip, he shouted, and the long-legged racer flew swiftly over meadows and forests, over mountains and lowlands.

III. THE GRAYBEARD AND HIS SON

All night the Minstrel rode wildly towards the South Country, never looking behind him, never pausing to rest. The day was breaking when he reached the end of the mighty forest. There, on the slope of a barren mountain, the road divided into three paths, and at the end of each path he saw a small house with smoke rising from the chimney. And now his pain increased, and the blood began to pour anew from his deep wound.

Weak and weary, he turned boldly into the lowest pathway and drove his steed up to the little homestead.

"Hail, ho!" he cried; and a piping voice inside answered, "Hail, ho!"

The door was open, and the Minstrel saw a little child sitting on the hearth beside the blazing fire.

"Hail, ho!" he cried again; and the child laughed and said, "Welcome, stranger!"

Wainamoinen sat upright in his sledge; his wound pained him; he was in much distress.

"Is there any one in this house that can heal the wounds of Iron?" he asked.

"No, no," answered the child. "All gone but me. Drive away, big man! Drive away to some other house."

The Minstrel pulled the reins and turned his sledge about. He cracked his whip, and the steed leaped forward. Soon he came into the middle pathway, and madly he drove to the second little cottage. He drove right up under the window and looked in. There he saw an old woman resting on a couch, while another woman was spinning by the fire. They were telling pleasant tales of their neighbors and of goblins and ghosts and unnameable things.

"Hail, ho!" cried the Minstrel, not too loudly.

The women jumped up in alarm; but when they saw his pale and weary face they answered, "Welcome, stranger! Alight, and rest thyself by our fireside."

Wainamoinen sat still in his sledge. The blood was pouring in torrents from his wound.

"Tell me," he said, "is there any one in this house that can stop the flow of blood, that can heal the wounds of Iron?"

"Ah, no!" answered the elder of the two, and her three teeth gnashed together. "Naught do we know about blood or iron. Drive away to some other house. Speed thee, rash man!"

Again the Minstrel pulled the reins and turned the sledge about in the narrow pathway. Again he cracked his whip, and the steed rushed onward. With furious speed he drove into the upper pathway, and paused not until he reached the highest cottage. There he drew up before the doorway and called as before, but very feebly:

"Hail, ho! Hail, ho!"

"Welcome, stranger!" was the answer from within. Then an old Graybeard opened the door and repeated, "Welcome, stranger!"

"Welcome, stranger!" echoed the Graybeard's son, peeping over his father's shoulder. "Alight and rest yourself and your steed."

"First tell me," said the Minstrel feebly, "tell me if you can stop this flow of blood and heal this wound of Iron."

"Three magic words may stop the flood, three magic drops may heal the wound," answered the Graybeard.

And the young man added, "Come in and let us see what can be done."

The Minstrel climbed out of his sledge slowly, painfully. He staggered into the house. He lay down upon the couch by the fireside. The wound was bleeding sorely.

"Ah, save us!" cried the Graybeard. "What hero is this? Bring something to catch the flowing blood."

His son ran quickly and fetched a golden goblet; but it was far too small to hold the gushing blood. He ran for other vessels.

Seven pails he brought, then eight, and all were filled to over-flowing. The Graybeard shook his head; he lifted his eyes; he clinched his fists. Then he spoke harshly to the crimson flood:

"Hear me, O thou blood-stream! Cease thy flowing. Fill no more pails. Flow not upon the floor. Stay in the veins of this hero and give him strength. Stay in his heart and give him courage. Hear me, O thou blood-stream!"

Forthwith the red stream grew smaller; but still the drops trickled from the wound. All the strength of the Minstrel was gone.

The Graybeard looked upward, he turned his face towards heaven. He spoke in tones that were soft and pleading:

"O thou great Creator, thou lover of heroes! Come down and help us. Stop this rushing red river. Heal this gaping wound. Restore to this hero the strength that is rightfully his."

Then he grasped the Minstrel's knee just above the place where the wicked axe had struck it. He pressed the sides of the wound together firmly, gently. The bleeding ceased; and now not even the smallest drop escaped. The Graybeard bound soft bands of linen around the limb, he laid the Minstrel upon his own rude bed, he covered him with warm robes and bade him rest quietly.

"The flow of blood is stanched," he said; "we must now heal Iron's bitter bite, we must close up the gaping, ugly wound."

Then turning to his son, he said, "Go now to our smithy on the mountain. Take with you a supply of healing herbs, as I have taught you. Bake them, boil them, mix them, brew them into a magic ointment that will heal all manner of wounds. When you have finished the mixture and tested it, bring it hither to me."

"That I will do, father," answered the young man; and with a basket on his arm and a glad song rising from his lips, he hastened away.

Half-way up the mountain side he came to a gnarly old oak.

"Friend oak, so good and strong," he said, "have you any honey on your branches?"

"Look and see," answered the oak. "Yesterday I had such plenty that the bees came to carry it away."

The young man gathered many handfuls of slender twigs from the tree, and saw that on each twig was a tiny drop of dew. Then he wandered hither and thither among the rocks, seeking all kinds of healing herbs and putting them in his basket. When, at length, the basket was filled, he went on, whistling, to the little smithy on the mountain top.

Soon a fire was roaring in the furnace. A pot was filled with the herbs and twigs and set to boiling on the coals. The pungent odor of the mixture pervaded the air; every corner of the smithy was lit up with the glare of the flames; the smoke rolled in clouds from the smoke hole in the roof.

For three sunny days and three lonely nights the youth stood over the furnace and stirred the magic mixture. He threw fuel upon the flames, he poured fresh spring water into the seething pot. And all the while he sang weird songs and muttered strange charms such as his father had taught him. Then for nine nights he caught the moonbeams and mingled them with the mixture; and for nine days he entrapped the sunlight and added it to the magic ointment.

On the tenth day he looked into the pot and saw that all was of a rich golden color, bright and sparkling, with pretty rainbows mingled here and there in many a curious pattern.

"It is done," he said. "I will test its power."

He lifted the pot from the fire and allowed the mixture to cool, still singing his songs of magic. Then he went out to find something that had been wounded and might be healed.

Half-way down the mountain side there was a giant pine tree which the lightning had split from crown to roots. Its two halves gaped wide apart; its torn and broken branches hung dangling in the wind.

"Ah! here is a case to test," said the young man. Then, with the greatest care, he took a small portion of the ointment upon his finger; he smeared it gently upon the trunk and branches of the wounded pine; he sang softly a little song of magic:

> "Make it whole and make it strong,
> Heal it all its length along;
> Join part to part, restore its heart,
> And make it straight as hunter's dart.
> Thus your magic power show,
> And let all men your virtue know."

As he spoke the last words he clapped his hands together and shouted; and lo! the parts of the pine tree came suddenly into their right places, and it stood there as whole and as beautiful as it had been before the lighting smote it.

"Good!" cried the young man. "The ointment is as it should be. None could be better."

Then, with the pot balanced carefully on his shoulder, he started homeward. Every now and then, as he went down the slope, he paused to try the healing mixture on splintered rocks and broken bowlders; and he smiled as he saw the rough stones knit themselves together and the gaping fissures close up and disappear.

When at length he approached his father's cottage he heard loud groans within—groans of some one suffering deadly pain. He listened and knew that they came from the wounded Minstrel; he knew that now there was great need of his magic ointment.

The Graybeard met him at the door. "What news, my son?"

"Good news, my father," he answered. "Never was there better salve than this. I could fuse the hills together with it if I had the mind to try."

The father took the pot and carried it into the house. He dipped his finger gently into the ointment; he touched it to the tip of his tongue.

"The mixture seems perfect," he said. "Now we shall see wonders."

The Minstrel was lying upon the bed and groaning at every breath. True, the bleeding had ceased, but the fever of Iron was upon him. He knew not where he was. He had forgotten his family, his home, and his sweet country. The madness of Iron had clouded his mind.

The Graybeard smeared a little of the ointment on the Minstrel's wounded knee; he stroked the poor man's back, his hands, his head. He waved his palms slowly to and fro before his eyes. And all the while he softly muttered a little song of wisdom and power.

The groans of the wounded man waxed louder and louder. He turned this way and that, seeking ease; but at each moment the pain grew greater, and he writhed in anguish. Then the Graybeard raised his voice and angrily commanded the pain to depart.

"Hear me, pitiless pain!" he cried. "Go away from this house! Depart! Vanish! Leave this worthy stranger and betake yourself to your own place. Hide yourself in the Hill of Tortures. There, if you choose, you may fill the stones with anguish; you may rend the rocks with torment. But now let this hero rest in peace. Depart! Depart! Depart!"

As he uttered the last word the pain vanished. The Minstrel's mind grew clear; he felt his strength returning; he laughed right joyfully and rose from his bed. The wound was healed, the ugly gash had disappeared, every trace of pain had vanished from his body.

"I never felt so well in my life!" he shouted as he danced about the room. Then remembering himself, he threw his arms around the Graybeard's neck and thanked him for his exceeding kindness.

"No thanks are due to me," said the old man, leading him to a seat by the fireside. "I have done nothing myself; Jumala did it all. Give praises to Jumala, the great Creator, from whom all good things come."

Thereupon the Minstrel raised his hands towards heaven, and cried, "To thee, O Jumala, the gracious, I humbly offer thanks. To thee I owe my life, my strength, my all—accept my gratitude."

"Jumala only is good," said the Graybeard. "He only is merciful and kind. But what shall we say of Iron—of Iron, the spiteful, the treacherous, the wicked? Tell me, my friend, why should Iron bear a grudge against you? Why should he seek to destroy your life?"

Wainamoinen, first of minstrels, answered, "Iron has no grudge against me. He wounded me, it is true, but not purposely. Had it not been for a wicked hornet, Iron would never have harmed me—would never have harmed any one. Blame not Iron. Blame the hornet that made him what he is."

"Pray tell me how that can be," said the Graybeard.

Then, sitting by the pleasant fireside, the Minstrel answered him by telling a story—a story as old as the race of man on earth.

IV. THE WICKED HORNET

This is the tale[1] which Wainamoinen, old and truthful, told to the listening Graybeard while the fire blazed and crackled on the hearth between them. It is a tale which he himself had learned from the minstrels of a former age.

The first of all mothers was Air, and she had three daughters. Of these three maidens there is much to be said. They were as lovely as the rainbow after a storm; they were as fair as the full moon shining above the mountains. They walked with noiseless feet among the clouds and showered gifts upon the earth. They sent the refreshing rain, the silent dew, and the nipping frost, each in its season. They gave life to the fields, and strength to the mountains, and grandeur to the sea. And because of their bounty the earth was glad and the stars twinkled for joy.

"What more can we do to make the land fit for men to dwell in?" asked the eldest of the sisters.

And the youngest said, "Let us send down iron—iron of which tools may be made, iron of which sharp weapons may be shaped. For without tools man will not be able to plough, to reap, or to build; and without weapons he cannot defend himself against the savage beasts of the forest."

So, when the sun was about going down, the sisters went forth in trailing robes of purple and crimson and gold; and in their hands they bore mighty vessels of foaming milk. The eldest

---

[1] See Note D, at the end of this volume.

sprinkled red milk in the brooks and marshes and along the banks of the rivers. The middle one scattered white milk on the wooded hills and the stony mountains. The youngest showered blue milk in the valleys and by the gray seashore. And on the morrow, where the red milk had been sprinkled, red and brittle ore of iron flecked the ground; where the white milk had been scattered, powdery ore of a yellow hue abounded; and where the blue milk had been showered, flaky masses of crude iron, tough and dark, lay hidden beneath the soil.

Thus came Iron into the world—Iron, the youngest of three brothers. Next older than he was Fire, a raging, dangerous fellow when free, but loving and faithful when held in bonds. Older still was Water, terrible in strength but, when not aroused, as gentle as a mother's caress.

Years upon years went by, and at length one day Iron set out to visit his brothers. He found Water at home in the deep sea, and by him he was welcomed kindly enough. But when he climbed a mountain to see his second brother he had quite another reception. Fire was in a raging mood. The terrible fellow leaped and roared, and stretched out his long red fingers as though he would devour his visitor.

Iron was so terrified that he turned and fled down the steep slopes, never stopping nor pausing to look behind. He ran on, hiding in clefts and chasms, creeping under rocks, and lurking in the dry beds of mountain torrents. When, by and by, he reached the level plain, he glanced backward. The hills and the whole mountain top were aflame.

Wild with terror, he hurried on, hiding himself in the woods and under the roots of trees, and resting at last in reedy marshes where swans build their nests and wild geese rear their young.

For ages and ages—nobody knows how many—Iron lay hidden in bogs and forests and lonely caverns. Fear of his raging brother made him lurk in lonely places, made him cover up his face. Lazy bears went ambling through the rocky places; wolves rushed madly over the oozy marshlands; and timid deer ran and leaped among the trees. In time the hiding-places of Iron were uncovered. Where the paws of bears had plodded often, where the feet of wolves had pattered, where the sharp hoofs of deer had trodden, there the timid metal, red, gray, yellow, black, peeped shyly out.

At length, into that same land there came a skilful Smith. He carried a hammer of stone in one hand and tongs of bronze in the other; and a song of peace was upon his lips. On a green hillock, where the south wind blew, he built him a smithy, and in it he placed the tools of his craft. His anvil was a block of gray granite; his forge was carefully builded of sand and clay; his bellows was made of the skins of mountain goats sewn together.

The Smith heaped live coals in his forge and blew with his bellows until the flames leaped up, roaring and sparkling, and the smoke rose in dense clouds over the roof of the smithy. "This forge will do its work well," he said. Then he checked the bellows and smothered the flames and raked ashes upon the fire until the red coals slumbered unseen at the mouth of the forge.

Out into the forest the Smith wandered. Closely he scanned the hillsides and the boggy thickets and the paths among the trees. And there, where the bears had trailed and the wolves had rushed and the deer had left their footprints, he found ruddy Iron, dusky Iron, yellow ore of Iron peeping, trembling, hiding. The heart of the Smith was glad. His eyes danced merrily, and he sang a song of magic to the timid metal:

> "Iron, Iron, hearken while I call you!
> Let no false and foolish fears appall you,
> Come from out the crevices that hide you,
> Leave the worthless stones that are beside you,
> Leave the earth that lies around, above you,
> And come with me, for I do dearly love you."

Iron moved not, but timidly answered, "I dare not leave my hiding-places; for Fire, my brother, waits to devour me. He is strong and fierce. He has no pity."

The Smith shook his head and made reply, still singing:

> "No! your brother does not wish to harm you,—
> Willingly he never would alarm you.
> With his glowing arms he would caress you,
> Make you pure and with his kisses bless you.

> So come with me, my smithy waits to greet you;
> In my forge your brother waits to meet you—
> Waits to throw his loving arms around you,
> Glad indeed that thus, at last, he's found you."

These words made Iron feel much braver; and they were spoken in tones so sweet and persuasive that he was almost minded to obey without another word. But he asked, "Why should I leave these places where I have rested so long? What will become of me after I have made friends with Fire?"

The Smith answered:

> "Come with me, for kindly we will treat you.
> On my anvil gently I will beat you;
> With my tongs, then, deftly will I hold you;
> With my hammer I will shape and mould you
> Into forms so fair that all will prize you,
> Forms so rare that none will e'er despise you:
> Axes, knives (so men will wish to use you)
> Needles, pins (so women too, will choose you).
> Come with me, your brother will not harm you,
> Come with me, my smithy sure will charm you."

Hearing this, Iron came out of his lurking-places and without more ado, bashfully followed the cunning Smith. But no sooner was he in the smithy than he felt himself a prisoner. The tongs of bronze gripped him and thrust him into the forge. The bellows roared, the Smith shouted, and Fire leaped joyfully out of the ashes and threw his arms around his helpless younger brother. And bashful, bashful Iron turned first red and then white, and finally became as soft as dough and as radiant as the sun.

Then the tongs of bronze drew him forth from the flames, and twirled him in the air, and threw him upon the anvil; and the hammer of stone beat him fiercely again and again until he shrieked with pain.

"Oh, spare me! spare me!" he cried. "Do not deal so roughly with me. Let me go back to my lonely hiding-places and lie there in peace as in the days of old."

But the tongs pinched him worse than before, and the hammer beat him still harder, and the Smith answered: "Not so, not so! Be not so cowardly. We do not hurt you; you are only frightened. Be brave and I will shape you into things of great use to men. Be brave and you shall rule the world."

Then, in spite of Iron's piteous cries, he kept on pounding and twisting and turning and shaping the helpless metal until at length it was changed into many forms of use and beauty—rings, chains, axes, knives, cups, and curious tools. But it was so soft, after being thus heated and beaten, that the edges of the tools were quickly dulled. Try as he might, the Smith did not know how to give the metal a harder temper.

One day a honeybee strolled that way. It buzzed around the smithy and then lit on a clover blossom by the door.

"O bee," cried the busy Smith, "you are a cunning little bird, and you know some things better than I know them. Come now and help me temper this soft metal. Bring me a drop of your honey; bring the sweet liquor which you suck from the meadow flower; bring the magic dew of the wildwood. Give me all such things that I may make a mixture to harden Iron."

The bee answered not—it was too busy with its own affairs. It gathered what honey it could from the blossom, and then flew swiftly away.

Under the eaves above the smithy door an idler was sitting—a mischief-making hornet who heard every word that the Smith said.

"I will help him make a mixture," this wicked insect muttered. "I will help him to give Iron another temper."

Forthwith he flew to the thorny thickets and the miry bogs and the fever-breeding marshes, to gather what evils he might. Soon he returned with an armload—the poison of spiders, the venom of serpents, the miasmata of swamps, the juice of the deadly nightshade. All these he cast into the tub of water wherein the Smith was vainly trying to temper Iron.

The Smith did not see him, but he heard him buzzing, and supposed it was the honeybee with sweets from the meadow flowers.

"Thank you, pretty little bird," he said. "Now I hope we shall have a better metal. I hope we shall make edges that will cut and not be dulled so easily."

Thereupon he drew a bar of the metal, white-hot, from the forge. He held it, hissing and screeching, under the water into which the poisons had been poured. Little thought he of the evil that was there. He heard the hornet humming and laughing under the eaves.

"Tiny honeybee," he said, "you have brought me much sweetness. Iron tempered with your honey will be sweet although sharp. Nothing shall be wrought of it that is not beautiful and helpful and kind."

He drew the metal from the tub. He thrust it back among the red coals. He plied the bellows and the flames leaped up. Then, when the metal was glowing again, he laid it on the anvil and beat it with strong, swift strokes; and as he worked he sang:

> "Ding! Ding! Ding-a-ling, ding!
> Of Iron, sharp Iron, strong Iron, I sing.
> Of Iron, my servant, of Iron, my king—
> Ding! Ding! Ding-a-ling, ding!"

Forthwith, Iron leaped up, angry and biting and fierce. He was not a soft and ductile metal as before, but Iron hardened into tough blue steel. Showers of sparks flew from him, snapping, burning, threatening; and from among them sprang swords and spears and battle-axes, and daggers keen and pointed. Out of the smithy and out through the great world these cruel weapons raced, slashing and clashing, thrusting and cutting, raging and killing, and carrying madness among men.

The wicked hornet, idling under the eaves, rejoiced at the mischief he had wrought. But the Smith was filled with grief, and the music of his anvil became a jangling discord.

"O Iron," he cried, "it was not for this that I caused you to leave your hiding-places in the hills and bogs! The three sisters intended that you should be a blessing to mankind; but now I greatly fear that you will become a curse."

At that moment the honeybee, laden with the sweets of field and wood, came buzzing into the smithy. It whispered hopefully into the ear of the Smith: "Wait until my gifts have done their work."

Here the Minstrel paused.

"Is that all?" asked the Graybeard.

"Yes, it is all," was the answer; "for now I can think of nothing but my dear home land. My sweet country calls me, and I must hasten on my journey. So, let my sledge be made ready and the steed harnessed before it, and I will bid you good-bye."

"In the morning you may go," said the Graybeard.

V. THE TREE OF MAGIC

Very early in the morning the Minstrel rose from his couch. He opened the door and looked out. The sun was not yet up, but a tinge of yellow in the eastern sky foretold the coming of brilliant day. The stars of the Great Bear were still visible, twinkling dimly above the pine trees. The air was sharp and biting; the frost lay thick on the hilltops and the barren moorland; patches of newly formed ice glared white in the marshes.

"What a fine day for my journey!" said the Minstrel.

Presently the Graybeard's son brought the red reindeer to the door and harnessed it to the birchwood sledge.

"You will have a fine day for your journey," he said.

The Graybeard helped the Minstrel into the sledge; he wrapped the robes of fur around him and threw over his shoulders a bearskin cloak that was both ample and warm. Then he packed beneath the seat a store of food for the long journey— eight large jars of bread and deer meat, yes, nine great jars of toothsome victuals.

"Farewell, kind host and skilful surgeon!"

"Farewell, great guest! My blessings go ever with you!"

Thus the good-bye words were spoken. Then the Minstrel seized the reins and cracked his long whip. The reindeer leaped forward; the journey was begun.

Swift as the wind the well-built sledge glided on its course. Loudly the birchwood runners rang upon the frozen ground, smoothly they sped over the hoarfrost and the glistening ice. Through fens and woodlands, across the meadows and the moorlands, the red reindeer rushed unwearied, never pausing to rest, never thinking of food.

For one whole day the Minstrel held the reins and shouted urgently to his faithful steed. Yes, for two days and two long, silent nights he sat in the sledge and drove onward with no slackening of speed—so impatient was he to reach his dear home land, to behold his own fireside. The third day came, and still onward flew the tireless reindeer. The fourth day came; it was half gone when the Minstrel uttered a shout so joyful that the woodlands rang with the sound, and the wild geese in the marshes answered it gleefully.

He shouted again and again, for now he was among familiar scenes. Here was the forest road which he had often travelled in his youth and later manhood. Here was the long, rough causeway across the treacherous fen land—he knew it so well that it seemed like the face of a friend. Straight ahead, only three leagues farther, the little village of Wainola was nestling warmly in a wooded glen close by the sea; in that village was the snug cottage which the Minstrel called his home; and in that cottage was the fireside around which his friends were sitting and bewailing his absence. What wonder that he shouted so joyfully!

All at once, however, his joy was dimmed; the memory of something unpleasant came into his mind. A cloud passed over his face, and the last shout died, half-uttered, on his lips. The birchwood runners bumped hard on the rough causeway. The reindeer slackened its speed; it seemed ready to sink in its tracks. The Minstrel's mind was far away; it was with the grim, gray Mistress of the Frozen Land. For suddenly he had thought of the promise he had given her—"I will send you Ilmarinen, the skilfulest of smiths; he will forge the Sampo for you."

In another hour—yes, in half that time—he would meet Ilmarinen face to face. Would he be able to redeem his promise?

"I am a wizard; I can do wonderful things by magic," said the Minstrel to himself. "If my friend, the Smith, will not be persuaded, I will prevail upon him through other means."

Then he chuckled to the reindeer, and the birchwood runners glided more smoothly over the causeway.

On the farther side of the great fen there was a grove of pine trees, and in the midst of the grove was a green, grassy space as round as the moon and as level as the sea. At this spot the Minstrel paused; he brought the reindeer to a sudden stop. He leaped from the sledge and began to draw magic circles upon the ground. He muttered strange words which only wizards and magicians know. He lifted his arms above his head, and sang a song so weird and wild that the pine trees shuddered and shrieked.

He ceased; and instantly in the centre of the green space a slender twig sprang out of the ground and grew. It grew and grew, unfolding leaves and buds and blossoms. It grew and grew until it became a flower-crowned tree which seemed to pierce the clouds and sweep the solemn sky. No one knows how tall it might have grown. It might have grown till it touched the stars had not the Minstrel bidden it to cease expanding.

Then he sang another song quite different from the first—a song so sweet, so persuasive, that the wild creatures in the forest and the fen came out of their dens and listened to it. The white-faced moon heard, and sat herself down among the branches of the tree of magic. The seven stars of the Great Bear also heard; and they came circling from the sky and began to dance and play amid the leaves and blossoms.

Cunning, indeed, was Wainamoinen, cunning and old; and when he saw the work of his magic, he was pleased beyond measure. He clapped his hands together in triumph; he leaped and danced around the tree like one gone mad. Then he climbed into the sledge and sat down upon the furry robes; he shook the long reins and spoke gently to his steed. Slowly and thoughtfully, as one well contented with himself, he drove onward along the well-known pathway that led towards the village. His sharp gray eyes looked first this way and then that; his ears were open to the slightest sound; all his senses were alert.

VI. THE SMITHY

As the Minstrel journeyed onward the road gradually became broader and there were more signs of travel. Wainamoinen remembered every object; he knew every shrub and tree and every hummock and bog-hole. A sunny smile overspread his face, and his eyes twinkled for joy; for was he not again in his own dear home land, and would he not soon grasp the hands of his kinsmen and friends whom he had not seen for many months?

At every turn in the road the country became more open, and little by little the forest gave way to fields. Then in the distance thin wreaths of smoke could be seen rising above the crest of a hill—and the Minstrel knew that at the foot of that hill his own little village of Wainola was nestling in peace and quietude. His heart beat fast and his hands trembled as he thought of the welcome that was waiting for him there.

Suddenly, as he rounded a turn in the road, he came in full view of a grove of poplar trees in the middle of a field. He drove forward slowly, cautiously. He approached the field and paused quite near to the grove, listening, smiling as though he expected something. Then suddenly, from among the poplars, came well-remembered sounds—the sound of a hammer, cling-clanging upon an anvil, and the melodious tones of a manly voice singing in unison therewith. The Minstrel had heard that song a thousand times before; nevertheless, it seemed strangely new to him, and he leaned forward to listen to the words:

"Cling, cling, clinkety cling!
With Iron I labor, of Iron I sing;
I heat it, I beat it, I make it ring, ring,
I scold it, I mould it—my hammer I swing—
Cling, cling, clinkety cling!

"Ding, ding, dinkety ding!
O honeybee, hasten, come hither and bring
Your sweets from the wildwood, the flowers of spring,
Help make of this Iron some beautiful thing—
Ding, ding, dinkety ding!

"Cling, cling, clinkety cling!
Beware of the hornet, beware of his sting,
Beware of the evils he surely will bring;
In all things be gentle, O Iron, my king—
Cling, cling, clinkety cling!"

The Minstrel from his sledge could see the smithy from which the music came—a long, low building of logs in the very centre of the grove. It was dark and dingy and begrimed with smoke, but through the open door the fire of the forge glowed brightly, lighting up the whole interior and revealing even the smallest object; and there, before his anvil, stood the Smith, swinging his hammer and twirling his tongs and thinking only of his pleasant work.

Wainamoinen leaped from his sledge and ran forward; he stood in the doorway and called loudly to his busy friend:

"Hail, ho, Ilmarinen! Hail, dearest brother!"

The astonished Smith dropped his tongs; he threw his hammer down; he ran to greet his unexpected visitor.

"O Wainamoinen!" he cried. "Wainamoinen, prince of minstrels, wisest of men, best of friends—welcome, welcome! How glad I am to see you!"

"And how sweet it is to grasp your hand again," said the Minstrel warmly. "Oh, what joy to see home and comrades and country once again!"

Ilmarinen led the Minstrel into the smithy; he made him sit down on the edge of his workbench; and all the time he kept his arm around his neck in loving, brotherly embrace. Each gazed into the other's eyes, and for a time not another word was spoken—the hearts of both were so full of joy.

At length the Smith made out to stammer, "Tell me, my brother, where have you been these many months?"

"Far from home, Ilmarinen—yes, very far," answered the Minstrel. "I have been tossed on the sea; I have been in many countries; I have seen the whole vast world."

"Tell me about it," said the Smith. "You were gone so long that we gave you up as lost. Where have you been these many weeks, these long, long months? Tell me all about it."

Then, in a few words wisely spoken, the Minstrel told of his shipwreck, and how for eight days—yes, for nine long, wearisome days—he had been carried hither and thither on the crests of the waves.

"I see! I understand!" said the impatient Smith. "Hard, indeed, was your lot, and fraught with danger. Tell me quickly, how did you escape from the seething waters? To what place did the mad waves carry you? On what savage shore were you cast?"

"Have patience, brother, and I will tell you all," answered the Minstrel. "Never did I think that Fate would carry me to the cold and misty shores of Pohyola, the Frozen Land; but it happened even so. There, for three months—yes, for four long and dismal months—I was forced to tarry. I learned wisdom from the Mistress of that land; and indeed it was she who snatched me from the jaws of the sea and nursed me to health and strength. Never saw I a wiser woman, although she is not strikingly fair. I sat by her fireside; I listened to her words; I ate at her table. On her snowshoes I skimmed hither and thither over her cheerless land. In her boat I went fishing in the quiet inlets of the shore. But no matter where I went, no matter what I did, my heart was always sick for my home land; I sighed for the dear friends I had left behind me."

"O great Wainamoinen!" cried the Smith, embracing him again. "O cunning magician, sweetest of singers! Tell me now about your escape from that dismal land. Tell me about your journey homeward. I am anxious to hear."

"There is not much to say," answered the Minstrel. "The jour-

ney homeward was easy—it was delightful. As for my escape—
well, I escaped by promising to send you to the Frozen Land,
my dear brother."

"What do you say?" cried the Smith in wonder. "Send me to
the Frozen Land! Never will I go—no, not even to please my
best friend."

"Indeed, you *must* go," said the Minstrel curtly and decisively.
"I have promised, and you know the penalty of a broken
promise."

"Nay, nay, great Wainamoinen!" and dismay was pictured in
the face of the Smith. "Is this your love for me, that you cause
me to perish in order to save yourself?"

"Calm yourself, young brother," said the Minstrel soothingly.
"You shall not perish. I have arranged it all. You are to do some
skilful blacksmithing—use a little of your wondrous magic—and
your reward shall be the loveliest wife in the world. The
Mistress of Pohyola has promised."

The Smith spoke quickly, angrily: "You may make bargains for
yourself, not for me. I want no wife. My own mother is queen of
my house, and none other shall enter my door. Our dear village
of Wainola is my home; it is the place of all places; I will never
leave it."

"But if you could know how lovely she is—this Maid of
Beauty—you would do as I desire, you would go to Pohyola,"
said the Minstrel with increasing earnestness.

"Never! never!" shouted the Smith, trembling with anger.

"Yes, I am sure you would go," said the cunning Minstrel.
"There is no other maiden like unto this daughter of the Frozen
Land. She is wise, industrious, brave. Her face is fairer than the
moonlight on a midsummer eve; her eyes are like two suns; her
lips are like twin berries, red and luscious; her voice is sweeter
than the song of the meadow lark. All the young men in the
countries of the North have sought to win her."

"And win her they may!" shouted the Smith. "Now say no
more about her; change the subject; tell me a new story. I am
sick of such twaddle."

"Come, come, dear brother!" said the Minstrel gently, as
though conceding all. "Let us not quarrel. You are wise, your

judgment is good, and I love you. Forgive me if I have offended you. Come and sit by me again, and we will talk of other things."

The Smith forgot his anger; he threw his arms about the Minstrel's neck and burst into tears.

"There! there!" said his old friend kindly, coaxingly. "Think no more of my words. I was hasty; I was rash. Come now and let us hasten home, for I long to see my own dear fireside—to hear the voices of my kinsmen."

"Yes, let us go," said the Smith joyfully; and he hastened to cover the fire in his forge, to put his tools in their places, to remove his sooty apron.

"We will ride together in my birchwood sledge," said the Minstrel. "My reindeer steed will carry us briskly over the hill. But I wish first to drive back to the end of the causeway and show you a wonderful tree that I saw standing there."

"I will go with you willingly, gladly," answered the Smith, "but I know every tree in the forest and the fen, and I call none of them wonderful. Indeed, I passed by the end of the causeway yesterday, and I saw only whispering pines and dwarf oaks and a few stunted poplars."

"Well, but the tree which I saw there is the most wonderful sight in the world," said Wainamoinen. "Its topmost branches brush the sky. It is full of gorgeous flowers. The white moon sits on one of its branches; and the seven stars of the Great Bear play hide-and-seek among its leaves and blossoms. I saw it all with my own eyes not an hour ago."

The Smith laughed loudly, merrily. "Oh, my wise and truthful brother, tell me a story, two stories tell me! Travellers' tales are wondrous, pleasing; but only fools believe them."

They climbed into the birchwood sledge; they sat down on the furs; they talked of this thing and of that as the reindeer drew them swiftly back towards the fen and the long causeway. The road seemed short to both, and both were surprised when they found themselves in the grove of pine trees beside the green and magic circle.

"Wonderful! wonderful!" cried the astonished Smith as he gazed upward at the flower-crowned tree of magic. "Forgive me, my best of friends, sweetest of minstrels. You spoke the truth; you always speak the truth. I will believe whatever you say, I will do whatever you bid—only, I will never go to Pohyola."

"Well then," said the cunning Minstrel, "let us make what we can of this wonderful tree; for it may disappear as suddenly as it came. I am old, my legs are stiff, my arms rheumatic. It is long since I climbed a tree. But you—you are young and nimble, strong and supple, and spry as a squirrel when the nuts are ripening. You can climb and never grow tired."

"Yes, dear Minstrel, but why should I climb?" asked Ilmarinen.

"To gather those gorgeous blossoms," answered Wainamoinen; "to pick the rare fruit which you see; and, most of all, to bring down the white-faced moon and the seven golden stars that are playing among the branches. O Ilmarinen, skilfulest of men, if you are not afraid, climb quickly up and fetch down those matchless treasures."

"I am not afraid," cried Ilmarinen; and he began at once to climb the tree of magic.

VII. THE TEMPEST

With painful labor, Ilmarinen climbed from branch to branch. He looked upward and saw the moon with silver face smiling from the topmost boughs. He saw the seven stars of the Bear glittering like gold amid the leaves and blossoms. They seemed almost within his grasp. They beckoned to him, called to him; and he, with right good-will, climbed up, up, towards the moonlight and the starlight.

"Foolish fellow!" he heard a voice whispering. "Foolish fellow! foolish fellow! foolish fellow!"

"Who is it that calls me names—me the prince of all smiths?" he said in anger.

"It is I," came the answer. "I am the tree which you are climbing—foolish fellow, foolish fellow! The moon which you are after is only a shadow, foolish fellow. The stars are false as jack-o'-lanterns, foolish fellow. Even I, the tree, am a delusion. Save yourself while you may, foolish fellow, foolish fellow!"

The Smith heard, but he heeded not. The moon was just a little above him; the stars were right at his fingers' ends; in another moment he would grasp them all. On the ground far below him, the Minstrel was working his spells of magic, Ilmarinen saw him dancing, heard him singing, but understood him not.

> "Come storm wind, come whirlwind,
> Come swiftly, I say now;
> Pick up the wise blacksmith
> And bear him away, now.

> "Seize on him, and into
> 　　Your flying boat lay him;
> Then far to the Frozen North,
> 　　Gently convey him.

> "Blow storm wind, blow whirlwind,
> 　　Let nothing delay you.
> Blow swiftly, blow fiercely,
> 　　Blow, blow, I pray you!"

Suddenly there was a roaring in the air and in the tree tops, and the sky grew dark and very dark. Then a mighty tempest came hurtling over the land. In a moment the tree of magic melted into nothingness, and the fairy moon and the dancing stars vanished in the murk and gloom. The winds lifted the venturesome Smith in their arms; they laid him softly in their swiftly sailing cloud boat; they hurried him over forests and marsh lands, over mountains and sea, and at the hour of midnight dropped him gently on the frozen shores of Pohyola.

Wise old Louhi, gray and grim and toothless, was standing in her doorway. She heard the roar of the tempest and the shrieks of the night wind. She saw the inky clouds swiftly sailing from the South Land and the gray wolves of the air racing madly over the sea. Then in the misty darkness she heard footsteps; but the watch dogs lay sleeping in the sledgeway, their ears were closed, they did not bark. She listened, and presently a voice—a strange and manly voice—was heard above the storm wind's roar; but still the watch dogs slept and gave no alarm.

The Mistress, grim and fearless, spoke up bravely in the darkness, heeding not the dreadful turmoil. "Who goes there?" she cried. "Who is it that comes on the storm wind's back, and yet so quietly that he does not rouse nor waken my watch dogs?"

Then the voice answered from out the turmoil and the gloom, and a young man tall and handsome stepped into view. "I am a wayfarer and a stranger," he said, "and I am not here through my own choice. Nevertheless, I beg that I may find in this place some shelter till this fearful storm has passed."

"You have no need to ask shelter of me," answered the

woman; "for when did the Mistress of Pohyola turn a stranger from her door? When did she refuse to give a wayfarer the warmest place by her fireside?"

Forthwith she led him into her long, low hall; she gave him a seat by the pleasant fire. She brought food in plenty and set it before him. She did everything that would take away his weariness, everything that would add to his comfort.

At length, when he had warmed and rested himself and had satisfied his hunger, she ventured to ask him a question. "Have you ever in all your travels met a minstrel, old and steady, whom men call Wainamoinen?"

"Oh, yes, surely," answered the Smith. "He is an ancient friend of mine, dear as a brother, precious as a father. He has just returned home from a long visit to this North Country. He tells wonderful stories of the good people of Pohyola—pleasant tales of a pleasant land."

"How glad I am," said the Wise Woman. "Now tell me if in all your travels you have ever met a certain smith, young and wondrously skilful, whom men call Ilmarinen."

The stranger leaped to his feet and answered, "Surely, surely, I have often met that famous workman. Indeed, I myself am he; I am Ilmarinen, the Prince of Smiths, the maker of beautiful things, the skilfulest of men."

"Then welcome, welcome!" cried Louhi, grim and gray; and she grasped the stranger's hand. "We have been waiting for you a long time. We expect you to forge the Sampo for us. I know you will do so, for Wainamoinen the Minstrel promised me."

"The Sampo! the Sampo! What is the Sampo?" stammered Ilmarinen. "The Minstrel spoke of skilful smithing, but he mentioned not the Sampo. Never have I heard that name, although I have travelled wide."

"Oh, you shall hear enough about it, and you will forge it for us, I know," said the Mistress, grim but joyful. And then she turned and left him—left him standing by the hearth-side and gazing sadly, thoughtfully, into the flames.

"Now I understand it all," he softly muttered to himself. "Wainamoinen has betrayed me. He has sent me to this dreary Frozen Land to do a task too great for his skill, too wonderful

for his magic. He is old, he is cunning, he has outwitted me,
shall I do the thing which he sent me to perform?"

Meanwhile the gray Mistress of the Frozen Land hurried
from the long hall. She paused not till she reached her daughter's chamber. Briskly she went in, and softly she closed the door
behind her.

"My child, my beautiful child," she cried, "he has come at last.
He is young and tall and handsome. He will forge the Sampo for
us; he will put the wonderful mill together; henceforth we shall
want for nothing."

"Yes, mother," said the Maid of Beauty.

"Dress yourself, now, fair daughter. Put on your finest rai-
ment and deck your hair with jewels. Don't forget the golden
chain that goes around your neck; nor the belt with copper
buckle; nor your earrings; nor the silken ribbons for your hair;
nor the jewelled band that goes upon your forehead. And oh, my
dear child, do look pleasant, pretty, comely, and let your face be
bright and cheerful."

"Yes, mother," said the dutiful daughter.

VIII. THE RECIPE

S mith Ilmarinen stood thoughtfully, silently, beside the fire. The low, dark hall was full of shadows; dim figures lurked in the corners and danced among the rafters; the air was grimy with smoke; the flames burned blue and fitfully on the ash-strewn hearth.

Out-of-doors the storm was raging. The winds whooped and howled in savage combat. They reached their chilly fingers down through the chimney-hole as though they would snatch up the luckless Smith and bear him still farther away into regions untraversed and unknown.

He stood and listened. He heard the shrieking of the tempest demons; he heard the hail pelting upon the roof and the rain dashing and splashing upon the half-frozen ground; he heard the sea roaring fearfully in the darkness and the mad waves pounding upon the dumb and patient shore.

"In such a storm as this, any shelter is sweet," he said; and he stirred the fire logs till the sparks shot upward and filled the hall with the sound of their merry snapping. Then the thought came to him of his own fireside at home—of his mother and sister and the friends whom he loved—and he groaned aloud in anguish.

"O Wainamoinen, prince of minstrels!" he moaned. "Why have you treated me so unkindly? Why have you betrayed me—me your friend and brother? Never could I have believed that your magic power was so much greater than my own. Never——"

He paused suddenly, for he heard a rustling which was not the rustling of leaves, a breathing which was not the breathing

39

of the South Wind, a pitty-pat of soft footsteps upon the floor. He turned and looked, and lo! a radiant vision appeared before him in the firelight. It was the Maid of Beauty, the peerless daughter of the grim Mistress of Pohyola. Right winsomely she came forward to greet him, her cheeks blushing red, her eyes sparkling and joyous. The Smith's heart was beating hard and fast like a sledge-hammer beneath his waistcoat. He trembled and grew pale. Never had he seen, never had he imagined, a maiden so wondrously fair.

"O Prince of Smiths," she said in tones more sweet than the warble of birds, "I welcome you to our pleasant land of Pohyola."

Not even when the storm winds seized him had Ilmarinen felt so helpless and utterly overcome. He could scarcely say a word in answer; he could hardly lift his eyes; his hands hung as though palsied at his side; his feet were rooted to the floor. Then, ere he could recover from his confusion, he saw the Mistress herself advancing—the grim and toothless Mistress of the Frozen Land. She spoke, and her voice was cracked and harsh and grating.

"O master of smiths," she said, "this is my daughter, the fairest of all maidens. Now say, will you not forge the Sampo? Will you not hang its weights, adjust its levers? Will you not hammer its lid of many colors, even as your brother, the Minstrel, assured me you would?

"Yes, yes, yes!" stammered the poor Smith, scarcely knowing what he said. "I will do anything, everything that lies in my power. But I have never seen a Sampo, and I know not what it is. Tell me what it is like; tell me of its various uses."

"The Sampo," answered the Maid of Beauty—and her voice was like the ripple of wavelets on the shore of the summer sea— "the Sampo is the mill of fortune—the magic grinder that will grind whatever its owner most desires: money, houses, ships, silver, flour, salt—everything!"

"Silver, flour, salt—everything!" echoed the Smith.

"Yes. Do you think you have the skill to forge it?"

"Well, I have done greater things than that," he answered boastingly. "Long ago, when the world was young, I found Iron, ruddy Iron, hiding in the bogs, skulking in the woods, basking in the sunlight of the hills. I caught him and subdued him; I taught him to serve me; I gave him to the world to be a joy forever."

"We have often heard of your skill, and your praise is in all men's mouths," said the eager Mistress. "But the Sampo can be forged only by a great master of magic. Your friend, the Minstrel, although he was able to do many very wonderful things, would not undertake a task so difficult."

"Truly, I have performed harder tasks," answered the boaster. "Why, it was I that forged the blue sky that bends over the earth in summer. I hammered it out of a single piece of metal. I fashioned it into a dome-shaped lid to shut down over the earth and air. I painted it pale blue and azure and murky brown. Nothing is too great for my magic. Give me but one hint regarding its shape and nature, and I will make the Sampo—yes, a hundred Sampos—for you."

Toothless though she was, the wise old Mistress smiled—she smiled fearfully, cunningly, as one pleased and plotting.

"I cannot describe its shape," she answered, "for it is still uncreated and therefore formless; but its composition is quite simple and its ingredients are of the commonest kind. If by your power in magic you can mix these ingredients properly, the mill is made—it will do its work. But talk not of a hundred Sampos; the world can never hold but one."

"And I promise that with my magic skill I will put that one together," said the Smith; "but what can you tell me about its ingredients? Tell me all you know about its composition."

"I have a recipe which has come down through the ages," said the woman, "a recipe for making the Sampo; but no magician has ever yet been wise enough, strong enough to make use of it. Here it is, written in runes on a white whalebone:

"*Take the tips of two swan feathers;*
Add the milk of a young heifer;
Add a single grain of barley;
Mix and stir with wool of lambkin;
Heat the mixture, quickly, rightly;

> *In a magic caldron boil it;*
> *On a magic anvil beat it;*
> *Hammer its lid of many colors;*
> *Furnish it with wheels and levers;*
> *Set it up, and start it going.'"*

Ilmarinen listened. "The directions are plain and easily followed," he said. "To a smith who has shaped the mountains and hammered out the sky it will be an easy task, the pleasant pastime of a few fleeting days. But it must not be undertaken in the winter time. We must wait till the sky is clear and the sun shines warm on land and sea."

"And will you then forge the much-desired Sampo?" inquired the Mistress.

"I promise you," answered the Smith.

Thus the boasting Ilmarinen, having come suddenly, unexpectedly, unwillingly to the land of Pohyola, was conquered by the power of beauty. And thus he promised, not once alone, but thrice, promised solemnly on his honor, that he with his magic power would forge the wondrous mill of fortune and shape its lid of rainbow colors. And the cunning Mistress grimly smiled and joyfully gave him a home in her broad, low dwelling—she gave him food and lodging, the softest seat beside her hearth, the warmest bed beneath her rafters. And he, forgetful of his home and kinsmen, sat content in the glow of the blazing fire logs, and counted the days till the storm should pass, the weeks till the winter should end.

IX. THE CALDRON

All through the long and dreary winter, Ilmarinen waited idly by old Louhi's hearth-side. "No great thing in magic can be done in stormy weather," he said. "Summer and fair days of sunshine are the wizard's time for action."

The wise men of the North Land came often to see him. Herdsmen from the frozen meadows, savage fellows from the forest, fishermen from the icy inlets—these also came to hear the words of the wizard Smith and be taught by him. They came on snowshoes and in reindeer sledges, battling with the wintry storm winds and heeding not the cold. Singly and by twos and threes they came and squatted round Dame Louhi's fireplace, rubbing their hands together, warming their shins, and staring into the face of the marvellous stranger. And Ilmarinen sat in their midst and told them many tales of wonder, chiefly tales of his own rare skill and cunning.

He told them how he had broken the mountains with his hammer, how he had conquered wild Iron and imprisoned him in his smithy, and how, from a single lump of metal, he had hammered out the sky and set it up as a lid to cover the land and the sea. "All these things," said he, "were done by me—me, the prince of smiths, me, the skilfulest of men."

Then all his listeners, wise men, herdsmen, fishermen, wild men, looked up at him with awe and admiration. They drew up closer to the fire, they threw fresh logs into the flames, they turned their faces towards him and asked a thousand curious questions.

"Who painted the sky and gave it its blue and friendly color?" asked the wise men.

"I painted it—I, the first of smiths." answered Ilmarinen. "And when I swept my brush across from east to west, some drops of blue fell into the sea and colored it also."

"What are the stars that glitter so brightly above us when the nights are clear?" asked the herdsmen.

"They are the sparks from my forge," was the answer. "I caught them and fixed them securely in their places; I welded them into the vast sky-lid so they should never fall out nor fly away."

"Where is the home of the Great Pike, the mightiest of all the creatures that swim in the water?" asked the fishermen.

"The Great Pike lurks in the hidden places of the deep sea," said Ilmarinen; "for he knows that I have forged a hook of iron that will some day be the cause of his undoing."

"Ah! ah! ah!" muttered the wild men. Their mouths were open and their eyes were staring at the rafters where hung long rows of smoked salmon, slabs of bacon, and dried herbs of magic power. "Ah! ah! ah! What shall we do when we are hungry and there are no nuts to be gathered, no roots to be digged, no small beasts to be captured, no food of any kind? Ah! ah! ah!"

"Forget to-day, think only of to-morrow—for then there will be plenty," answered Ilmarinen. "Go back to your old haunts in the forest, and to-morrow I will send you so many nuts and roots and small beasts that you shall grow fat with the eating of them."

Thus, all through the wintry weather, Ilmarinen dispensed wisdom to the inquiring men who desired it, and there was no question which he could not answer, no want which he could not satisfy. And at length, when every mind was filled with knowledge, and every stomach with food from Dame Louhi's bountiful stores, the visitors departed. Singly, or by twos and threes, in sledges, on snowshoes, on foot, they returned to their respective haunts and homes. "We have seen him, and there is nothing more to be desired," they said.

And now the snow was melting, the grass was green on the

hillsides, the reeds were springing up in the marshes, and the birds were twittering under the eaves.

Forthwith, brave Ilmarinen sallied out to find a smithy. Ten men, willing and strong, followed him, prepared to do any sort of labor, to undergo any sort of privation. Long did he seek, and far and wide did he travel, and many were the vain inquiries which he made; but nowhere in all the Frozen Land could he discover forge or chimney, bellows or tongs, anvil or hammer. In that dismal, snowy country men had never needed iron; they had no tools save tools of fish-bone; they had no weapons save sticks and stones and fists and feet. What wonder, then, that they had no smithy?

Some men would have given up in despair, but not so Ilmarinen. "Women may lose their courage," he said; "fools may give up a task because it is hard; but heroes persevere, wizards and smiths conquer."

So, still followed by his serving-men, he set out to find a fit place in which to build a smithy. For nine days he sought—yes, for ten long summer days he wandered over the brown meadows and among the gloomy hills of Pohyola. At length, deep in the silent forest he found a great stone all streaked and striped in colors of the rainbow.

"This is the place," he said, never doubting; and he gave orders to build his smithy there.

The first day's task was to build the furnace and the forge with yawning mouth and towering chimney. On the second day he framed the bellows and covered it with stout reindeer hide. On the third he set up his anvil, a block of hardest granite for ten men to roll.

Then he made his tools. For a hammer he took a smooth stone from the brook; for tongs he cut a green sapling and bent it in the middle, forcing the two ends together. Thus his smithy was completed; but how was he to forge the magic Sampo? With what was he to form its iridescent lid?

"Only weaklings say, 'I cannot,'" said he. "Only want-wits say, 'It is too difficult.' Heroes never give up. Nothing is impossible to a true smith."

Then from a secret pocket he drew the things most needful

for his forging. He counted them over, giving to each a magic number—two tips of white swan feathers, a bottle of milk from a young red heifer, a grain of barley grown in a land beyond the sea, and the fleece of a lambkin not one day old. These he mixed in a magic caldron, throwing upon them many bits of precious metals, with strange wild herbs and rank poisons and sweet honey dew. And all the while, he kept muttering harshly the spells and charms which none but smiths and skilful wizards understand.

At length the mixture was completed. Ilmarinen set the caldron firmly in the furnace, he pushed it far into the yawning cavern. Then he kindled the fire, he heaped on fuel, he closed the furnace door and bade the serving-men set the bellows to blowing.

Tirelessly the ten men toiled, taking turns, five by five, at the mighty lever. Like the fierce North Wind sweeping over the hills and rushing through the piney forest, the heaving bellows roared. The flames leaped up and filled the furnace and the forge. The black smoke poured from the chimney and rose in cloudlike, inky masses to the sky. Ilmarinen heaped on more fuel, he opened the draughts of the furnace, he danced like a madman in the light of the flames, he shouted strange words of magic meaning. Thus, for three long summer days and three brief summer nights, the fire glowed and the furnace roared and the men toiled and watched unceasingly. And round about the feet of the workmen lichens and leafy plants grew up, and in the crannies of the rocks wild flowers bloomed, nourished by the warmth from the magic forge.

On the fourth day, the wizard Smith bade the workmen pause while he stooped down and looked into the caldron far within the fire-filled furnace. He wished to see whether anything had begun to shape itself from the magic mixture, whether anything had been brought forth by the mighty heat.

As he looked, lo! a crossbow rose from out the caldron—a crossbow, perfect in form and carved with figures fantastical and beautiful. On each side it was inlaid with precious gold, and the tips were balls of silver. The shaft was made of copper, and the whole bow was wondrously strong.

"This is a beautiful thing," said Ilmarinen, "but it is not the Sampo."

Forthwith the crossbow leaped from the caldron; it flew out of the furnace; it stood humbly bowing before the wizard Smith.

"Hail, my master!" it said. "Here I am, ready to serve you as you command. My task is to kill, and I love it, I love it! Send me forth quickly, and let me begin. On every work-day I'll kill at least one. On every holiday I'll kill more—sometimes two, and sometimes very many. Oh, yes, I will kill, I will kill!"

"What will you kill?" asked Ilmarinen.

"In war, men; in peace, singing birds and timid deer. Oh, I can kill, I can kill!"

And having said this, the crossbow began to shoot arrows recklessly about to the great peril of the ten serving-men. This made Ilmarinen angry. "You are bad!" he cried. "You love only evil. I have no use for you!" and he seized the bow and threw it back into the boiling caldron. Then he bade the workmen blow the bellows as before; and he heaped on more fuel and more fuel, singing meanwhile a wild, weird song which made the flames leap out from the very top of the chimney.

All day, all night, the bellows roared; all day again, and again all night, the furnace glowed, white-hot, and furious. Then, just at sunrise, the Smith called to the bellows-men, "Halt!" He stooped down and gazed steadfastly, curiously, into the magic caldron. As the flames subsided and the furnace began to grow cool, behold a ship rose from the mixture—a ship complete with pointed beak and oars and sails, all ready to be launched upon the sea. Its hull was painted blue and yellow, its ribs were golden, its prow was of copper, and its sails were of white linen whereon were depicted most wonderful figures of dragons and savage beasts; and on its deck and within its hold were all manner of weapons of war—axes and spears, bows and arrows, sharp daggers and gleaming swords.

"Here I am, my master!" said the ship. "I am ready for your service, if you please. You see that I am well fitted for war, well fitted to plunder and rob the seaports of other lands. Send me out, that I may help you slay your enemies and make your name a terror throughout the world."

The wizard Smith drew the ship toward him. Beautiful and well-laden though it was, he was by no means pleased with it. "I like you not!" he cried. "You are a destroyer and not a builder. You love evil, and I will have no part nor parcel of you," and he broke the ship into a thousand pieces, and threw the fragments back into the caldron. Then he bade the serving-men blow the bellows with all their might, while he heaped fresh fuel upon the flames and sang wild songs of wizardry and enchantment.

On the fourth morning Ilmarinen looked again into the caldron. "Surely something good has been formed by this time," he said.

From the caldron a mist was slowly rising, hot, pungent, fog-like; within it, the magic mixture could be heard bubbling, seething, hissing. The Smith looked long ere he could see what was forming. Then suddenly the mist cleared away and a beautiful young heifer sprang out into the sunlight. Her color was golden, her neck and legs were like the wild deer's, her horns were ivory, her eyes were wondrous large, and on her forehead was a disc of steely sunshine.

The Smith was delighted, his heart was filled with admiration. "Beautiful, beautiful creature!" he cried. "Surely, she will be of use to mankind."

Scarcely had he spoken when the heifer rushed out of the smithy, pausing not a moment to salute her master. She ran swiftly into the forest, bellowing, horning, fighting, spurning everything that came in her way.

"Ah, me!" sighed the Smith, "she, too, has an evil nature. Alas, that one so wickedly inclined should be blessed with so beautiful a form!"

Then he bade the serving-men bring her back to the smithy; and when, with infinite labor, they had done this, he cut her in pieces and threw her back into the caldron. And now the bellows was set to blowing again, and it roared like a tempest in a forest of pines; the smoke rolled darkly from the chimney; and the fire glowed hotter than before around the seething caldron. And all that day, and through the midsummer night, the master and his men toiled unceasingly.

At sunrise on the fifth day, Ilmarinen looked again into the caldron. As he stooped and gazed, a plough rose suddenly from the magic mixture. Like a thing of life it glided softly through the furnace door, bowed low before the wizard Smith, and waited to receive his judgment. It had been shaped and put together with great skill, and every line was a line of beauty. The frame was of copper, the share was of gold, the handles were tipped with silver.

"Here I am, my master," it said. "Send me forth to do your bidding."

"What good thing can you do?" asked Ilmarinen.

"I can turn things over, tear things up," answered the plough. "Nothing in the fields can stand against me. I will overturn the sod, I will uproot all growing things whether good or bad. I will go into gardens, meadows, cornfields, and stir the soil; and woe to the plant that comes in my way, for I will destroy it."

"You are beautiful and you are useful," said the Smith; "but you are rude and unkind. You do not know how to discriminate between the evil and the good. You give pain, you cause death, and therefore I do not love you."

He waited not for the plough's answer, but struck it with his hammer and broke it into a thousand fragments; then he threw the fragments back into the magic caldron and closed the door of the furnace.

Long and thoughtfully he sat, silent but not despairing. His elbows rested upon his knees, his head was bowed upon his hands. And he repeated to himself his favorite saying: "None but cowards say, 'I cannot,' none but weaklings say 'Impossible,' none but women weep for failure."

At length he rose and called to his serving-men; he dismissed them, every one, and summoned the winds to come and be his helpers.

X. THE FORGING OF THE SAMPO

The four winds heard the magic call of Ilmarinen, and they hastened from the corners of the sky to do his bidding. First came the East Wind, riding over the sea, combing the crests of the waves with his clammy fingers, and rushing with chilly breath through the dank marshes and across the lonely meadows. He knocked at the door of the smithy, he rattled the latch, and shrieked down the chimney:

"Master of wizards and prince of all smiths, what will you have me do?"

And Ilmarinen answered, "Set my bellows to blowing that I may forge the wondrous Sampo."

Next there was heard a joyous whistling among the pine trees, and a whir-whirring as of the wings of a thousand birds; and there was a fragrance in the air like the fragrance of countless wildflowers, and a soft breathing like the breath of a sleeping child. The South Wind crept softly up to the smithy door, it peeped slyly in, and said merrily:

"What now, old friend and companion? What will you have me do?"

And Ilmarinen answered, "Blow into my furnace, and blow hard, that I may forge the wondrous Sampo."

Then came the jolly West Wind, roaring among the mountains, dancing in the valleys, playing among the willows and the reeds, and frolicking with the growing grass. He laughed as he lifted the roof of the smithy and peered down at the furnace and the forge and the tools of the Smith.

"Ha, ha!" he called. "Have you some work for me? Let me get at it at once."

And Ilmarinen answered, "Feed my fire, so that I may forge the wondrous Sampo."

He had scarcely spoken when the sky was overcast and heavy gray clouds obscured the sun. The North Wind, like an untamed monster, came hurtling over the land, howling and shrieking, as fierce as a thousand wolves, as fleet as the swiftest reindeer. He filled the air with snowflakes, he covered the hills with a coating of ice. The pine trees shivered and moaned because of his chilly breath, and the brooks and waterfalls were frozen with fear.

"What do you wish, master of wizards?" he called from every corner of the smithy. "Tell me how I can serve you."

And Ilmarinen answered, "Fan the flames around my magic caldron, so that I may forge the wondrous Sampo."

So, the chilling East Wind, the whistling South Wind, the laughing West Wind, and the blustering North Wind, joined together in giving aid to the wizard Smith. From morning till evening, from evening till another morning, they worked with right good will, as their master directed them. The great bellows puffed and groaned and shook the very ground with its roaring. The flames filled the furnace; they wrapped themselves around the caldron; they burst out through a thousand cracks and crevices; they leaped, in tongues of fire, through the windows of the smithy. Showers of red sparks issued from the chimney and flew upward to the sky. The smoke rose in clouds of ink-like blackness and floated in vast masses over the mountains and the sea.

For three anxious days and three sleepless nights the winds toiled and paused not; and Ilmarinen sang magic incantations, and heaped fresh fuel upon the fire, and cheered his helpers with shouts and cries and words of enchantment which wizards alone can speak.

On the fourth day he bade the winds cease their blowing. He knelt down and looked into the furnace. He pushed the cinders aside; he uncovered the caldron and lifted the lid slowly, cautiously. How strange and beautiful was the sight that rose before him! Colors of the rainbow, forms and figures without number, precious metals, floating vapors—all these were mingled in the caldron.

Ilmarinen drew the vessel quickly out of the furnace. He thrust his tongs into the mixture, and seized it with the grip of a giant. He pulled it bodily from the caldron, writhing, creeping, struggling, but unable to escape him. He twirled it in the air as blacksmiths sometimes twirl small masses of half-molten iron; then he held it firmly on his anvil of granite, while with quick and steady strokes he beat it with his heavy hammer. He turned it and twisted it and shaped it, and put each delicate part in its proper place. All night and all day, from starlight till starlight, he labored tirelessly and without ceasing.

Slowly, piece by piece and part by part, the magic Sampo with its wheels and levers grew into being. The wizard workman forged it with infinite skill and patience, for well he knew that one false stroke would undo all his labor, would be fatal to all his hopes. He scanned it from every side; he touched up the more delicate parts; he readjusted its springs and wheels; he tested its strength and the speed of its running. Finally, after the mill itself was proved satisfactory, he forged the lid to cover it; and the lid was the most marvellous part of all—as many-colored as the rainbow and embossed with gold and lined with silver and ornamented with beautiful pictures.

At length everything was finished. The fire in the furnace was dead; the caldron was empty and void; the bellows was silent; the anvil of granite was idle. Ilmarinen called to his ten serving-men and put the precious Sampo upon their shoulders. "Carry this to your Mistress," he said, "and beware that you touch not the lid of magic colors."

Then, leaving the smithy and all his tools in the silence of the forest, he followed the laborers to Pohyola, proud of his great performance, but pale and wan and wellnigh exhausted from long labor and ceaseless anxiety.

The Wise Woman was standing in the doorway of her smoke-begrimed dwelling. She smiled grimly as she saw the working men returning. She welcomed Ilmarinen not unkindly, and he placed before her the results of his long and arduous labors.

"Behold, I bring you the magic Sampo!" he said. "In all the

world there is no other wizard that could have formed it, no other smith that could have welded its parts together or forged its lid of many colors. You have only to whisper your wishes into the small orifice on the top of the mill, and it will begin to run— you can hear its wheels buzzing and its levers creaking. Lay it on this side and it will grind flour—flour for your kitchen, flour for your neighbors, flour for the market. Turn the mill over, thus, and it will grind salt—salt for seasoning, salt for the reindeer, salt for everything. But the third side is the best. Lay the mill on that side and whisper, 'Money.' Ah! then you will see what comes out—pieces of gold, pieces of silver, pieces of copper, treasures fit for a king!"

The Mistress of Pohyola was overcome with joy. Her toothless face expanded into a smile—a smile that was grim and altogether ill-favored. She tried to express her feelings in words, but her voice was cracked and broken, and her speech sounded like the yelping of a gray wolf in the frozen marshes. Without delay she set the mill to grinding; and wonderful was the way in which it obeyed her wishes. She filled her house with flour; she filled her barns with salt; she filled all her strong boxes with gold and silver.

"Enough! enough!" she cried, at length. "Stop your grinding! I want no more."

The tireless Sampo heard not nor heeded. It kept on grinding, grinding; and no matter on which side it was placed, its wheels kept running, and flour or salt or gold and silver kept pouring out in endless streams.

"We shall all be buried!" shouted the Mistress in dismay. "Enough is good, but too much is embarrassment. Take the mill to some safe place and confine it within strong walls, lest it overwhelm us with prosperity."

Forthwith she caused the Sampo to be taken with becoming care to a strong-built chamber underneath a hill of copper. There she imprisoned it behind nine strong doors of toughest granite, each of which was held fast shut by nine strong locks of hardest metal. Then she laughed a laugh of triumph, and said: "Lie there, sweet mill, until I have need of you again. Grind flour, grind salt, grind wealth, grind all things good for Pohyola, but do not smother us with your bounties."

They closed the strong doors and bolted them and left the Sampo alone in its dark prison-house; but through the key-hole of the ninth lock of the ninth door there issued a sweet delightful whirring sound as of wheels rapidly turning. The Sampo was grinding treasures for Dame Louhi's people, and laying them up for future uses—richness for the land, golden sap for the trees, and warm and balmy breezes to make all things flourish.

Meanwhile Ilmarinen sat silent and alone in the Mistress's hall, thinking of many things, but mostly of the reward which he hoped to receive for his labor. For an hour he sat there, waiting—yes, for a day of sunlight he remained there, his eyes downcast, his head uncovered.

Suddenly Dame Louhi, the Wise Woman, came out of the darkening shadows and stood before him. The flames which darted up, flickering, from the half-burned fagots, lighted her grim features and shone yellow and red upon her gray head and her flour-whitened face. Very unlovely, even fearful, did she seem to Ilmarinen. She spoke, and her voice was gruff and unkind.

"Why do you sit here idle by my hearthstone?" she asked. "Why, indeed, do you tarry so long in Pohyola, wearing out your welcome, and wearying us all with your presence?"

The Smith answered her gently, politely, as men should always answer women: "Have I not forged the Sampo for you—the wondrous Sampo which you so much desired? Have I not hammered its lid of rainbow colors? Have I not made you rich—rich in flour, rich in salt, in silver and gold? I am now waiting only for my reward—for the prize which you promised."

"Never have I promised you any reward," cried the Mistress angrily. "Never have I offered to give you a prize"; and her gaunt form and gruesome features seemed truly terrible in their ugliness.

But Ilmarinen did not forget himself: the master of magic did not falter.

"I have a friend whose name is Wainamoinen," he answered. "He is the first of all minstrels, a singer of sweet songs, a man of honor, old and truthful. Did you not say to him that you would richly reward the hero who should forge the magic Sampo—that you would give him your daughter, the Maid of Beauty, to be his wife?"

"Ah, but that was said to him and not to you," said the Mistress, and she laughed until her toothless mouth seemed to cover the whole of her misshapen face.

"But a promise is a promise," gently returned the Smith; "and so I demand of you to fulfil it."

The features of the unlovely Mistress softened, they lost somewhat of their grimness as she answered: "Willingly would I fulfil it, prince of wizards and of smiths; but I cannot. Since Wainamoinen's visit, the Maid of Beauty has become of age. She is her own mistress, she must speak for herself. I cannot give her away as a reward or prize—she does not belong to me. If you wish her to go to the Land of Heroes with you, ask her. She has a mind of her own; she will do as she pleases."

She ceased speaking. The firelight grew brighter and suddenly died away, and the room became dark.

"I will see her in the morning," said Ilmarinen.

XI. THE HOMESICK HERO

The sunlight was streaming white and yellow, over sea and land. The wild geese were honking among the reeds. The swallows were twittering under the eaves. The maids were milking the reindeer in the paddock behind Dame Louhi's dwelling. Ilmarinen had slept late. He rose hurriedly and hastened to go out, not to listen to the varied sounds of the morning, but to ponder concerning the great problem that was soon to be solved.

He opened the door, but quickly started back, trembling, and pale. What had he seen to give him pause, to cause him to be frightened? Right before him, so near that he might have touched her with his hand, stood the Maid of Beauty. Her cheeks were like the dawn of a summer's morning; her lips were like two ripe, red berries with rows of pearls between; her eyes were like glorious suns, shining softly in the midst of heaven. Who would not have trembled in the presence of such marvellous beauty?

Ilmarinen was overcome with bashfulness. He stammered, he paused, he looked into those wonderful eyes and was covered with confusion. Then he spoke to his own heart and said, "Why am I so cowardly—I who have hitherto feared nothing under the sun? I will be brave. I will ask her the momentous question and abide by her answer."

So, with quivering lips and downcast eyes he spoke: "Fairest of maidens, my task is done. I have forged the Sampo, I have hammered its marvellous lid, I have proved myself worthy to be

called the Prince of Smiths. Will you not now go with me to my
far distant home—to the Land of Heroes in the sunny south?
There you shall be my queen; you shall rule my house, keep my
kitchen, sit at the head of the table. O Maid of Beauty, it was for
you that I forged the Sampo and performed those acts of magic
which no other man would dare to undertake. Be kind, and dis-
appoint me not."

The maiden answered softly, and she blushed as she spoke:
"Why should I leave my own sweet home to go and live with
strangers, to be a poor man's wife in a poor and distant land? My
mother's hall would be desolate; her kitchen would be cold and
ill-cared for were I to go away. She herself would grieve and die
of loneliness."

"Nay," said Ilmarinen, "she is not the sort of woman to feel
sorrow; her heart is too hard to be crushed so easily."

"But there are others who would miss me," said the maiden
softly. "If I should go away, who would feed the reindeer at the
break of day? Who, in the early springtime, would welcome the
cuckoo and answer his joyous song? Who, in the short summer,
would caress the wildflowers in the wooded nooks and sing to
the violets in the meadows? Who, in the autumn, would pick the
red cranberries in our marshes? Who, at winter's beginning,
would tell the songbirds to fly southward, and who would cheer
the wild geese on their way to summer lands?"

The Smith had now grown bolder, and he answered wisely:
"The cuckoo comes to my country as well as yours. There are
flowers in the forests of Wainola more beautiful than any in this
chilly land. There are cranberries in our marshes also, redder
and larger than any you have ever picked. The songbirds live in
the Land of Heroes half of every year, and the wild geese tarry
there and build their nests in the sedgy inlets."

"All that may be true," said the Maid of Beauty, "but your
cuckoo is not my cuckoo, and so how could I welcome it in the
springtime? All things in Wainola would be strangers to me,
while all things in Pohyola are friends. The North Country, the
Frozen Land as you call it, would be very lonely if I were
to leave it; the meadows would be joyless, the hills would be

forlorn, the shores would be desolate. Were I not here to paint the rainbow, the storm clouds would never vanish. Were I not here to note the change of seasons, the songbirds would surely forget to come, the flowers would neglect to bloom, the cranberries would perish ungathered. No, Ilmarinen, I must not go with you. You are skilful, you are wise, you are brave, you are the prince of wizards and of smiths—but I love my native land. Say no more; I will not go with you."

The Smith was speechless; his tongue was motionless, and he could not make reply. He turned slowly away, and with head bowed down and cap pulled over his eyes, he sought his favorite place by the side of the smouldering hearth-fire.

All day he sat there, pondering, wondering how now by any makeshift he could escape from Pohyola and return to his native land. The longer he thought, the larger his troubles appeared. He had no boat to sail by sea, no sledge nor reindeer to travel by land, no money in his purse, no knowledge of the road. Would not magic avail him? Could he not call upon the winds to carry him, as they had once done against his will? Alas, no! All his magic lore, all his magic power, had been exhausted in the forging of the Sampo; he was utterly bankrupt.

While he sat thus, homesick, disappointed, and forlorn, Dame Louhi came suddenly into the hall. She was white with flour and laden with silver, and she wore a look of triumph on her grim and unlovely face.

"Ha! forger of the Sampo!" she cried. "Why do you sit here moping day after day? What ails you—you, who hammered out the sky and set the stars in their places—you, the prince of wizards, the king of boasters?"

Ilmarinen groaned and pulled his cap still lower over his eyebrows; but he answered not a word.

The Mistress went on with her bantering; she laid salt on the poor man's wounds and briskly rubbed it in. "Why do you groan so like an ice-floe breaking up at the end of winter? Why do you weep salt tears, extinguishing the fire on my hearth? Have you the toothache, earache, heartache, stomach-ache? Did you eat too much at dinner? Surely, the prince of wizards ought to curb his appetite."

The Smith's heart was filled with anger; his brain burned, his cheeks were flushed with shame. Much had he suffered from this woman's greed and cunning; painfully was he stung by her bitter words. Yet he answered her with becoming gentleness— for was she not the mother of the Maid of Beauty?

"I have no ache nor bodily pain," he said; "but I am sick of this wretched country, this Frozen Land. I am sick of its mists, of its storms, of its long nights and its cheerless days. And, most of all, I am sick of its thankless people."

"Ah! I understand," answered the woman; and she closed her toothless jaws tightly, restraining her anger. "In other words, you are homesick; your heart is filled with longing for your own country and your own fireside."

"You speak rightly," answered Ilmarinen. "My heart is in the South Land, in the Land of Heroes. Unwillingly did I come to your bleak and chilly Pohyola; unwillingly have I remained here, cheered by a single hope which has at last been blasted. And now my only wish is to return home, to see once more the friends whom I love, to cheer my mother in her loneliness."

"Surely, the lad who cries for his mother should be comforted," said the Mistress derisively. "At what moment would you like to start on your homeward journey?"

"At the break of day?" answered the Smith, his face brightening as his hopes were strengthened.

"It shall be as you wish," said the woman, and her tones were uncommonly tender and kind. "I will see that everything is in readiness. At the break of day a boat will be waiting for you at the landing. Delay not a moment, but go on board and ask no questions. You shall be safely carried to the haven that is so dear to you."

Ilmarinen stammered his thanks. His eyes grew brighter, his heart was cheered with hope.

Very impatiently the hero waited through the short hours of night, and gladly did he hail the first gray streak of dawn that heralded the morning.

He hastened out to the shore. The promised boat was there, moored to the landing by a hempen rope. It was a small vessel, but roomy enough for one passenger who would also be captain and crew. Its hull was of cedar and the trimmings were of maple. Its prow was tipped with copper, sharp and strong. The oar also was of copper, and the sail was painted red and yellow.

In the boat a great store of food was packed—deer meat, smoked herring, cakes of barley, toothsome victuals enough for many days.

Ilmarinen asked no man any questions, although many persons were gathered on the shore, wondering whence came the strange vessel and whither it was going. He climbed over the polished gunwales and stepped boldly on board. Then, as the sun was peeping out of the sea, he raised the square sail of red and yellow. He cut the mooring rope, and took the copper paddle in his hands; he sat down in the stern to do the steering.

A gentle wind filled the sail, and the boat glided smoothly, swiftly away from the land. Ilmarinen looked back; he saw all the folk of Pohyola standing along the shore, and he heard them shouting their good-byes and bidding him god-speed. He looked again, and saw the Maid of Beauty among them; she was waving her hand, and her face seemed to him tenfold more beautiful than before; her cheeks were wet with tears, and there was a look of great regret in her wonderful eyes.

And there also stood the Mistress of Pohyola, gray and grim and toothless, but noble in mien and of queenly appearance. She lifted her arms, she raised her eyes towards heaven, and called to the North Wind to prosper the voyage for her departing guest:

> "Come, thou North Wind, great and strong,
>   Guide this hero to his home;
>   Gently drive his boat along
>   O'er the dashing white sea-foam.
>
> "Push him with your mighty hand;
>   Blow him o'er the blue-backed sea;
>   Carry him safe to Hero Land,
>   And let him ne'er come back to me."

The North Wind heard her, and he came, strong, swift, and steady. Like a waterfowl in some sheltered cove, the boat glided with incredible smoothness over the chilly waters. Joyfully the prince of smiths handled the oar, and loudly he shouted to the wind as he saw the red prow cleaving the waves and knew that he was speeding homeward.

Three days the voyage lasted. As the morning of the fourth was dawning, Ilmarinen beheld on his left the lofty headland and pleasant shore of his native land, green with summer-leafing trees and odorous with the breath of wildflowers. The sun rose above the eastern hills, and then his eyes were rejoiced with the sight of the weather-stained roofs of Wainola, and curling clouds of smoke rising from the hearths of many well-known dwellings.

Gently, then, the glad voyager guided his boat into the harbor. He dismissed the North Wind with warm thanks for his friendly service; and then with a few skilful strokes of the oar, he drove his stanch little boat high up on the sloping beach.

"Home! home at last!" he cried as he leaped out. He paused not a moment, he took no care to tie his little vessel to the mooring-post, but with eager, impatient feet he hastened towards the village.

Scarcely had he walked half-way to the nearest dwelling, when a man stepped suddenly into the road before him. It was Wainamoinen, the cunning wizard, the first of all minstrels.

"O Ilmarinen, dearest of brothers!" shouted the aged man, so wise, so truthful, so skilled in tricks of magic. "How delighted I am to behold your face again! Where have you been hiding through all these anxious months?"

The Smith answered curtly, coldly, yet politely: "You know quite well my hiding-place, for it was you who sent me thither. I thank you for the journey; but it will be long ere I climb another one of your magic trees."

"Wisest and skilfulest of metal workers, why do you speak in riddles?" asked the Minstrel, appearing to be hurt. "Never have I sought to harm you; but all that I did was for your own good. Now, I welcome you back to Wainola. Let us be brothers as in the days of yore. Come! here is my hand; let us forgive and forget!"

The generous Smith could not cherish ill-feeling in his heart. He loved the aged Minstrel as he would have loved a father. So he grasped the proffered hand, gently, warmly; he embraced his friend twice, three times, as had been his wont whenever fondness prompted his warm heart. Then he said, "I forgive you, sweetest of minstrels."

Side by side, arm in arm, the two old comrades walked homeward.

"Tell me, Ilmarinen," asked the Minstrel, "did you perform my errand? Did you fulfil my promise and forge the magic Sampo? Did you win the prize?"

"Yes, I forged the Sampo," answered Ilmarinen; "and I hammered its rainbow cover. Therefore your debt is paid, and you are freed from your promise. But as for me—well, as you see, I have not won the Maid of Beauty."

XII. THE UNFINISHED BOAT

Never were two pledged lovers more stanch and true than the ancient Minstrel and the youthful Smith, and their affection for each other grew stronger and stronger as the days went by. The brief summer waned, and the long winter came with its sleet and snow and furious storms; but through all the weather changes and the varying fortunes of the year, the mutual devotion of the two heroes remained steadfast. Ilmarinen toiled daily in his smithy, hammering out chains and hoes and axes, and shaping things of beauty and of use for his kinsfolk and neighbors in Wainola. And the Minstrel also toiled, composing new songs of love and conflict, retelling old tales of mystery and magic, and studying to discover the secrets of nature and of life.

"Come and live with me," said the younger hero to the older. "My cottage is roomy, my table is large, and my hearth is cozy and warm. My mother, Lokka, will welcome you; she will serve you and prepare toothsome victuals for your meals. Your sweet songs will enliven the hours of evening, and we will converse often together concerning those things that are nearest to your heart and mine. Come! Come and be my eldest brother!"

"I thank you," answered the Minstrel. "We shall both be happy."

And so, without further persuasion, he took up his abode in the home of his friend; and Dame Lokka the Handsome, the best of all the matrons in Hero Land, kept house for them both.

"What have you wrought in your smithy to-day?" old Wainamoinen would ask as they met at the evening meal.

63

Then the master Smith, grimy with soot and gray with ashes, would begin to tell of a hoe he had beaten out, or a gold ring he had fashioned; but ere he had spoken a dozen words his mind would wander far away to a low-roofed dwelling in the Frozen Land, and the rest of his speech would be a burning discourse in praise of the Maid of Beauty.

"Now, sing us your newest song, sweetest of minstrels," the younger hero would say as they sat together beside the evening fire.

And the Minstrel would begin with a hymn of creation, or a tale of mighty strife and heroism; but at the end of the strain he would forget his subject and begin to chant a ballad of love or a ditty recounting the charms of the matchless maiden of Pohyola.

Thus, ere long, it came about that the two friends were constantly and forever recalling the sweetest memories of their lives—memories which, strange to say, were also mingled with thoughts of experiences that had been unpleasant, painful, humiliating. They talked daily of their strange adventures in Pohyola; and now, in the halo of long absence, the Frozen Land was remembered only as a land of spring showers and summer sunshine, and their days of sadness and gloom were forgotten in contemplation of the blessedness which they had felt in the presence of the Maid of Beauty. And now her image seemed always before their eyes, and her voice seemed calling to them through the misty and frost-laden air of the desolate North Land.

Gradually, and by a process unknown to himself, Ilmarinen came to think of her as he thought of the sun and the stars and the wonderful sea, as something mysterious, sublime, incomprehensible, which he might worship from afar but never hope to possess or understand. She was his deity, his Jumala, as far superior to him as he, the prince of smiths and wizards, was superior to the beasts of the fields and woods.

But the Minstrel, old and steadfast, was more worldly-minded. He remembered how the maiden had laughed at him and twitted him as she sat on the rainbow plying her magic shuttles and weaving the web of the unmeasured sky; and as he thought of her words and her taunting manner, his feeling of reverence for her was tempered with a desire for some sort of revenge. Therefore he resolved that he would get even with her; verily he would show her that he, too, was one of the mighty— a magician unexcelled in power, a master of things seen and unseen. And having done this, what would be easier than to make her his own?

Long did he ponder, and many were the thoughts that came into his old, experienced mind. Day after day, week after week, he sat by Dame Lokka's fireside, thinking, thinking, thinking— yet keeping all his thoughts to himself.

"He is composing some new, sweet song," said the motherly matron; and she refrained from disturbing him.

At last, when the wild geese were again honking in the quiet fjords and the frogs were making the marshes musical, he perfected a secret plan by which he hoped to win the object of his desires, and at the same time add much to his already matchless fame. He told no one of his project, but he clenched his hands together and shut his teeth hard with determination.

"None but women say, 'I cannot'; none but cowards say 'I dare not,'" he repeated to himself again and again as though he would bolster up his courage.

Then, unknown to Ilmarinen—unknown to all his friends and neighbors—he set to work to build a boat, roomy and stanch and shaped for swiftest sailing.

It was his intention, when this boat was finished, to make a secret voyage to the Frozen Land and boldly make known his suit to the Maid of Beauty. If she would listen to him and accept the high place of honor which he had once before offered her— if she would consent to be the mistress of his kitchen, to bake his honey cakes and sing at his table, well and good; the fame of Wainamoinen, prince of minstrels, would be carried to the ends of the earth.

But what if she should scorn him as before? Was he not a magician? Through the power of magic he would subdue her; he would carry her aboard his vessel; he would bring her, willy nilly, to the Land of Heroes; she would have no choice but to be the queen of his dwelling in Wainola.

The boat itself was to be built by magic. By magic spells the beams were to be hewn and properly placed, the keel was to be laid, the hull was to be made stanch and shapely. No hammer was to be used in the work of building, but every nail and spike must be driven in the right place by a magic word that was known only to the prince of wizards, the first of all minstrels.

The place which Wainamoinen chose for the building of his boat was on the shore of a shady island well concealed behind a lofty headland. Trees grew along the shore, and there were thousands of them covering the hillside; but they were small trees, mere saplings, and would be of little use in boat-building. Where could the Minstrel find fit timber for his vessel? Who would cut it for him? Who would saw the boards, and who would carry them to the shore? The Minstrel could not do these things by magic alone. He must have help.

In a cave on the hillside there dwelt a brown dwarf, the last of the ancient race of earth men. He was small of stature, wrinkled, and old—so old that he himself had lost all reckoning of his age. Men called him Sampsa, and they told many a tale of his wisdom and cunning, and how in former times he had guarded the treasures of kings. His days were spent in the forest and his nights in the unexplored chambers of his cavern home. He knew by name every tree and shrub that grew in the Land of Heroes, and he understood the language of birds and of beasts and of every living thing. Who better than he could be the Minstrel's helper?

With a golden axe upon his shoulder Sampsa sauntered, singing, through the forest. To each slender sapling and to every beast and bird he said, "Good-morning!" and every bird and beast and growing tree returned the salutation. Presently the little man paused beside an aspen, smooth of bark, and tall and graceful. The tree trembled and every leaf upon it quivered when he held before it his sharp-edged axe with golden poll and copper handle.

"O master! O man of earth," it whispered, "what do you wish of me?"

"I am seeking timber for a boat," answered Sampsa. "The Minstrel is building a magic vessel to cruise on northern seas, and he has sent me to find a tree from which to make the beams and keel. May I have your trunk, my friend?"

The aspen groaned, and every one of its thousand leaves seemed to have a tongue as it softly murmured: "Surely, I am not fit for boat timber. My branches are hollow; a grub has eaten my heart. My wood is soft and pithy; it would never float upon the water. I pray you, pass me by, O master!"

"You speak well," said the dwarf; "stay where you are and enjoy the soft breezes from the sea. Whisper your light songs to the birds, and let them nest among your branches. I will look elsewhere for boat timber."

He shouldered his golden axe and trudged onward, deeper and deeper into the forest. In a secluded valley between two mountains, he found a pine tree, green and slender and beautiful. He struck it lightly with his sharp axe-blade, and every needle on its branches shrieked as though in sudden terror.

"Why so rough, good Sampsa?" asked the tree, bowing its head and bending before the little master.

"Friend pine tree," he answered, "how will your trunk do for boat timber? The prince of minstrels, Wainamoinen, has sent me to find some for the magic vessel he is building."

"My trunk is not fit for such use," said the pine tree, speaking loudly. "My wood is knotty, gnarly, scraggy, hard to fashion in any manner. It is brittle, unsmooth, easily split and broken. It would make but a poor boat."

"It would make good beams and a fine mast," said Sampsa.

"But very unlucky, very unlucky," answered the pine. "Three times this summer a crow has sat on one of my branches, croaking misfortune and foretelling disaster."

"Then fare you well, my evergreen friend," said the dwarf, kindly; "I will look elsewhere for my boat timber"; and again he shouldered his axe and resumed his walk through the forest.

It was noon and the sun shone hot on land and sea when he came to a giant oak tree on the summit of a green hill. This oak tree had long been the monarch of the woods. Its branches reached out on every side nine fathoms from the trunk, and its topmost twigs seemed to brush the sky.

"Good-morning, friendly oak tree!" said Sampsa; and a tremor of joy ran through every leaf and branch as the noble tree answered, "Good-morning, master!"

"Our friend, the Minstrel, is building a boat," said the dwarf. "He wants good timber with which to make the beams and the keel and the boards for the hull. He would have it broad and high and very swift. He would have it beautiful and graceful and strong. But as yet he has found no wood that is fit."

Then from every leaf of the great tree there came a sound of music, a song of joy; and the acorn-bearer answered, "O master, I will gladly give him of my wood. It is tough and stout and free from knots and worm holes. The grain of it is straight, and no other wood can equal it for withstanding the weather and the salt sea-water."

"That is good," said the dwarf; "but what omens of good or evil are yours?"

"Omens of good fortune are written on my branches," said the oak. "Three times this summer a cuckoo has rested on my topmost bough. On every clear day, sunbeams have danced among my leaves. On every clear night, the silver moon has looked down and smiled upon me. And so I pray you to take me for the Minstrel's magic vessel. I long—oh, I long! to float on the blue-backed sea, to carry treasures from land to land, to fight with the storm and conquer the waves."

Forthwith, the earth man smote the oak with his magic axe, and the tree uttered a cry of joy as it fell prone upon the earth. Then with skill and great patience Sampsa hewed and cleaved and shaped it into beams and boards, more in number than he could reckon. He planed them, he sawed them, he fashioned them with infinite care until each was of the proper length and thickness. And when, at last, all were finished, he carried them out of the forest, one by one, and laid them on the beach where the Minstrel had directed.

"Behold, O singer of songs!" he said. "Here is the wood for your magic boat. These are for the beams, these for the keel, and these for the well-shaped hull. May the fairy ship float lightly upon the waves and bear you whithersoever you desire to go! May it be a joy to the sea and a wonder to all the world!"

The Minstrel thanked him and then began to chant the magic spells by which to put the beams and boards in their places. These, one after the other he sang, and he recited the runes whereby to shape the whole into a stanch and swift-sailing vessel. With one song the keel was fashioned; with a second the gunwales were laid; with a third the boat's ribs were fastened in their places; with a fourth the rudder was hung at the stern. No hammer was used, no axe nor mallet; but every nail and spoke and bolt was driven by a word of magic from the lips of the prince of minstrels.

At length every spell was recited, every rune was sung, every magic word was spoken, and the wonderful vessel was completed—all except the nailing down of the three long boards at the bottom of the hull. The Minstrel stood aghast—without three words more his boat could not be launched; it could not be made water-tight; it would never skim the foam-capped waves of the northern seas. He stroked his chin, he tapped his forehead with his forefinger; no word of magic, not even the shortest, could he call to memory.

"How unlucky I am!" he cried. "Misfortune follows me, and all my wisdom is in vain. Never can my task be finished unless I can find the three words of power that are lacking. My plans will fail utterly."

He sat down upon the white sand and pondered upon the troubles that confronted him. For five summer days he sat there—yes, for six long days he tarried by the shore not knowing what to do. And the little ripples on the beach laughed at him, and the sea birds flapped their wings in his face, and he felt himself to be helpless.

On the seventh day a white swan flew down as though inspecting his boat, a gray goose made its nest under the well-hung rudder, and a flock of swallows sat twittering upon the gunwales. "Ah! Perhaps the words that I need so badly have been stolen by some of these birds. Perhaps they are concealed in the head of a swan, in the brain of a goose, or under the tongue of a swallow. I will examine into this matter and see."

The next day, therefore, he took his bow and arrows and went hunting. He slew a whole flock of swans; he killed great numbers of geese; and hundreds of swallows fell, pierced by his unerring weapons. But in the brains of all these creatures he found not a single word, nor yet so much as the half of one;

and under the tongues of the swallows, there was nothing uncommon.

The Minstrel was not wholly discouraged. "Perhaps the missing words are beneath the tongue of some four-footed animal," he said. "Perhaps a squirrel, perhaps a summer reindeer, or perhaps a gray and skulking wolf is hiding the precious secrets in its throat or between its jaws. I will search and find out if this be true."

So, for nine days—yes, for ten days of terror—he went stalking hither and thither through the woodlands and the meadows and the boggy thickets, shooting every timid creature that his eyes could see. He slew an army of squirrels; he killed a field full of reindeer; he slaughtered gray wolves without number. Cruelly, as one devoid of pity, he filled the forest with sorrow and death. He found strange words in plenty, groans and shrieks and cries of pain, but among them all there was not one syllable of magic.

At length he ceased his bloody work, he laid his weapons down, grief overcame him, and sorrow for the destruction he had wrought. All night long he sat on the sand beside his unfinished boat and bemoaned his evil fortune. All day he wept—but his mind was strong within him, and he would not give up his undertaking. On the second day, as the sun rose red above the hilltops, a raven flew croaking among the trees. "Caw! caw! caw!" cried the bird of ill-omen.

"Stop your cawing! Stop your crying!" shouted the Minstrel, full of anger. "Did Tuoni send you hither to taunt me? Begone! Return, I say, to your master, Tuoni!"

The bird flapped its wings, and Wainamoinen heard from far in the forest the echo of his words, "Tuoni! Tuoni!"

Then a strange thought came into his mind. He leaped to his feet, he clapped his hands, he shouted his oft-repeated maxim: "None but cowards say, 'I dare not!'"

"You speak truly," said a voice beside him—it was the voice of Sampsa, the little man of the woods: "You speak truly; and since you are not a coward, what will you next dare to do?"

"Far away, on the world's edge," answered the Minstrel, "there is a land of silence and fear, the Land of Shades, the kingdom of Tuoni. Many men have travelled thither—heroes not a few, woodsmen, fishermen, even fair women and tender children—but never has any one returned to tell of that land. All things that are lost, all things that are forgotten, are stored away there; they lie in King Tuoni's treasure house waiting for the day when all things will be remembered. The three magic words that I desire are hidden there—the raven, Tuoni's bird, has reminded me of it by his croaking."

"And will you dare to go thither and get them?" asked the dwarf.

"I will dare," answered the Minstrel.

XIII. THE LAND OF TUONELA

Tuonela—the Land of Shades! Does any one know where that country lies? On what chart is its location shown? Where are its boundary lines, and what is its extent?

Many are they who have gone thither—some by land, some by sea—yet none have returned to tell others of what they have learned. They who once enter that mysterious land may not hope to depart therefrom, neither must they send word home to their kindred and friends. They are thenceforth the subjects of King Tuoni, and must abide forever with him.

Is the place very far? Is the road thither a long one? Is it difficult to find?

Oh, the distance is great, but all roads lead to that land. You may arrive there quickly, in a day, in an hour, perhaps even in the twinkling of an eye—and quite before you expect to do so. You need not inquire the way nor ask about the road—you cannot fail to find it; and sooner or later you must walk in it, whether you wish or not.

The Minstrel's journey was both long and hard,[1] for he had undertaken it of his own free will. The road was exceeding rough, and perils beset him at every step. Dark were the forests through which he passed; broad and deep were the rivers which he crossed; high and rugged were the mountains which reared themselves before him. For six days—yes, for seven painful days he

---

[1] See Note E, at the end of this volume.

toiled through the thickets of thorns; for seven eventful days he cut his way through a magic wilderness of hazel; for seven other days he groped through dark hedges of juniper and tangled masses of wild briars; and then, for three times seven days he wandered through desert lands and wide wastes of snow where there was no shelter from the storm and no place to rest his weary feet.

Three score and ten days, three score and ten nights, were the measure of his journey; and at length he found himself on the shore of a mighty river, deep, dark, and sluggish. He looked, and on the farther side he saw a gray castle and a long white shore, and he knew that it was Tuoni's land—the land of silence and of mystery. He walked up and down the river bank, hoping to find some way to cross, but the water was everywhere deep, and the current, although sluggish, was everywhere strong. At length, however, he saw a sort of landing-place, where was a post for mooring a boat, and at the top of the post was a sign-board with words painted upon it:

FERRY TO TUONELA

CALL TO THE KEEPER ON THE FARTHER SHORE;
THE KEEPER WILL QUICKLY FERRY YOU O'ER.

Wainamoinen stood upon the sand and shouted with all his might:

"Ho! Keeper of the ferry! Bring thy boat quickly. Here is a traveller who desires to be carried over the water. Haste thee hither!"

The unwonted sound of a human voice rolled thunderously across the river, stirring the sluggish stream to its very depths; it awakened the echoes in the distant colorless hills of Tuonela, and with deafening roar broke the silence of ages.

The water-door of the castle opened, and a dwarfish maiden came forth, looking inquiringly across the river. Very small she was, but well-shaped and comely. Her eyes gleamed like lightning and her face was stern and pitiless. She was the daughter of Tuoni, and to her belonged the duty of keeping the ferry whereby the shades of mortals were carried to her father's kingdom. Sharply, and in shrill, cutting tones, she answered the call of the Minstrel:

"Who are you who calls so lustily? Why have you come to this river with body so strong and active? Tell me truly if you would be ferried to Tuonela."

The Minstrel was old and cunning, and because he feared to tell the maiden the truth, he answered her with guileful words: "I am a poor woodsman from the Land of Heroes. Yesterday, as I was felling a tree, your father, Tuoni, smote me. He smote me and made me his thrall; he made me his thrall and bade me come hither to his kingdom. This is why I stand on the shore and call to you so lustily."

"You speak falsely!" cried the dwarfish maiden, with anger in her tones. "If my father had made you his thrall, he would be with you now. His hat would be on your head and his gloves would be on your hands. His mark would be on your forehead and your voice would not resound like thunder upon the water. Tell me who you are, and tell me truly, or never will I ferry you to Tuonela."

But Wainamoinen still trusted in his cunning, and he made up another guileful story to deceive her. "Perhaps it was not Tuoni who sent me," he said. "Now that I think of it, it was Iron who smote me. Sharp Iron, pitiless Iron in shape of a sword pierced my heart, and I was forced unwillingly to seek the kingdom of Tuoni. So come, I pray you, and ferry me over the river."

The dwarfish maiden could scarce contain herself for anger. She smote the air with her fists and shouted, "Now I know that you are a liar! If Iron had smitten you I would see blood trickling from your wounds; your face would be scarlet; your hands would be crimson. But there you stand unscarred, unmarked, with the hue of health upon your cheeks. What do you hope to gain by trying to deceive me?"

"Far be it from me to deceive you," said the artful hero, foolishly and without judgment. "O daughter of Tuoni, I will tell you the truth! Now that I think of it, I am quite sure that it was Water that sent me hither. I was a fisherman, and I sailed too far from the shore. The deep sea overcame me, and the raging waves seized me, and when my breath failed me and my strength was gone, Water commanded me to come quickly to Tuonela. So, hasten, I pray you, and row me over the river."

The sharp-eyed daughter of the king was furious. With savage looks and threatening gestures, she answered the cunning Minstrel: "O foolish fellow, why do you tell such falsehoods? Do you think that I will believe you? If the waves had overcome you, if Water had sent you, your coat would be wringing wet and your wan face would be overspread with moisture. How, then, do you stand so proudly, your hair dry, your cheeks glowing, and your clothing untouched by dampness? Tell me the truth, for you will gain nothing by falsehoods."

The foolish Minstrel listened, and his heart grew stubborn. Then he answered her with flattering words, deeming that thus she would be pleased and therefore easily deceived. "O lovely keeper of Tuoni's ferry, speak not so harshly to a lone, weary, traveller! Never have I seen such beauty as yours; never have I heard a voice so sweet. And now I will tell you truly why I have come hither. I am the victim and the thrall of Fire. Three days ago I was seized by Fire, the elder brother of Iron. Very roughly did he handle me, and little mercy did he show. And this is why my clothing is dry and my hair untouched by dampness. So, sweet lady, hasten to be kind and carry me over the ferry."

Tuoni's daughter trembled now with rage and shame. Her patience was wellnigh gone, she no longer felt pity for the aged traveller. Yet she answered him once again and in tones decided and severe:

"O foolish, foolish fellow!" she said. "If Fire had seized you and sent you hither, your hair and beard would be singed, your eyebrows would be scorched, your feet would be blistered. Three falsehoods you have told me—yes, four barefaced lies you have shouted across the water. Now, beware that you tell me not another. Speak with clean lips and say truly why you have come hither with healthy body and with red heart beating lustily."

Then Wainamoinen saw that it was vain to practice deceit with one so skilled in the ways of life and death. So he

answered her truthfully and half-ashamed: "I pray you, pardon
the slippings of my tongue, for my heart does not lend itself to
falsehood. Months ago I began to build a magic vessel in which
to sail the northern seas. With one song I laid the keel, with
another I framed the gunwales, with a third I fastened the ribs
in their places. All my tools, my hammer, my auger, my saw, my
chisels, were words of magic. But, when my work was almost
finished, lo! my tools failed me. Three smooth holes still
needed boring, three strong bolts still needed driving, three
broad planks still needed fastening—and I lacked the three
mystic words with which to do these things. So I have come
boldly to Tuonela to borrow the tools which I desire so
greatly—the three lost words that shall make my boat seaworthy and safe. This, fair maiden, is the truth!"

"Stupid fellow!" cried Tuoni's daughter. "You have neither
wit nor wisdom. Have you lived to be an old, old man and yet
never learned that the liar is sure to be discovered? And now
that you speak the truth, do you think that you deserve any
favors from me?"

"I deserve nothing," answered the Minstrel, humbly, con-
tritely, yet cunningly. "I only pray you to do me a great, although
undeserved, favor. Come and ferry me over the water."

The dwarfish maiden hesitated, standing beside her boat.
Then in half-sad tones, as though in pity, she said, "You do not
know what you ask, foolish hero. Never has any one who came
to my father's palefaced country returned to home or friends.
This river being once crossed by you, you can never cross again.
Turn back while you can, and think not to visit my father in his
strong castle. Hasten away, and seek your own home and kindred ere it is too late."

The Minstrel heeded not her warning; for never had he abandoned a task once begun.

"I am old," he said, "and many are the perils I have faced and
many the dangers I have escaped. I am not a woman that I
should say, 'I cannot'; I am not a coward that I should say, 'I dare
not!' So, come now, tiny daughter of Tuoni. Come, and quickly
row me over your ferry."

The maiden said not another word. She leaped into her boat, she seized the oars, and with lightning speed she crossed the river. The broad, flat-bottomed vessel grated against the shore where the Minstrel was standing; he saw that it was roomy and large, and he stepped quickly aboard, not looking behind him. Then, instantly, and without sound, ten thousand shades who had been waiting unseen and intangible on the shore, glided also into the boat and stood beside him. The tiny maiden received each one silently, taking note of every mark or sign or other means of recognition. When all were safely aboard, she again seized the oars and with swift and sturdy strokes rowed her strong craft across the stream.

"Farewell, brave but foolhardy hero!" she said as the boat touched the farther shore and Wainamoinen leaped out upon the beach. "None but the prince of wizards could thus have come to Tuonela; and yet there is no magic strong enough to save you from your doom."

But the Minstrel was undaunted. He buckled his girdle about him, and with long strides hastened toward the great house which he knew must be King Tuoni's palace.

At the door the queen met him and softly welcomed him. "Come in, most honored of guests!" she said. "Never before has a living hero dared to cross this threshold."

She led him into the broad hall, she seated him on soft cushions, she threw a mantle of finest cloth over his shoulders. Then she brought him food and drink, and bade him refresh himself and be joyful. But when he lifted the covers of the enticing dishes, and when he looked into the foaming pitchers, what did he see? Vile things in plenty—the poison of serpents, the spawn of toads, shiny lizards, squirming worms—a medley of horrors indescribable and foul.

"I thank you, mighty queen," the Minstrel said politely, "but my errand in Tuonela permits neither eating nor drinking. No morsel of food will I taste until I have made known the business that brings me hither."

Then in a few words wisely spoken he told her plainly, truly, the object of his visit.

The queen listened, and her ashy-pale face grew palor still and an unpitying smile overspread her joyless countenance. When he had finished she answered him briefly and sternly:

"Truly there are magic words in plenty stored up in Tuoni's treasure houses; but they are neither sold nor lent nor yet given away. The king imparts his knowledge to none; the secrets of his kingdom remain unknown forever. Rash man! You have come hither uninvited; you shall not soon depart."

Even while she was speaking she began her spells of enchantment. She waved her wand of slumber and chanted strange runes never heard on this side of the dark water. Softly, very softly, she began to sing a weird lullaby—a song of the silent land. And Wainamoinen neither spoke nor made resistance, but, wrapping his cloak about him, he laid himself down to sleep on the dread couch of King Tuoni.

XIV. THE HAG OF THE ROCK

Silently, stealthily, Tuoni's queen glided from the room in which the Minstrel lay asleep. Hastily she went out from the castle, furtively she glanced backward over her shoulder as though fearful of pursuit. Down to the river-side she went, nor did she pause or slacken her speed until she came to a sudden turn in the shore where a huge ledge of rock jutted far out into the stream.

An old, old woman, gray-eyed, hook-nosed, wrinkled, was sitting on the rock and busily spinning.

"Hail, O Hag of the Rock!" said the queen. "What are you spinning to-night?"

"What am I spinning?" answered the Hag. "I am spinning the thread of many a man's life. For those who are honest and true and deserving, I spin joy and honor and length of days; for those who are false and cruel and selfish, I spin grief and punishment and an early journey to Tuoni's kingdom."

"Yes, yes, I know!" cried the queen impatiently; "but what kind of thread do you spin to-night for that rash, foolhardy man who has come into our kingdom unbidden and before his time?"

The old woman paused in her spinning; her fingers twitched uneasily, her thin lips grew thinner still, and her gray eyes shone with phosphorescent light. Then she asked hoarsely, "Is there such a man?"

"There is," answered the queen; "and he sleeps now on Tuoni's couch, in the great hall of our dwelling. He is old, his hair is snow-white, wrinkles are beneath his eyes; yet he is wise and fearless, and his limbs are strong. He would fain return to

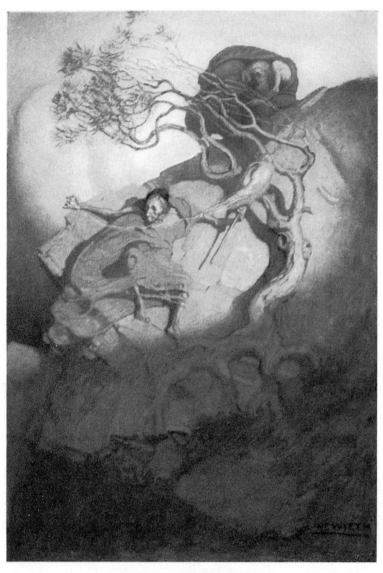

THE HAG OF THE ROCK
An old, old woman, gray-eyed, hook-nosed, wrinkled,
was sitting on the rock and busily spinning.

his own country, carrying with him the secrets that none should know save those of Tuoni's household."

"That he shall never do!" cried the old woman, fiercely, savagely. "No man, whether hero or slave, shall ever recross our river to tell his friends and countrymen how matters fare on this side of the stream."

"But he is very wise; he possesses many powerful runes; he is master of many magic spells," said the queen. "My cunning may detain him for a while; Tuoni may hold him for a season; but it is not given to us to destroy him. I would that we might keep him here forever—one hero in the flesh among a myriad of formless shades!"

"Leave that to me, sweet queen," said the spinner soothingly. "I will hedge him about with prison walls and perils through which he can never escape. His doom is fixed."

Then, without deigning to speak another word, she resumed her spinning. But the threads were not of the sort she had spun before. She twirled her spindle to the right, and drew out threads of iron; she twirled it to the left, and wires of copper, small but exceeding strong, ran through her fingers; she twirled it upward, downward, and a thousand coils of twisted metal soon lay in the moonlight beside her.

Higher up, on the same ledge of rocks, an old wizard was sitting—a grisly, misshapen creature who, in times long past, had been a counsellor of kings. This wizard had but one hand, and on it were three long and crooked fingers, fearful to behold, which he used in weaving nets. As fast as the Hag of the Rock spun threads of iron, wires of copper, or coils of twisted metal, he would gather them up and intertwine them together, making a fabric both pliable and strong. Thus, in that short silent night of summer, he wove a hundred broad nets of iron—yes, a thousand small-meshed nets of twisted metal.

At length the Hag of the Rock cried, "Enough!" and the Wizard of the Rock ceased his weaving.

"Now spread your nets cunningly wherever a fish may attempt to swim," said the hag.

So the wizard, with his hard and crooked fingers, stretched them, one by one, across the river; he stretched them, this way and that, along the sullen stream; he stretched them all around the gray-peaked island, the kingdom of Tuoni. Nowhere in the darksome water did he leave an open space through which a shiny fish could wriggle. How, then, would it be possible for a living man, a breathing hero, to escape through this wall of nets so closely woven and so cunningly spread?

By and by the day began to dawn. The sun rose pale and sickly above the ashy-gray hills, the lonely woodlands, and the empty plains. Its garish light fell upon the face of the Minstrel and woke him from his slumber. He sat up and looked around, scarcely remembering where he was.

How fearful was the silence! How ghost-like seemed the very air! A dreadful horror seized him, his blood ran cold, his heart seemed frozen.

Then suddenly and with great effort he leaped to his feet and fled from Tuoni's hall. The gates were open and unguarded, and he ran out into the fields, into the vast unknown beyond. Terror pursued him, and new horrors came into view at every moment of his flight. On each side of the way he beheld yawning chasms filled with yellow flames. From beneath rocks and from crevices in the earth snakes peeped out, licking with fiery tongues. From every tree hideous creatures looked down and grinned at him.

The wind blew strong and cold, yet made no sound. The trees swayed back and forth as though rocked by the fiercest of storms, yet there was silence everywhere. The Minstrel could not hear his own footfalls as he ran blindly, aimlessly, among traps and snares, and through a wilderness of perils. At length, however, his tongue was loosened in prayer; it moved in his mouth, but uttered not even a whisper.

"O Jumala, the mighty!"—these were the words which the Minstrel tried to frame. "O Jumala, the mighty! O Jumala, ruler over all! O Jumala, Jumala! Help me, save me!"

And Jumala heard where there was no sound; for he led the hero straight to the river's bank, he showed him how to avoid every snare, and how to escape every peril. With the courage of despair, Wainamoinen leaped into the dark water and swam with hasty, sturdy strokes toward the shore of safety. He swam not far, however, for the nets of wire rose up against him—the nets of twisted metal which the three-fingered wizard had spread to catch him. He tried to avoid them. He turned this way and that, he dived into the black depths of the stream, he sought everywhere for an opening through which he might pass. But the meshes were fine; the nets were laid close together; there seemed to be no way of escape.

Again he called upon Jumala the mighty; and then he bethought him of all the magic he had practised erstwhile in the Land of Heroes. His voice came to him, and he muttered a spell of enchantment; he recited the runes which no other wizard knew; in the midst of the whelming waters he cried aloud and sang weird songs to charm the evil powers that were seeking to entrap and destroy him.

The old net weaver, the three-fingered wizard, heard him and came swimming out into the sluggish stream; with his gaunt and hideous fingers he seized one net after another and tore the meshes apart; he made a way between the wires through which the Minstrel might squeeze his by no means slender body.

Why did the grim Wizard of the Rock thus undo his own work? In the spells and songs which Wainamoinen uttered, the maker of nets had found his master; the power of magic had overcome him; naught could he do but obey the will of the mighty Minstrel.

And the Minstrel was glad when he saw that his enchantment had worked his deliverance. He uttered still another magic spell, and suddenly his body became slender and sinuous like that of an eel or water-serpent. Then, with ease and quickness, he squirmed and glided, this way, that way, through the broken meshes and between the nets so cunningly spread. Across the broad stream he labored; through a thousand narrow holes he squeezed and clambered; and, at length, wearied exceedingly, he reached the shore of safety and climbed panting upon the dry, warm, throbbing land of the living.

"O Jumala, I thank thee!" he cried. "Grant, mighty Jumala, that no other man shall be so rash, so foolhardy, as I have been. Grant that no other hero may ever see the sights that I have seen, or feel the fear that I have felt. Not for gold, nor for power, nor for lost words of magic, should any mortal dare to trespass upon the forbidden realms of King Tuoni."

XV. THE HERO'S RETURN

It was midwinter in Wainola, and the shortest day of the year. The sun had not been able to rise above the horizon and short was the interval between night and night. The North Wind came hurtling over the sea, carrying the storm spirit in his arms. He buried the earth in snow and filled the air with blinding frost. He roared on the hill-tops, and shrieked in the tree-tops, and threatened to overwhelm everything that stood in his way.

But, safely sheltered in their low-roofed dwellings, the villagers thought but little of the turmoil out-of-doors. They sat gossiping and nodding beside their cheerful hearth-fires, and were glad that their lives had been cast in the pleasant Land of Heroes. To sleep, to eat, to rejoice together in the hour that was their own—this, to them, was the sum of all happiness—and this, too, is wisdom.

Suddenly, far down the snow-drifted road, a sound was heard which was not the noise of the wind, a cry was heard which was not the voice of the storm spirit. It was repeated again and again, each time a little nearer. Men heard it and ran to their doors to look out and listen. Women left off their knitting, they forgot their baking, and peered out wonderingly, into the gloomy twilight. Again the call was heard. It was the call of a human voice; but by whom was it uttered? Was it the cry of a stranger, or was it the shout of a home-coming hero?

Presently, some of the watchers saw in the distance a dim figure battling with the storm, struggling through the heaped-up snowdrifts. Friend or stranger, it mattered not, this man needed help. A dozen heroes ran forward to save him, a dozen strong arms were stretched out to succor him—and lo! to the wonder and joy of all, they perceived that it was Wainamoinen, their honored neighbor, their best-loved countryman. His face was haggard and worn, and his body was bent with weariness from long journeying and much buffeting with the storm.

"O sweetest of singers! Is this indeed you?" cried his rescuing friends.

He could answer them not a word, so feeble had he become; his eyes grew suddenly dim, and he fainted away in their arms.

They lifted him gently; they carried him to Ilmarinen's dwelling and laid him on his own bed. There the master Smith and his mother, Dame Lokka, did all that they could for his comfort. They covered him with soft robes, they wrapped his half-frozen feet in warm flannels and chafed his icy hands between their own cheer-giving palms. Then, as he gradually came to himself, the good matron brought him that which would satisfy his hunger. She fed him warm milk of the reindeer, food most nourishing; soups and gruels she also gave him till his strength revived. All this and more did these kind people do for the returning hero—gave him rest and quiet, asking no questions, saying nothing, suffering no one to disturb him.

On the third day the poor man rose and sat in his old accustomed seat by the fire—he seemed quite well and strong. Then the neighbors flocked in to see him. They came by twos and threes—men, women, and children—and each one brought him some gift to cheer him in his illness.

"Why did you leave us, O best of singers?" they asked. "We have missed you sadly, and great was our fear that we should never see you again."

"O my friends," answered the hero, "it is only through Jumala's goodness that I am here! For surely I have been in dreadful places, I have seen dreadful sights, I have suffered dreadful hardships."

"Tell us about it," cried both men and women. "Tell us of the dreadful places in which you have been. It will ease your mind and make you stronger."

"My friends," then answered the Minstrel, "I have been to the land of Tuonela. Oh, whisper not that name, breathe it not to your children or to one another! For it is a land indescribable, full of terrors, full of fearful creatures. Many heroes have gone unwittingly to Tuoni's kingdom, but none have ever returned. O my friends, pray now to Jumala, the almighty! Pray that the day may be far away when you shall cross the dark river into that unnamable region."

He could say no more. His friendly neighbors saw how sadly the memory of his journey distressed him, and they asked no more questions. They talked of the storm, of their household affairs, of their children, of Ilmarinen's latest work in smithing; and all thoughts of the dark river and Tuoni's kingdom were banished from their minds.

Days passed, and strength returned to the hero minstrel. Soon all his ancient courage came to him again, and the happy habits of by-gone days were resumed. Again he sat with the master Smith through the evening hours, and pleasantly discussed the charms of the Maid of Beauty; again in every dwelling he was a welcome visitor, and his voice was heard singing the sweet songs of the older times; and again the children of the village clustered round him to listen to his words of wisdom and to be taught the lore of the ancients.

"Now, every child of Hero Land, listen to me," he would say. "Here are five rules for you to remember—yes, six which you must write down in your hearts and never, no, never, forget:

> Honor father, honor mother;
> Kindly bear with one another;
> Help the helpless, cheer the friendless;
> Let your deeds of love be endless;
> Cheat your trusting neighbors never;
> Speak the truth, and speak it ever.

Obey these rules, my children, and you will be happy. And when the time comes for you to cross the dark river you need have no fears of King Tuoni, for messengers of light will lead you into the valley of rest prepared for the good and the true. Pray earnestly to Jumala to help you."

XVI. THE WISDOM KEEPER

At length the South Wind came again and stripped the earth of its white snow mantle. The wild geese returned to their old haunts in the sheltered inlets and reedy streams, and the voice of the cuckoo was heard in the groves of poplar. Joyful then were the voices of the children as they sought for the first wildflowers in the woods, and jocund were the songs of maid and matron as they bustled hither and thither, caring for the house, caring for the garden, caring for the lambs and the young reindeer.

Very early one morning, the Minstrel went out secretly to the place where he had sought to build his magic boat. There, high on the shore, the unfinished vessel lay, its hull of oakwood smooth and flawless, its prow of copper gleaming in the sunlight. Only three things were lacking to make it ready for the launching—three magic strokes to drive the three bolts that would fasten the three planks which still hung loose at the bottom of the hull. The Minstrel looked at the fair boat steadfastly; he viewed it from this side and from that, and then hot tears came into his eyes and trickled down upon his beard. He threw himself headlong upon the ground, and groaned with anguish.

"Ah, my beautiful, my beautiful one!" he murmured. "Who would believe that for the lack of only three words thou shouldst lie here forever, unnoticed, unfinished, forgotten? Alas! I shall never see thee skimming over the waves; thou wilt never carry me to Pohyola's dreary shores; thou wilt never bring the Maid of Beauty hither to be queen of my house and the joy of my heart!"

Suddenly he sprang up, startled by a voice. He looked around him, and, half hidden among the brushwood, he saw the dwarfish earth man, Sampsa, standing with cap in hand, his small eyes twinkling.

"Master, why do you grieve so sorely?" asked the little planter of the forests.

"O friend and gentle helper," answered Wainamoinen, "I grieve for the lack of three words with which to finish my magic vessel. Do you know where they are? Can you tell me how to find them?"

The little man came out of the brushwood and stood on the sand beside the unfinished boat. He pointed with his right hand towards the forest and the blue hills beyond it, and spoke in low, half-whispered tones as if revealing a forbidden secret:

"Far away, near at hand, in his own large realm of mystery, lies the giant Wipunen, the Wisdom Keeper, whom men sometimes call Nature. He is wiser than all wizards and stronger than all strong men. From him you may learn a hundred wisdom words—yes, a thousand volumes of wisdom words—if you will only do that which is required to earn such great knowledge. Go, find him and ask him for what you need."

"But how shall I go, not knowing the road? Where is he to be found?"

"The footpath to his kingdom is a magic highway," said the earth man. "It lies deep, deep in the forest, and you must travel far upon it. First, you must walk long leagues upon the points of needles. Then your feet must press upon the sharpened blades of a thousand swords. Lastly, you must pick your way between the points of glistening spears and the edges of gleaming battleaxes. Have you the courage to undertake the journey?"

"Courage!" cried the Minstrel. "Did I not once venture even to cross the dark river that divides our world from Tuoni's kingdom? Why should I talk of courage?"

"But Wipunen will not tell you his secrets willingly," said the dwarf. "You must overcome him in fair battle, and then he will whisper sweet words of magic into your ear. If you fail in the contest your life will be forfeited. Will you take the risk?"

"Trust me for that," said the Minstrel fearlessly. Then he

thanked the earth man heartily for his counsel, and with hopeful steps hastened to the smithy where Ilmarinen was toiling beside his flaming forge.

"Friend and brother," he said, breathing fast with eagerness, "I have come to ask your help. I am going on a journey to find some lost words that are very necessary to a minstrel. I am going to seek the mighty giant, even Wipunen, the all-knowing. He it is who understands every secret and who keeps the key to all the mysteries of earth and sky. I doubt not but I may obtain the words from him."

"You need not travel far," answered the Smith. "Wipunen the giant lies all around us, under us, above us. He dwells in the fields, he rests in the forests, he sings in the brooks, he abides in the deep sea. You are a wise man, my brother. It is strange that you should have lived so long without becoming acquainted with this mighty power."

"Nay, nay!" cried Wainamoinen impatiently. "The Wipunen that I seek dwells in his own kingdom, far from the haunts of men. I know him, and I know of the footpaths which lead to his distant abode. Waste no more time in idle talking. Ask me no questions; but if you love me make for me the things I must have for my journey. Make two shoes of iron for my feet, and a pair of copper gloves for my hands, and a slender spear of strongest metal to be my weapon. Do this for me promptly, quickly, for I am impatient to be gone."

Ilmarinen answered not a word, but hastened to obey. He heaped fresh fuel upon his fire and turned again to his bellows and his forge. All that day and all that night the smoke rolled black from the smithy chimney, and the hammer and anvil sang continuously their sweetest song. And lo! at sunrise time on the second day the work was done.

"Here, my dearest brother, are the shoes, the gloves, and the slender spear—the best that were ever made," said the Smith. "Take them, and may they speed you on your way!"

The Minstrel thanked him; and when he had donned his strange armor of iron and copper he started on his perilous journey. With the aid of Sampsa, the forest planter, he found the footpath to Wipunen's kingdom. Narrow indeed it was, and crooked, and intricate; but for one whole day—yes, for two days and even three—he followed it, never swerving. On the fourth day, he ran for leagues upon the sharpened points of needles; but his shoes of iron protected him. On the fifth day he toiled over the upturned edges of mighty swords; but his gloves of copper turned them aside that they did him no harm. On the sixth day he dodged one way then another to escape the cruel points of spears and the gleaming blades of battleaxes. And lo! on the seventh day, he came suddenly upon the great giant himself, lying prone upon the earth amid the vast, eternal solitudes— lying prone upon the earth and gazing upward into the solemn sky and the unmeasured depths of infinity.

Old, yes older than all other things, was this mighty Wipunen, the Wisdom Keeper, the guardian of the world's secrets. On each of his shoulders an aspen tree was growing; his eyebrows were groves of birches; willow bushes formed his matted beard. His eyes were two crystal lakes of wondrous depth and clearness. His mouth was a yawning cavern flanked by teeth of the whitest marble. And from his nostrils came a sweetness like that of the gentle South Wind after it has passed over vast gardens of early violets.

Filled with wonder and awe, the Minstrel drew nearer. Then he saw that in one of the giant's hands was a casket wherein were contained the magic songs of all the ages, while in the other lay the golden key to the mystic house of knowledge. He peered into the half open, cavernous mouth of Wipunen, and lo! on the tip of his tongue were the wisdom words of every people and clime.

"Rise, O master of magicians!" cried Wainamoinen, boldly, loudly. "Rise, O fountain of knowledge! Make me a partaker of your wisdom. Give me I pray you three words of magic power— three words that I lack and greatly desire."

But the giant heeded not. He lay motionless and silent, gazing steadfastly into the heavens and framing new thoughts of beauty and power to add to the treasures of wisdom that were in his keeping.

Then the Minstrel grew impatient and shouted his prayer still louder. He raised the sharp spear which Ilmarinen had fashioned, and struck the giant fiercely, forcibly. He struck him in the side, not only once, but twice—yes, nine times, ten times—without fear or pity. With the tenth stroke the Wisdom Keeper quivered and turned his head and, in tones mightier than thunder, began to sing.

He sang of the birds and the flowers, of the vast forest and the eternal hills, of the boundless sea and of still waters in sunny places. He sang of the heroes and the wise men of ancient days; he sang of youth and age, of good and evil, of life and death. Then he raised his voice still higher, and the music of his words was echoed from the four corners of the sky. He sang of the creation: how the earth arose in the midst of the waters; how the forests were planted and the wildflowers were taught to bloom; how the monsters of land and sea and the timid creatures of the fields and woods were given life; and lastly how the sky was shaped and the sun and moon and twinkling stars were set in their places.

All day, from dawn till evening twilight, and all night, from darkness till morning sunlight, the mighty Wipunen sang without ceasing. For two whole days—yes, for three long summer days—his singing continued. And such was the spell of his song that the moon stood still and listened, the stars danced in the northern sky, and the deep sea hushed its murmuring. Never before had such music been heard, never since has any song been sung that equalled it, and never so long as the world endures shall man again listen to words so sweet or to harmonies so divine.

And Wainamoinen? He sat entranced by the side of the mighty singer and laid each word of song deep down in the treasury of his memory. He learned not only the three wisdom words which he had sought so zealously, but a thousand others of rare beauty and splendid power.

"O mighty master!" he cried, when at length the singing ceased. "O matchless giant of the solitudes! I have found what I desired, I have received priceless gifts of which I never dreamed. Lie still now and rest again in the silent loneliness of your chosen kingdom. Rest till some other eager, earnest, querying learner shall venture hither in quest of wisdom. I give you thanks, thanks, thanks; for well I know that you desire no other fee. Farewell!"

Then, without more ado, he hastened homeward through the forest. Swiftly as a red deer when chased by wolves, swiftly as a sparrow on the wing, he glided over the hills and marsh lands till at last he came again to Wainola and the smithy of Ilmarinen.

"Welcome, welcome, daring brother!" cried the master Smith. "Did you find the Wisdom Keeper in his own mysterious abode? Have you learned the three lost words so necessary to your business?"

"Yes, yes, dear comrade!" answered the joyful Minstrel. "Not only three words have I learned, but a hundred; and a thousand wonderful secrets do I know—secrets which the master of knowledge whispered in my ear."

"How fortunate you are!" said the master Smith, "and your good fortune shall be ours also; for I know that we shall soon hear some wonderful new songs from your lips. Perhaps, also, you will tell us all about those strange bits of wisdom which you have acquired from the mighty keeper."

"Perhaps!" answered the Minstrel.

XVII. THE LAUNCHING

All night long the Minstrel lay open-eyed upon his bed, sleepless and alert. He called to mind all the wisdom words that he had learned from great Wipunen; he repeated them softly, one by one, and his heart swelled with pride when he thought of the power he had gained by listening to the song of wisdom. Then he thought of his neglected boat, lying high upon the shore and waiting for the finishing touches which he was now prepared to give. And when he remembered his object in building it he chuckled to himself, feeling that finally there was nothing to prevent the carrying out of the plans which he had cherished so long and so earnestly. Yes! he would finish the magic vessel, and he would sail forthwith to the Frozen Land and win the Maid of Beauty for his queen!

Very early in the morning he arose. The swallows under the eaves had not yet begun to twitter at the approach of day. The cuckoo was silent in her nest, and the cattle were slumbering in their paddock. Scarcely was there a tinge of yellow in the eastern sky—the day was so young.

The Minstrel rose quietly and stole out of the house very cautiously—so cautiously that the dogs who were sleeping by the doorway were not aroused. Hastily he made his way to the seashore, the day growing brighter with every step. Impatiently he ran to the secret spot where his magic boat was lying.

"O little ship, so stanch, so strong!" he cried. "You shall no longer lie there unfinished and useless. Soon you shall float on the waves, the South Wind will caress you, the deep sea will welcome you."

He walked slowly around the little vessel, looking at it lovingly from every side. Three times he walked around it, three times he drew a magic circle about it. Then, slowly and in commanding tones, he uttered the three words of power which he had learned at so great cost of time and trouble. Three times he pronounced them, and immediately the three holes were bored, the three bolts were fitted therein, and the three last planks were fastened in their proper places: the hull was finished, the boat was water-tight and seaworthy.

The Minstrel looked at his finished work and was pleased—but he was not yet satisfied. The hull was bare and unadorned, the copper prow was rough and unshapely, the deck was uneven and uninviting. The boat as a whole was not beautiful.

"O little ship," he said, "wherefore are you so crude, so rough, so ill-finished? Do you think that I know only three words of magic? I know a hundred—yes, I have a thousand which I caught as they fell from the tongue of Wipunen, the mighty master. You shall hear some of them and profit by them."

Thereupon he began to sing one of the strange, weird, wonderful songs that he had learned from the Wisdom Keeper; and as he sang, strange changes came over the magic vessel. First, the prow was overlaid with sunbright gold and its forward part was beautifully carved and shaped into the form of a swan with outspread wings. Then the deck was covered with plates of shining silver ornamented with figures of birds and beasts and little fishes. Finally, the broad, well-shaped hull and the gunwales, fore and aft, were painted in bright colors—blue and yellow and scarlet—and the slender mast was coated with snow-white enamel. And now, like a queen clad in her gorgeous robes, the little vessel sat upon the sandy beach and smiled at the morning sun and the rippling waves of the sea. She looked so beautiful, so grand, that the Minstrel clapped his hands and shouted for excess of joy, and the songs and words of the mighty Wipunen fell faster and louder from his lips.

Very earnestly did the Minstrel sing, and gradually his tones became sweeter and lower and more persuasive, like the murmuring of the waters on a peaceful summer morning. The song was of the sea, it seemed to come from the sea. It was as if the waves were calling gently, ever so gently, to the little vessel waiting on the shore:

> "Come, come, O magic boat,
> Come, and on the billows float!
> Come to the wrinkled sea and glide
> With swiftness o'er its rolling tide."

Soon there was a sound of creaking, rumbling, scraping—a sound not loud, but distinct and growing stronger. Then, gracefully and with dignity, like a princess on her wedding day, the little ship glided across the shelving beach and in another moment was floating lightly, smoothly, nobly upon the water.

The Minstrel, still singing and still reciting his magic spells, had already climbed upon the deck. He now lifted the mast in its place; he hoisted the sails—one red and one blue—and spread them to the winds. Gracefully and proudly, like a great swan on some quiet lake, the little vessel glided away from the shore and was soon moving swiftly along the borders of the boundless sea. Wainamoinen sat down at the stern, and with his long oar guided her northward, never losing sight of the land, never going far from the shore. As the magic boat speeded onward, cutting the waves with its gilded prow and dashing the white spray to left and right, the Minstrel's heart glowed with joy and pride. He lifted up his voice and sang a prayerful song to the mighty powers into whose keeping he had ventured to intrust himself.

> "O great Jumala let thy arm
> Protect this little ship from harm;
> Make its weak captain brave and strong,
> And listen to his humble song.

> "Sweet South Wind, whispering soft and low,
> Come fill these sails and gently blow—
> Breathe mildly while the storm winds sleep, *
> And waft us swiftly o'er the deep.

"O restless Waves, be kind, I pray
To this small craft while on its way;
Drive it along with gentle force,
Let nothing swerve it from its course."

Thus did the Minstrel sing as he sat at the boat's stern and guided it along its watery path. The sea was calm; the waves were sleeping; the winds breathed very softly on the sails of red and blue. The fairy vessel glided onward, steadily, proudly, towards its goal in the distant North.

XVIII. THE MAID OF THE MORNING

The voyage was scarcely begun. Close on the starboard side appeared the headland of Wainola; directly in front lay the bar, a long, narrow, pebbly beach, jutting far out into the deep sea. Like an old and skilled seaman, the Minstrel suddenly changed his vessel's course, veering sharply towards the west in order to pass round the low-lying barrier. But, just as the boat was gliding through the shallow water near the end of the bar, the wind ceased blowing. The sails hung useless from the mast; not a breath of air was stirring; scarcely a ripple could be seen on the face of the sea. The fairy vessel hesitated, then stopped stock-still not forty paces from dry land.

Was the South Wind angry? Why should she treat the prince of minstrels in this ungrateful manner? But Wainamoinen did not stop to argue; he was too wise to find fault with wind and weather. He looked on this side of the little ship—nothing but water, growing deeper and deeper and stretching away and away to the blue horizon. He looked on that side—the shallow water, the narrow bar, and beyond it the great northern sea and the winding shore which marked the way to the Frozen Land. Then quickly he seized his other oar, and thrust it out over the gunwales.

He was preparing to row the boat around the bar, when suddenly he was startled by hearing his name called, not harshly, but in tones of friendship and inquiry. He looked up. His face grew red with confusion, his lips trembled with vexation; for, right before his eyes, he saw one whom he by no means wished to see.

Midway between the boat and the sandy, pebbly bar a maiden was standing knee-deep in the quiet water. Her head was bare, save for the long, dark tresses that fell in profusion over her shoulders and dipped their ends into the wavelets that were playing modestly above her bare white ankles. Her cheeks were red—red as the dawn of a summer day. Her eyes were dark—dark as the midnight hour in winter. One of her fair hands was raised to shade her face from the glaring noonday sun; in the other she held a bundle of long silken ribbons which she had been washing in the sea.

"O Wainamoinen!" called the maiden. "O hero of the sea, do you know me?"

"Truly do I know you," answered the Minstrel; and, pulling in his oar, he dropped it with a crash upon the deck. "You are Anniki, the maid of the morning. You are the sister of my dearest friend, the master Smith. It was only yesterday that we sat together at the table of your good mother, Dame Lokka. So, why should I not know you?"

"Well," said the maiden, and she laughed while speaking, "memories are sometimes short, and even a minstrel may forget. Aren't you glad to see me?"

"Indeed, your face should make the surliest of men happy," answered the gallant Minstrel; "but, tell me, what errand has brought you hither? Why are you here, so far from home and all alone?"

"Oh, this is our wash day," laughed Anniki, and she danced in the water until the white bubbles floated all around her. "See these ribbons that I have just cleaned. See the clothes that are spread on the sandy beach to dry. There are still others hanging on the bushes a little way up the shore. Don't you think that I am *in-dus-tri-ous?*"

"Surely, Anniki; and you deserve to be the wife of an industrious man. I wonder how any maiden can do so much washing in one short morning."

"Well, I get up early," said the maiden, pirouetting in the shallow water. "I was here at the break of day, and not a minute have

I been idle since. But now my work is done and I'm going to play. Tra-la-la!"

The Minstrel stood on the deck of his becalmed and motionless ship and looked at her. His face betrayed both wonder and vexation, and he muttered to himself: "She is a witch and I know it. She has done more than wash clothes. It is she that has lulled the South Wind to sleep and halted my voyage at its very beginning. She will spoil all my plans."

Suddenly Anniki paused in the midst of her dancing and cried out, "O Wainamoinen! Where are you going in that fine boat?"

The Minstrel frowned, he pursed his lips, vexation filled his heart. Then he answered curtly, "I am going around to the great north bay to fish for salmon."

Anniki shrieked with laughter, "Do you think I'll believe that story?" she said. "I know something about salmon fishing. Father and grandfather used to go out often in the season for catching such fish. Their boat was a plain one—no golden prow nor silver-plated deck nor rainbow-colored sail. It was full of nets and snares and other tackle. The decks were littered with poles and lines and fishing spears. The smell of fish filled the vessel and floated thick in the air around it. Oh, I know something about salmon fishing!"

Then she danced another gleeful dance, splashing the water over herself and over the Minstrel, and making little waves that rocked the fairy boat to and fro but did not stir it from its place. At length, growing tired, she spoke again:

"O Wainamoinen! Everybody says that you are wise and truthful. Now tell me truly, where are you going in that beautiful boat?"

"I am on my way to the quiet inlets of yonder northern shore," said the cunning Minstrel. "In those pleasant waters many wild geese abound, and there they build their nests and rear their young. It is fine sport to lay traps for those red-beaked waterfowl, and better still to shoot them on the wing. I hope to fill my boat with the fat fellows, to carry a thousand home for winter eating."

"'Tis no such thing!" cried the maiden angrily, and she beat the water with her feet until the sea seemed boiling around her.

"Why, I know something about goose hunting. Father and grandfather used to go out often in the wild-goose season. Then their long bows stood ready, tight-strung, at the prow of their swift rowboat. They kept a fine bird dog always tethered at the stern, and three or four puppy dogs ran whining about the deck. But where are your dogs, and where is your long bow? If you are wise and truthful, don't be foolish. I know you are not going to hunt wild geese."

"Perhaps not," answered the Minstrel, growing somewhat ashamed; "perhaps I am going after larger game. In the North a war is raging, the strong are oppressing the weak, as is usual in wars. I am sailing thitherward, hoping to do my part in the struggle and to lend my aid to those who deserve it most. The wild geese that I shall capture are the foes that I shall overcome in battle."

"'Tis no such thing!" again cried the impatient Anniki. "Why, I know something about war and battle. Father used to go out to fight for friends and country, to help the weak and worry the strong. He went in a large ship which required a hundred men to row it. A thousand men stood beside him, fully armed. Their shields hung all round the hull of the mighty vessel and a black dragon floated from the masthead. Their sword-blades clanged against each other and glittered in the morning light, and their winged helmets were like golden birds of victory resting on their brows. Oh, yes, Wainamoinen, I know something about war and battle, and you are not going on any fighting errand, I'm sure. You have in mind some trick of cunning, and you shall sail no farther in your pretty boat until you tell me truly what that trick is."

The wary Wainamoinen was too proud to be outwitted by a simple maiden, and so he tried another subterfuge. He answered her gently, persuasively, and his words were full of guile: "O wise and beautiful maid of the morning, I have been speaking to you in riddles, trusting that you would understand their secret meaning. Fain would I make everything clear, but I dare not tell it to you where you stand: the fishes would hear me and carry the secret to every corner of the sea; the birds would hear me and convey the news to every land under the sun."

"Then speak out, and be famous," said Anniki disdainfully.

"Nay, nay, dear sister! I would whisper it in your ear. The water is not deep, so wade out hither and sit by my side on this shining, silvery deck, and I will tell you the plain truth and a wonderful secret. I know your power, Anniki. I know that you have chained the winds so that they will carry me no farther on my voyage until you have learned what you wish. So why should I try to deceive you? Come hither and see the treasures that I have in my boat, and listen to a wonderful story."

The maiden retreated to the shore, splashing the water angrily at every step. When she reached the dry sand she turned and looked back at the puzzled hero and his little ship. Then she raised both of her hands skyward and cried out, "Yes, the winds are mine and they obey me. If you try again to deceive me, I will command the East Wind to fall upon your pretty vessel and sink it in the sea. If you fail to tell me the truth, I will cause the waves to rise up and swallow you! Do you hear?"

Great and powerful wizard though he was, the Minstrel felt himself helpless before this slender girl. He was conquered, and well he knew the folly of trying further to deceive her. So, speaking softly, gently, as becomes a vanquished hero, he proposed this modest bargain: "If I tell you where I am going and for what purpose, will you promise to waken the South Wind that he may drive my ship forward on its perilous voyage?"

"Yes, yes, friend Wainamoinen," answered Anniki, very generous as becomes a conqueror. "You shall have a fair wind and a smooth sea and my best wishes to the end of your adventure."

"Listen, then," said the Minstrel. "This little vessel is a magic boat, built of strange runes and words of wisdom. On it I am hoping to sail to that distant, dismal country of which you have often heard me talk—to Pohyola, the Frozen Land, where wild men live under the ground and eat each other. My errand thither is to woo the Maid of Beauty and bring her, willy-nilly, to the Land of Heroes where she shall be the mistress of my dwelling and the joy of my heart——"

"Does my brother know about it?" asked Anniki, open-eyed, anxious, still suspicious. "Did you tell Ilmarinen about your plans?"

"I told no one," answered the Minstrel; "neither must you do so, Anniki, for this is a secret voyage and if any person should learn why I have undertaken it, all will come to naught."

"Take care of your boat! The South Wind is awake!" cried Anniki, and the next moment she was running to the mainland with the speed of a deer. Her washing was left behind, where she had spread the pieces to dry; her ribbons were scattered upon the sand; even her shoes were forgotten, so hasty was her flight. Before the astonished Minstrel could think of anything to say, yes, before he could call to mind a single magic word, she had reached the higher ground and was lost to sight among the stunted pines and cedars.

XIX. THE UNEXPECTED JOURNEY

In his smoky smithy Ilmarinen was toiling alone, fashioning crude bits of metal into forms most delicate and beautiful. His face and arms were begrimed with sweat and black soot, his eyebrows were gray with ashes, his shoulders and head were besprinkled with dust and flaky cinders. Like a weird elf, or some uncanny dweller in the underworld, he stood in the lurid light of his forge and deftly wielded his heavy hammer. His bellows roared and his anvil tinkled sweet music, and a song burst from his lips as he welded and wrought and gave shape to wonderful things.

So busy, indeed, was the master Smith that he heard nothing, saw nothing, thought of nothing, save the work which he had in hand; therefore, when his sister Anniki came suddenly to the outer door and called to him, he did not hear her.

"Ilmarinen, dearest brother!" she repeated. But the Smith, invisible in the midst of the smoke, did not hear her. He kept on singing and hammering and blowing his bellows, altogether forgetful of everything save the work in hand.

Anniki called a third time, a fourth, "Ilmarinen! O Ilmarinen!" But the hammer continued to strike, the anvil kept on singing, the fire in the forge flamed higher, and there was no pause in the Smith's sweet singing. His thoughts were centred on the trinket he was forging and shaping, but his song was of a maiden in a faraway land.

Anniki called a fifth time. Then, losing patience, she ran

through the thick of the smoke and seized her brother's arm just as he was taking a fresh bit of glowing metal from the fire.

"Ho! little sister of the morning!" he cried in surprise. "What now? Have you finished your washing? Have you brought me something from the shore?"

"Yes, yes, dear brother!" she answered, still breathless from running and excitement. "I've brought you a great secret. What'll you give me for it? It's about Wainamoinen and the Maid of Beauty. Would you like me to tell it to you?"

"Well, if it's anything important I will listen," said Ilmarinen. "So, out with it quickly, before this piece of metal gets cold. Tell me your wonderful secret."

"Oh, but it is too important to give away," said his sister. "It concerns you, and the Maid of Beauty, and the Frozen Land, and the Sampo, and, and—Well, wouldn't you like to know what it is?"

"Tell me about it, Anniki."

"What will you give me if I do?"

"A kiss, dear sister."

"Bah! kisses are for lovers. Will you make me a finger ring?"

"I will make you a dozen."

"Of gold?"

"No, of iron."

"Fie, fie! None of your jesting"; and Anniki stamped her foot angrily, while she gave her brother a look which told him more plainly than words that this was no unimportant matter. "I tell you that the Maid of Beauty is in great danger. Now, if you wish to know more you must make me a gold ring—yes, six gold rings to grace my pretty fingers."

Pouting and haughty, she turned as if going away; but Ilmarinen held her by the hand.

"You shall have the six gold rings, my sister," he said—"yes, I will make you seven this very day."

"And four or five pretty girdles inlaid with silver?"

"Oh, certainly, Anniki—anything that you wish. But make haste and tell me the secret."

"Will you make me a pair of gold earrings with blue stones in them?"

"If your secret is worth so much."

"And a brooch of woven silver?"

"I will make it."

"And a golden comb for my hair?"

"I promise it."

"Then, if you will surely keep your promise, I will tell you all that I know, and tell you truly. Is it a bargain?"

Ilmarinen looked down into his sister's dark eyes and answered, "If what you tell me is worth anything I will give you all that you have asked for—finger rings, earrings, brooch, comb, and five or six beautiful girdles. If you are fooling me, you shall have no trinket nor ring nor precious jewel—for I will teach you not to hinder me with trifles."

"I bring you no trifles," said Anniki; "and I shall hold you to your promise."

Then, in a few words plainly spoken, she told her brother all that she had seen and heard that morning. She told him of the Minstrel's magic boat, and of the voyage which he had planned, and of his cunning scheme to gain possession of the Maid of Beauty. "And now, brother," she added, "why do you toil here in the smoke and the heat while your false friend is hurrying northward to rob you of the treasure that ought to be your own?"

"He shall not rob me," said the Smith coolly, earnestly. Then he heaped some more fuel upon his fire and blew his bellows till the flames leaped up to the roof of his smithy. "Anniki, your news is worth the price. I will fashion the pretty girdles for you, I will make the rings and the earrings and the brooch and the comb, and I will bring them all to you before the sun goes down."

"That's a good brother!" cried the maiden. "I knew you would do it. Now I am sure that a great resolve is in your heart, and you will do something worthy of your name and fame. How can I help you?"

"Hasten home and heat the bath house for me," answered Ilmarinen. "Heap the wood around the big bath-stones; put plenty of dry kindlings underneath, then lay hot coals around and make a roaring fire. Fetch water and fill the pails and tubs, for I shall need not a little of it. Make a handful of soap, for nothing else will cleanse my smoky, grimy visage. Got everything ready, and tell mother that I am going on a long journey."

"Yes, brother," said Anniki. "I know what is in your mind, and everything shall be done as you desire"; and then with hasty steps, smiling and proud, she ran out of the smithy and hurried to her mother's house in the village.

"Mother!" she cried, "Ilmarinen is coming home early to-day. I think he must be going on a journey, for he wishes to take a bath."

"Well, then, my daughter," said good Dame Lokka, "it is for you to make the bath house ready. Put plenty of wood around the bath-stones and build a roaring fire. See that the water is ready, and put everything needful in the right place. And you should see that his clothes are mended and brushed and fit for him to wear."

"Yes, mother!" answered the dutiful maiden.

Anniki ran into the forest and gathered armloads of pine-knots, dry and resinous and impatient to be burned. She carried them into the bath house and heaped them up on the big hearth; she brought hot coals from the kitchen and made a roaring fire. She filled the pails and the great kettles with water. She placed the bath-stones where they would heat the quickest. She dipped some sprigs of white birches in wild honey and threw them into the water. Then she ran again to the kitchen and brought a handful of reindeer fat. She mixed this with milk and ashes, and thus made a magic soap that was pure and white and cleansing.

"My brother will have a good bath when he comes home," she said. "It will not be my fault if he doesn't come out of it clean."

Meanwhile the master Smith was toiling steadily at his forge, making the ornaments which he had promised to give to his sister. First, he hammered out the finger rings of gold and the precious earrings. Then he made six girdles of rare and most wonderful beauty; nor did he forget the comb and the brooch and some golden pins which he knew would please Anniki's fancy. He finished all these quickly, skilfully. Then he raked the coals from his forge; he laid his hammer down in its place beside the anvil; he took off his leather apron and hung it on a peg; he went out of his smithy and closed the door behind him. With long, impatient strides he hurried home and laid the precious gifts in his sister's hands.

"Here are your wages, Anniki," he said.

"Oh, brother, I thank you," she answered. "They are even more beautiful than I expected. Now make haste and take your bath. The bath-stones are hot, and the fire burns low; your soap, your brushes, your combs—all are ready. And your best clothes, they are hanging on the pegs, close by the bath-kettle."

Ilmarinen surely needed a washing. Grimy with soot and gray with ashes, he quickly obeyed his sister. He stepped into the bath house. Out of doors the sun was shining; by the window a cuckoo was calling; in the air sweet voices were sounding. He looked, he listened, his heart throbbed with joy as he disrobed himself and poured the water slowly upon the red-hot bath-stones. Soon the house was filled with a mighty steam; the Smith was lost to view in the dense hot vapor.

An hour passed by, the sun went down, and at length the Smith came forth from his bathing. Who would have known him? Who would have thought that a bath could work such wonders? His hair was a golden yellow; his cheeks were as ruddy as cranberries in the late days of autumn; his eyes sparkled like two full moons when the sky is clear and the winds are at rest.

And he was clothed, oh, so beautifully! His coat was of linen, dyed yellow and beautifully embroidered by his mother. His trousers were of soft flannel, scarlet-colored. His vest was of crimson silk. His stockings, too, were silken and very long. His shoes were made of softest leather—leather tanned from the skin of a reindeer. Over his shoulders he wore a sky-blue shawl, thick and soft. Around his waist was a magic girdle fastened with gold buckles. His hands were incased in reindeer gloves of wondrous warmth and beauty; and on his head was the finest cap that had ever been seen—a cap which his father and grandfather had worn in their youth when they went wooing.

Anniki clapped her hands for joy when she saw her brother thus arrayed, and Lokka, his mother, threw her arms around his neck and wept for very pride and happiness.

"O my beautiful boy!" she cried. "Never was your father more handsomely dressed. Never was any bridegroom more fitly arrayed. Good luck to you! Good luck to you!"

Ilmarinen put her off gently, kissing her on the cheek and thanking her for her words of praise. "Now bring me the horse," he said. "Harness my trusty steed and hitch him to my enchanted sledge. I am going to the North Country, to the Frozen Land and the dreary shores of Pohyola. Long will it be ere I again return to home and country."

"Which steed shall it be?" asked the serving-man. "There are seven racers in your stables, all trusty and true—seven fleet-footed steeds of rare strength and mettle. Which shall it be?"

"The gray is the best," answered Ilmarinen. "Hitch the gray steed to my enchanted sledge. Put in food and feed for seven days' journey—yes, for eight days of wintry weather. Remember, too, the big bearskin and the soft fur robes to be wrapped about me, for in the North Country the air is always chilly and the winds are always cold."

"Everything shall be done as you wish, my master," said the serving-man.

Very soon the fleet-footed gray steed and the enchanted sledge were brought to the door. The soft fur robes, the skins of two great bears, blankets in plenty were put in their proper places; a jar of reindeer meat, a string of smoked herring, food for many days, were stowed beneath the seat; everything was done to speed the traveller on his way.

The hero had bidden his mother good-bye, he had kissed Anniki's lips and whispered a word of magic in her ear, and he had sent messages of love to all his friends. Now he stepped out of the door, clad in his beautiful garments, princely in form and bearing. He climbed quickly into the sledge and sat down upon the great bearskins. They wrapped the warm robes around him and put the long reins in his hands. The last good-byes were spoken. The hero cracked his whip, and the gray racer bounded forward and sped swiftly away. Like the wind he flew through the woods and the marshes and along the pebbly shores of the sea; and the heart of the brave Smith was cheered with courage and hope.

Then in the dim evening twilight the hero perceived six

cuckoos perched on the dashboard before him, and beside them seven small bluebirds were sitting. They had been placed there by the trusty serving-man, and now they all began twittering and singing, and the faster they travelled the louder was their sweet music.

"They are omens of good fortune!" cried Ilmarinen. "'Tis thus that the merry springtime journeys to the Frozen Land! Good luck, good luck, good luck!"

Then he cracked his whip again and shouted loudly, joyfully. The gray racer neighed shrilly and flew onward with redoubled speed. The waves of the sea rippled with joy upon the sands, and the very stars in the sky twinkled and danced as the enchanted sledge glided like a swift meteor toward the frozen North Country.

XX. THE FRIENDLY RIVALS

Northward, northward, along the low-lying seashore, Ilmarinen pursued his course, never pausing, never faltering. All night long he travelled in the moonlight and the starlight. All day, from dawn till evening twilight, his brave gray racer flew over the half-frozen earth; and the cuckoos chattered on the dashboard, and the bluebirds sang their sweetest songs. For two short nights and one long day the journey was continued with never slackening speed. Then, as the sun was rising on the second morning, the hero looked out toward the gray sea, and what did he behold?

Quite close to the shore, so close that Ilmarinen might have thrown a stone upon its deck, a little ship was becalmed in the smooth waters. Its prow was like gold, its deck was plated with silver, and its sails were of rainbow colors. The Smith drew hard upon the reins; his racer ceased speeding, and the sledge runners grated on the beach. A pause was made in the journey.

"Hail, ho!" shouted Ilmarinen.

The captain of the fairy vessel looked up. His eyes were full of wonder and his face grew sour with vexation.

"Hail, ho!" he answered; but there was no heartiness in his tones, the words labored in his mouth before they could escape from his lips, they fell coldly, like ice on a stormy shore.

"Whither are you sailing, brave Minstrel?" asked the Smith kindly, but with a sense of victory.

The Minstrel was overcome with surprise. The winds would not serve him, the waves would not waft him away from the shore. He felt that he was at the mercy of his pursuer. All his magic would not avail him. So he dissembled his feelings and with his tongue made glad answer while his heart was burning with disappointment.

"O my dearest friend and brother, how happy I am to see you! I have long been thinking of you, wishing for you; and fain would I have you as my companion to sail with me up and down this pleasant coast. Leave now your sledge and your travel-worn steed and come hither and sit by me on the deck of this fairy little vessel. The voyage back to Wainola will be as pleasant as a summer holiday."

"Never will I sail in your enchanted vessel," answered the Smith half angrily, and he rose in his sledge and shook the furry robes from his shoulders.

"Ah, Ilmarinen, prince of wizards," said the Minstrel, still flattering, still dissembling, "how like a prince you appear! Whither you are journeying so gayly, so fleetly, so like a bridegroom going to his wedding?"

"You know where I am going," said Ilmarinen. "All your cunning is in vain, friend Wainamoinen. All your magic shall come to naught, for you shall never steal the Maid of Beauty from her home land, never put her in your magic vessel, never carry her over the treacherous sea."

The Minstrel saw now that he was beaten; he felt that all his secret plans had been discovered, and so he concealed his bitter feelings while he acknowledged defeat. "Wisest of smiths," he said, "we are friends and brothers, and therefore we must not fall out and quarrel. Let us still be lovers as of old. I assure you, I swear to you, I will do nothing to offend you. Ride on and woo the Maid of Beauty, and I will return alone to our dear home in the Land of Heroes."

The heart of the Smith was touched by the generosity of his friend. He felt that he must not be less generous, and in an instant all his anger vanished.

"O brother, tried and true!" he answered, "I know the thoughts of your heart, I know your great ambition. Let us agree each to woo this maiden honorably as a man and a hero would woo her. Let her freely choose one of us, or let her a second time refuse us both. Do you agree to this, my elder brother?"

"Truly, I do," said the Minstrel heartily. "I promise—yes, I swear to you that I will do naught that is dishonorable or unfair. If the maiden shall prefer you, I will not be envious; for your good luck will be my good fortune, and my success will be your triumph."

"I thank you, Wainamoinen!" shouted the Smith, waving his hand.

"I thank you, Ilmarinen!" returned the Minstrel, bowing to his friend.

Then with speed each resumed his journey, one travelling by sea, the other by land. Swiftly the gray racer flew along the shore; fleetly the boat of magic skimmed over the wrinkled waters. The hills and forests rang with the clattering hoofs of Ilmarinen's wizard steed. The white waves danced and trembled in the wake of Wainamoinen's gold-beaked vessel. The cuckoos twittered, the bluebirds sang merrily, and the birchwood runners of the enchanted sledge whizzed over the sand and then glided through the new-fallen snow. The South Wind breathed on the sails of blue and red, and the West Wind whispered joy in the nostrils of the fleeting gray racer.

"Good luck to my steed, good luck to my sledge, good luck to me!" shouted the hero Smith. "O Jumala, kind protector, helper, guide! Be my safeguard in this journey, lead me rightly on my way!"

And the Minstrel, standing at the prow of his fairy vessel, shouted words of magic to the winds and waves, while he too prayed for guidance and help. "O Jumala, just and true, think not hard of me if I have gone astray! Pardon me if I have been false to my friend. Give me fair winds and a gentle sea, and guide me safely to my journey's end. Good luck to me, good luck to my boat, good luck to everybody!"

Thus the two heroes journeyed onward, the one by land, the other by sea.

XXI. THE BARKING DOGS

Springtime had dawned in the Frozen Land. The sun was riding high in the sky, and the air was balmy with the breath of the south. The snow had melted on the meadows, and the ice had floated out of the inlets. The sea was no longer gray and shivering, but pale blue and motionless. The wild geese honked noisily in the marshy lakes and sought their nesting places by the creeks. Swallows twittered under the eaves and cuckoos called to each other among the budding bushes.

On her couch beside the door Dame Louhi, the Wise Woman of the North, sat reclining. Very ugly she was, toothless and grim, wrinkled with age and altogether unlovely. The Maid of Beauty was busy at her housework, sweeping, spinning, baking, weaving. The doors were open and warm breezes from southern seas breathed through the low-raftered hall, playing with the deerskin curtains and with the maiden's silken hair.

Suddenly an uproar was heard, a sound feeble at first but every moment growing louder. It was not an unusual sound, but it was unusually disturbing, unusually persistent and annoying.

"What is that, my daughter?" inquired Dame Louhi, sitting up and listening.

"Oh, it is naught but the dogs barking," answered the maiden. "They are over at the fishermen's huts by the shore. Perhaps they see some beggar or wild man coming down the path from the forest."

The noise increased, it was spreading. It sounded as though a score of watchdogs were barking in concert.

The Wise Woman was disturbed and growing nervous. "Daughter," she said, "I never heard such barking. Surely something strange is happening. Go out to the gate, look down the road, and see what is the matter."

The Maid of Beauty heeded not, but kept right on with her household duties.

"Mother," she said, "I am too busy to bother with barking dogs. The bread must be baked, and this pile of wool must be spun, and from its yarn six new blankets must be woven this very day. I have no time to stand gaping at the gate, listening to the noise of barking curs."

The uproar increased. The ancient house-dog, infirm and toothless as his mistress, rose from his place in the ashes; he dragged himself to the door and set up a mournful howling.

"O my daughter, what indeed can be the matter?" cried the Wise Woman.

"I know not," answered the maiden.

In his hut beside the reindeer paddock the keeper of the herds was sitting. He was old and fat and lazy, and the noise of the dogs awakened him from pleasant reveries.

"Wife, wife!" he cried. "Do you hear that barking? Go quickly to the door and see what is the matter!"

But the aged woman kept on with her knitting. "I am too busy to run to the door every time a dog barks," she said. "I must earn something to feed our children, to clothe them, to keep them neat. I have no time to listen to the prattle of dogs."

Still the clamor grew and grew. The black watchdog in the courtyard of Louhi's dwelling joined his voice to the general uproar. He pulled at his chain and howled most dismally.

By the smouldering fire in his own small hut the head serving-man was sitting; his eldest son was working beside the door. "My son," said the older man, "do you hear the black watchdog? Surely some stranger is coming this way. Run out to the road and see what manner of man he is."

The youth kept on with his work. "I am too busy to listen to watchdogs," he said. "My axe is dull and I must grind it. The wood must be brought for the kitchen fire; and who will split it if I go running after dogs? Let old Growler howl; I have no time to bother with dogs."

Louder and still louder waxed the tumult. All the puppies, all the house-curs, all the sledgedogs, all the watchdogs were barking, baying, yelping, howling.

The head serving-man was greatly disturbed, and yet he liked not to rise from his seat, for he was old and his limbs were stiff.

"In my lifetime I have heard much barking," he said, "but never such barking as this. Perhaps the dogs have scented a bear escaped from an ice-floe; perhaps they see a band of robbers coming up from the shore. Kuli, my little daughter, listen to me!"

"What is it, papa?" answered the child, sitting still on the floor.

"Run out to the turf pile, Kuli," said her father, "climb up on the very top of it and look around. See what the dogs are barking at, and then run back quickly and tell your tired father."

"O papa, I am too busy," answered Kuli. "I want to play with my dolly; I want to put her to sleep. I have no time to run after dogs."

The head serving-man was perplexed, he was uneasy and half-way angry.

"Everybody is busy to-day," he said. "Nobody has the time to do anything. Nobody cares for the dogs and nobody cares for me. But I must find out what all the noise is about."

He rose from his seat, grumbling because of the pains in his joints. He drew on his boots, he pulled his fur cap over his head. Then he went stamping out of the door and across the broad yard. The black watchdog was still tugging at his chain, still howling dolorously. The old serving-man took notice of his actions.

The brute first pointed his nose towards the sea, then he looked far away at the meadows and the misty, mysterious hills. The serving-man did likewise. He looked seaward, then landward—but naught did he behold save, on this side, the blue water and the sloping shore and the fishermen's huts, and, on that side, the brown marsh lands and the long, winding, indistinct roadway that led nowhere and came from everywhere.

"How now, old Growler?" he said angrily. "Why is all this clamor? Why is all this tumult? Hush your barking, I bid you." But the beast still tugged at his chain, and all the smaller dogs joined him in a chorus of howling. Then the serving-man looked again and with greater care. On the broad face of the sea he discerned a strange speck, white, yellow, and scarlet, gliding swiftly landward, glistening bright on the blue and silent water. On the winding meadow pathway he saw another speck, scarlet, yellow, and blue, moving fleetly towards Pohyola, smoothly gliding like a flying bird.

"Oh, surely the dogs are right!" said the astonished man. "Here is cause enough for barking; plenty of cause for yelping and snarling. One stranger comes by sea, another comes by land, and the poor beasts have scented them both while yet they are far away."

A third time he looked this way, then that. He put his half-closed right hand to his eye and looked through it as men sometimes in these later days look through a spy-glass. Now he could see quite clearly; soon he could discern what manner of wayfarers those were that had caused the doggish clamor.

The speck upon the meadows was a sledge of many colors drawn by a fleet and tireless racer. The speck upon the waters was a fairy ship, its prow all golden, its hull bright scarlet, its sails blue and red.

"How strange!" said the faithful man. "Be it war or be it peace, I must hasten and warn the Mistress."

He found the Wise Woman at her door, gazing sharply at the sky, the sea, the earth, to learn for herself the reason for the unusual uproar. To her he told his story quickly, briefly, adding also a word of warning. The face of the woman grew grayer, grimmer as she listened, and in her eyes was a look of puzzled apprehension.

She called loudly, shrilly to the Maid of Beauty, now busy with her weaving, busy with the wool and the blankets.

"Daughter, daughter, do you hear?"

"Truly, mother, I hear the dogs," answered the maiden. "Let them bark if it pleases them."

"They bark because they have scented some strangers coming.

A ship is approaching by sea, and a wonderful sledge is bringing some hero hither by land."

"Oh, how fine!" said the maiden.

"But who can these strangers be? How shall we receive them? Shall we welcome them as friends or flee from them as foes?"

"I know not," said the daughter. "I know not why such strangers should come to Pohyola."

"Try the rowan branch!" croaked a voice from the dark corner beyond the hearth. It was the voice of old Sakko, the dwarf, the last daughter of the race of earth men. No guest came oftener than she to Dame Louhi's dwelling, no other was more welcome to the Wise Woman's table and fireside. "Try the rowan branch," she repeated. "The rowan branch is the sure omen that never fails. If drops of red sap ooze from it, then look for foes and trouble. If only clear water bubbles, hissing, from its tiny pores, then be sure that friends are coming bringing rich gifts and joyful tidings. Try the rowan branch."

"Yes, let us try the rowan branch," said the Mistress, anxious, uneasy, trembling with alarm.

Quickly the Maid of Beauty ran to the woodpile beside the door. With much care she chose a stick of rowan, straight, smooth-barked, and full of sap. She carried it to the hearth and laid it on the coals; then all stood round to watch it.

The brown bark crackled with the heat, it shriveled and began to burn. The smoke curled lightly upward, the coals grew redder, the heat of the fire increased.

"O thou magic branch of rowan, tell us truly, tell us quickly, who those are who come so swiftly—friends or foes who come so swiftly!" chanted Sakko, the dwarfish wise one.

"O noble branch of rowan, bring only friends. Let naught but clearest water ooze from thy pores so tiny," muttered the Mistress of Pohyola.

"O thou pretty branch of rowan, bring good luck, bring fortune only, bring peace to all who dwell here—bring joy to our home and home land," softly murmured the Maid of Beauty.

The smoke grew blacker, it curled round the branch of rowan, the green wood was growing hot amid the heaped-up coals. Then there came a whistling, sizzling sound, and the sap began to trickle slowly from the tiny pores. The dwarf Sakku deftly seized the heated branch and held it aloft that all might see the oozing drops.

"They are not red!" cried the Mistress, Dame Louhi.

"They are not clear water!" said the Maid of Beauty.

"I see only common sap," said the head serving-man.

"Nay, nay!" muttered Sakko, the dwarf woman. "They are neither crystal nor crimson, but sweetest honey. And what do the honey-drops tell? They tell us that these strangers are better than friends, that they are suitors and have come hither as wooers."

"Look again and tell me whom they will woo," said Dame Louhi.

Sakko lifted the branch again and turned it this way and that, carefully examining the sizzling sap. She listened to the shrill little sound that came from it.

"Three women are in this house," she said, "and one of them is she whom the strangers seek. Is it the Mistress? Her youth has fled. Is it poor Sakko, the earth woman? Never has she known a lover. Is it the Maid of Beauty, the rainbow maiden? All the world adores her."

She twirled the rowan branch once, twice, thrice in the air above her head, and then cast it upon the hearth, scattering the ashes to right and left and sending a cloud of cinders upward through the smoke hole.

"The strangers will soon be at your door," she croaked. "Be ready to welcome them."

"Truly, my daughter," said Dame Louhi, "it becomes us to give these heroes joy after their perilous journey."

"Yes, mother," answered the Maid of Beauty.

XXII. THE OLD MAN'S WOOING

Arrayed in becoming garments, the Maid of Beauty stood beside her mother. Together they went out from their weather-worn dwelling. They walked across the courtyard to the dry ground beyond, and to the heap of stones beside the seashore. The young grass was upspringing beneath their feet. The sunlight was beaming around them. The swallows were flitting above them. The lonely sea was before them, the lonelier meadows were behind.

The Mistress looked out over the water, and then she bade her daughter look. Not far from the land they saw the strange boat gliding. Its gilded prow was gleaming in the sunlight; its sails were flapping loosely on the slender mast; and who was the sun-browned hero that stood on the deck guiding the vessel with an oar of copper?

"I do believe it is that old, old Minstrel from the Land of Heroes," said the Mistress in tones of surprise. "You surely remember him, my daughter—how he came to us from the sea, how he sat at our fireside, how he ate from our table!"

"Yes, mother, I remember," answered the Maid of Beauty. "And he grew homesick, he pined for his own fireside, he longed to return to his kinsfolk and friends, and notwithstanding our kindness he sang not one song during all his stay with us."

"Just so," rejoined the aged one; "and you surely remember the noble reindeer and the swift sledge that I lent him, so that he might return to his home land?"

119

"Certainly, mother, there are some things that I can never forget."

"Well, my child," said the mother, "this is surely the same great hero, the famous Wainamoinen, the first of all minstrels. He is rich, and no doubt his ship is filled with treasures. If he has really come to woo you, treat him kindly, listen to his words of honey, and answer 'Yes' to every question; for never will you have a nobler suitor."

"But, mother, I like him not," answered the Maid of Beauty.

Then she turned away from the sea, weary of looking at the approaching vessel. Her eyes wandered to the bleak, brown meadows, and she gazed wistfully towards the pathway which led from the distant hills. There she beheld the other visitor, speeding forward, drawing nearer, and now in plain view from the spot where she was standing.

Young and proud and strong seemed this landward comer. He was sitting in a sledge of scarlet and driving a steed of rare swiftness. Six cuckoos were sitting on the dashboard, all loudly calling; and beside them were seven bluebirds twittering blithely as birds are wont to twitter in the joyous springtime.

"See, mother, here comes the other stranger!" said the Maid of Beauty.

"Nay, nay, he is no stranger," answered Dame Louhi, speaking hoarsely. "He is the poor young Smith who forged the Sampo for me, and his name is Ilmarinen. He brings no gifts, he has no treasures, for his only wealth is his little smithy. What business has he in Pohyola?"

"Perhaps he comes to claim his wages that are due him," modestly answered the dutiful daughter.

Then with haste the two returned into their dwelling; they closed the door behind them; the mother sat down in her seat beside the fire, and the daughter resumed her weaving.

"My child," said the Mistress, "our visitors are close at hand, they will soon be at our door. When they come in and seat themselves beside the hearth-stones, you must come forward and greet them. Bring in one hand a bowl of honey, and in the other a pitcher brimming full of reindeer's milk. Give these to the one whom you choose to follow. Give them to the rich and mighty

Minstrel. He will understand you and will reward you with gold and jewels and fine garments and other costly presents."

"But he is old and I like him not," answered the daughter. "I care nothing for riches nor for a man of too great wisdom. I will give the milk and honey to the younger man, to Ilmarinen, if in truth he has come to woo me. He is poor, but he is handsome and strong. Once before at your bidding I refused to go with him, but now——"

"Foolish girl and disobedient!" cried the mother, the red blood of anger rushing to her face. "Why will you choose to go with that penniless fellow—to bake his barley-cakes, to wash his grimy clothes, to wipe the sweat from his sooty face, to sweep his kitchen floor, to keep his tumble-down hut in order?"

"It is my fancy," quietly answered the Maid of Beauty.

Meanwhile all of the people of Pohyola, men and women, boys and girls, and even the barking dogs, had run down to the waterside to watch the coming of the little ship. Skilfully, with his oar of copper, the Minstrel guided it straight towards the place of landing. Gently, smoothly, like a mother swan swimming among her cygnets in some sheltered cove, the vessel glided into the quiet inlet. The rope that dangled from the prow was seized by helping hands on shore and thrown over the mooring post. The ship trembled as it was drawn in, it stopped, it rested in deep water close by the shelving bank.

Without loss of time the Minstrel leaped ashore. He made his way quickly to Dame Louhi's well-remembered dwelling; he opened the door and entered; he stood beneath the smoky rafters and received the greetings of the grim and toothless Mistress.

"Welcome, welcome, O sweetest of singers!" she cried. "Much have we missed you, long have we waited for you. Now you shall sit again at our fireside; you shall eat again at our table; you shall rest and rejoice by the sunny shores of Pohyola."

"I thank you for your welcome, wise queen of the North," responded the Minstrel; "but I cannot sit at your fireside, I cannot eat at your table, I cannot rest by your shores until I tell you the object of my visit, the reason for my coming."

"Speak then, most honored friend, and I will listen," said the cunning Mistress.

Wainamoinen bowed and smiled and thus made known his errand: "It is for your daughter, the Maid of Beauty, that I have come. Three years ago I saw her sitting on a rainbow and spinning threads of silver. I asked her then to go with me to the Land of Heroes, to be the queen of my kitchen, to bake my honeycakes, to fill my cup with barley water, to sing at my fireside. Now, I am here to receive her answer."

The Maid of Beauty rose from her weaving and came towards the hearth. In one hand she carried a bowl of honey and in the other a yellow pitcher brimming full of reindeer's milk; but she offered neither of these to the Minstrel. She smiled and said, "Have you built the boat that I required? Is it made from the splinters of my spindle and the fragments of my shuttle?"

"I have built a boat, but not that one," answered the Minstrel. "With the help of magic I have constructed a vessel more wonderful than your eyes ever saw—more beautiful than your dreams ever pictured. It is strong to resist the waves; it has two broad sails that it may fly swiftly before the wind; its prow is of copper overlaid with gold; its deck is floored with silver; in its hold are treasures more precious than I can tell. Will you not come and sit beside me on the deck of this fairy vessel? Will you not help me guide it over the trackless sea—guide it safely to the haven of Wainola?"

"I care naught for old men," replied the Maid of Beauty; "riches tempt me not; the magic vessel may never reach its haven. But wait a day, and——"

She looked up. Ilmarinen was at the door.

XXIII. THE FIELD OF SERPENTS

Yes, the master Smith was standing at the door. A hero, indeed, he appeared—tall, handsome, and brave. Over his shoulders was the sky-blue shawl which his mother had woven for him. On his head was the cap of his ancestors, and around his waist a golden girdle was buckled. His shoes of reindeer leather were highly polished and his stockings of silk were long and black. His embroidered coat was of yellow linen, very fine, and his trousers were of scarlet-colored flannel.

The Maid of Beauty blushed when she saw him; then her face grew white again, and again suddenly red. Her heart beat hard and fast, her hands trembled. Never in her life had she beheld a hero so finely clad, so perfect in form, so noble in feature. She would have swooned had not pride prevented.

"Poor men are always fond of gaudy garments," whispered the mother; and then remembering the law of the hostess she hastened to greet the unwelcome guest. She led the hero into the low-raftered hall and gave him a seat beside the smouldering fire. She stirred the coals and threw on wood; the flames leaped up and filled the room with brightness.

Then the Maid of Beauty came forward with the bowl of honey and the pitcher of milk, a smile on her lips and a sparkle in her eye. "Welcome, weary traveller!" she said. "Eat, drink, and be refreshed."

"Nay, nay," answered the hero. "Never under the silver moon will I taste of food till my desire is granted me—till I have leave to take and wed the maiden who is the desire of my heart."

The grim old Mistress grew grimmer still as she answered him: "When wilful maidens choose 'tis folly for mothers to refuse. But never should suitor win his bride too easily, lest doing so he prize her too lightly. The Maid of Beauty is waiting for you, Ilmarinen, but before you take her your courage must be tested, you must perform the task that I require of you."

"Name the task, and I will do it," said Ilmarinen boastfully as of yore. "Was it not I who hammered the sky? Did I not forge the Sampo and shape its lid of rainbow colors?"

"But this task is different," responded the Mistress, "and if you fail your life is endangered."

"Tell me what it is and I will perform it," answered the hero. "I will drain the sea, I will level the mountains, I will snatch the moon from its place in the sky if you so command me. I will do anything to win from you the great treasure, the priceless Maid of Beauty."

"No doubt the feats you name are easy," said the Mistress; "but I shall require a harder one. Before you are permitted to take the Maid of Beauty you must plough the field of serpents that lies in the barren lands beyond the forest of pine. Twelve furrows you must make lengthwise of the field, and twelve furrows you must make crosswise; and you must plough it deep, without touching either beam or handles."[1]

"I have heard of that fearful field," said Ilmarinen. "No man has ever yet gone into it and lived. It is more dreadful even than Tuoni's silent kingdom."

"Yes, one man has lived," then spoke the Maid of Beauty. "One man, in the old, old times, furrowed the field with a copper ploughshare drawn by horses of fire. The beam was of red-hot iron and the handles were of living flame. The name of that hero was Piru, and after he had performed his task he came from the field of horrors unbitten and unharmed. Surely, the task which he performed was hard, but if he succeeded why may not another hero do likewise?"

Ilmarinen made no answer. He rose silently, and with eyes

---

[1] See Note F, at the end of this volume.

downcast went out of the hall. His sledge was standing beside the door; the fleet-footed racer was pawing the ground; the cuckoos were calling, and the bluebirds were singing. He sat down upon the soft robes and took the reins in his hands. Then he looked up.

The Maid of Beauty was standing before him, her eyes were full of tears, her face betrayed the grief that was in her heart. Softly then the hero spoke to her:

"Tell me, princess of the rainbow, do you remember when I forged the Sampo and hammered out its lid of many colors? Then it was that I vowed a solemn vow. I swore by anvil and tongs, by hammer and smoke, by forge and fire, that I would some day win you to be my bride. Now, by the token of honey and milk, you have promised yourself to me. But your mother has set me a task that is full of peril. So, come now, maiden of the twilight. Come sit beside me in my sledge of magic, and I will carry you swiftly, safely to my own country, to my own dear fireside."

The Maid of Beauty drew back; her cheeks blushed crimson and her eyes flashed fire as she answered:

"Never will I wed a coward. Never will I wed without my mother's consent, for just punishment surely waits for disobedient daughters. You must plough the field of serpents, or I will never, never be your bride."

"The task is a hard one, it is full of peril," said Ilmarinen, as his courage came slowly back to him. "But I will perform it; I will plough the field of serpents, and no man nor maiden shall call me a coward."

"Then let me tell you something," said the Maid of Beauty. "You are a great smith and skilled in working with all sorts of metals. You are a cunning wizard and wise in magic. Your smithy still stands deep in the silent forest—the smithy which you built when you forged the Sampo. Go thither and make for yourself a golden plough wherewith to furrow the field of serpents. Make its beam of silver and its handles of red copper, and strengthen it throughout with spells of magic. Then go and do the task my mother requires of you."

"I thank you, maiden of the twilight," answered Ilmarinen.

Then he hastened to the gloomy forest and to the smithy strong and roomy, in which he had forged the magic Sampo. Again the bellows roared, again the flames leaped up in the ample forge, again the black smoke poured from the chimney top. And the Smith, with many a magic incantation, hammered out a golden ploughshare, he shaped the handles of copper and the beam of shining silver. A wonderful thing it was, slender and strong and well fitted for the work it was designed to do.

"Truly, with such a plough I shall not fail to stir up a host of hissing serpents," said Ilmarinen; "but how shall I protect myself from their fury while I am furrowing the field?"

He threw both fuel and metal into his forge, and while he recited one magic rune after another he thrust his long tongs into the roaring fire. Presently, when the smoke subsided and the coals were white with heat, he drew forth a great mass of half-melted iron. This he laid upon the anvil. With short, quick strokes he hammered it; he turned it and twisted it; he shaped it according to his will. He separated it into parts, and of each part he formed something that would be of use in the great task that was before him.

First he made a pair of iron shoes to wear upon his feet; then he forged ten long chains, slender and delicate, and these he wove together and shaped into pliant greaves to cover his legs. After this he wrought for himself a coat of mail, and gauntlets of iron, and strong gloves which no tooth nor sting could pierce. Then he made a belt of hardest iron, sky-blue and brilliant, to be buckled around his waist.

Lastly, in its place within the furnace, he hung the magic caldron from which he had once drawn the wonderful Sampo. Into this caldron he threw many strange and potent things: the hoof of a reindeer, the tail of a hare, a bag of wind, a flash of lightning, a shooting star. With these he made a mixture such as no other wizard had ever compounded, and as he stirred it he repeated the runes, the songs of mystery that he had sung while forging the Sampo.

All day and all night and far into another day the master Smith toiled and sang, blew his great bellows, and threw fuel into the furnace. Then with caution he drew the caldron from the flames, he lifted the lid and looked warily inside. At first nothing but boiling vapor, scalding steam, shapeless white clouds could be distinguished. The next moment a horse sprang out, beautiful, shapely, and strong. Its body was glittering bright like fire, its mane and tail were glowing red like the sun when it shines through the mists of the morning. It leaped out and stood, docile and obedient, beside the mighty wizard, the master Smith.

"What will you have me do, my master?" it asked.

"Draw my plough through the field of dreadful serpents," answered Ilmarinen.

"I am ready," said the horse.

Forthwith the hero harnessed the fiery steed to his plough of magic. He donned his coat of mail and drew on his greaves and his shoes of iron and his wonderful gloves which no weapons could pierce. Then he drove with speed, out through the shadowy pine woods and across the desolate plains, till he came to the field of serpents—a barren waste lying cold and dreary under the empty sky.

The field was full of horrid reptiles, crawling, writhing, hissing. They reared their heads high and looked at the hero, they licked out their tongues and threatened him. But he, no whit afraid, paused in the midst of them and spoke these words of warning:

"O ye snakes, so vile, so wise! Jumala made you, and therefore you are not wholly bad. Put your proud heads down, quit your hideous hissing, cease your wriggling and your writhing. Creep away into the bushes, hide yourselves in your loathsome dwellings. Dare not touch me, dare not threaten me, lest Jumala smite you with his swift and flashing arrows!"

Then fearlessly he drove his steed of fire through the dreadful field, and skilfully he guided his golden plough, touching neither beam nor handles. On this side and on that the earth was heaped up, nor did rocks or roots stand in the way of the cleaving ploughshare. The serpents were lifted from their holes, they were torn in pieces, they were buried deep in the ground. Twelve mighty furrows did the hero plough lengthwise of the field, then, turning, he made twelve other furrows across the width of it. No barren spot nor stony space was left unturned, no blasted shrub nor baneful vine was unuprooted. Thus the haunts of the serpents were broken up, and the field of dread was made fertile and safe, a fit place for trees to grow and grass to flourish.

The last furrow was completed, and Ilmarinen rested from his labor. He loosed the long reins with which he had guided his steed and lifted the plough from the ground. He spoke lovingly to his faithful helper:

"O wonderful plough-horse of fire! Your task is finished and you are free. Go! Fly away! Henceforth you may wander unrestrained in the boundless pastures of the North."

The horse bounded away. It rose in the air, higher, higher, until it looked like a cloud of fire-dust floating in the sky; then it faded away and Ilmarinen saw it no more. But it did not remain invisible; for often, even in our own times, it may be seen during the silent winter nights leaping and prancing, shaking its fiery mane and shooting beams of golden light athwart the northern sky.

Ilmarinen tarried not a moment. With long, impatient strides he hastened away from the field of victory. For two weary days he travelled through trackless ways and along forgotten paths where bears used to amble and wolves pursued their prey. For three long and painful days he toiled among bogs and fens and across the lonely, never-ending meadows. On the sixth day, however, his eyes were gladdened by the sight of the shores of Pohyola and the weather-stained dwelling of the Wise Woman of the North. Pale and wan and weak from hunger and long exposure, he approached the house and opened the door.

The Mistress was reclining upon her couch beside the hearth.

XXIV. THE GREAT PIKE

"Ah! Who is this?" cried the Wise Woman, rising quickly. Surprise leaped from her narrow eyes, disappointment sat in her loveless face. "Is this the young man who went out to plough our field?"

"The field is ploughed," humbly answered Ilmarinen. "I have performed my task and now I come to claim my own—the Maid of Beauty for whom I have waited and toiled."

"Who saw you plough the field of serpents? Who saw you perform the dreadful task? Am I to believe your word alone?" And wise Dame Louhi spoke harshly, gruffly, as one who has never been defeated or denied.

Then, from the dark corner beyond the hearth-stones, suddenly a voice croaked like the voice of a sea-bird breasting the storm. And out of the gloom emerged the dwarfish form of old Sakko, the last and the wisest of all earth women.

"I will be the hero's witness," she croaked. "Unknown to him, I was hidden close beside the field of deadly serpents. I saw the young man perform his task, and he performed it well. Twelve broad furrows he made towards the east, towards the west; twelve other furrows he made towards the north, towards the south. The ground was heaped up, deep trenches were made. The serpents reared their heads, they ran out of their holes, hissing and dismayed; they were overwhelmed and destroyed; not one remains. Give the hero his prize. Give him the duckling for whom he has risked so much."

"No, no!" answered Dame Louhi, graver, grimmer than ever

before. "Any man can kill snakes. Shall this poor Smith have my daughter for performing so paltry a task as that? No! no! But there is another task which perhaps he would like to try—an undertaking worthy of a hero, although I fear too difficult for this young man!" She spoke tauntingly, bitterly, unkindly.

Then Ilmarinen's boastfulness returned, and he answered proudly, fearlessly: "Never yet was there anything too difficult for me. Did I not hammer out the sky and set the stars where they belong? Did I not find Iron in his hiding places and subdue him? Did I not forge the Sampo and shape its lid of rainbow colors? Harder things than these will I do if only you will surely give me your daughter."

"Listen then," said the cunning Mistress. "In the dark and sluggish river that surrounds the land of Tuonela there lives a monstrous fish, a pike so huge, so scaly, so fierce that all the fishes of the sea obey him. Hundreds of brave fishermen have sought to snare him, but not one has lived to tell his story. Go, now, and capture this king of fishes. Take him without using net or tackle and bring his head to me. Then I will surely give you my daughter; you shall have the blue-winged duckling; you shall wait no longer, toil no longer, but be at once rewarded with your prize."

The hero heard and deep dejection came upon him. He hung his head, he turned away and walked slowly, silently out into the darkening twilight. He sat down on the rocks by the shore and looked out over the cold and pitiless sea.

"Now, I may as well die," he said. "This last task is impossible. For how can any one, without net or tackle, catch and subdue the Great Pike? and how can I hope to drag him from the sluggish water and bring his head hither to the Mistress of Pohyola? Vainly have I lived, vain have been all my valiant deeds, vain indeed is life with all its empty victories; there is naught that is worth the doing."

Suddenly he heard light footsteps behind him, suddenly the darkness was dispelled and the smiling Maid of Beauty laid her hand upon his shoulder.

"O Ilmarinen, prince of wizards, smith of all smiths!" she said, "Why are you so despondent? The task is not so hard as you imagine."

"But I cannot perform it," said the hero. "I dare not attack the Great Pike in the dismal stream of Tuonela."

"Only women say, 'I cannot,' only cowards say, 'I dare not,'" laughed the maiden cheerily. "You see I have learned a lesson from your elder brother, the prince of minstrels. Now I will tell you how to catch the Great Pike of Tuonela. Go at once to your magic smithy and forge a fiery eagle with flaming wings and iron talons. Then sally forth upon your errand; have no fear, but be wise and valiant."

Ilmarinen would have replied, but she had vanished. He buckled his armor about him and with right good courage hastened to his smithy. There for many days he toiled at his forge; for many days he watched the magic caldron in the midst of his glowing furnace; for many days he tried all his wizard arts, singing strange songs and reciting secret runes which only the wisest may ever know. At length one morning he drew the caldron from the fire and lifted the lid.

"Art thou there, my eagle?" he cried.

Quickly from the clouds of scalding vapor a wonderful bird leaped into being. Her wings were as large as the sails of a ship, her claws and beak were of the hardest iron, her eyes were like flaming fire.

"Here I am, my master, what will you have me do?"

"O, my eagle," answered the Smith, "carry me swiftly towards the land of Tuonela, fly with speed and pause not till the sluggish, silent river is beneath you. Then find for me the Great Pike, so huge, so scaly, the king of all the fishes. Help me take the slippery monster from its lair beneath the waters."

The wonder bird spread her wings and Ilmarinen leaped up between them and seated himself upon her back. The bird screamed and began her flight. Up, up, up into the high air she soared. Then, swifter than the wind, she sailed straight onward, towards the mystic island and the dark and dismal river. How far did she fly? No man can tell; for none can know whether Tuonela be in this place or in that, whether it is one day's journey distant or an hundred. From the graybeard it is only a step, a stone's throw, a short walk at most; from the babe upon the floor it may be a thousand weary leagues removed.

At length, however, the goal was reached and the flaming eagle stayed her flight. She swooped down and perched herself upon a rock which overhung the shore. Beneath it flowed the sluggish river, dark and dismal and deathlike; beyond lay the shores of the silent land where Tuoni reigns; above it was the ashy-gray sky where no bird flies and no star has ever twinkled. Upon this rock the eagle sat and watched for her prey, and Ilmarinen waited patiently beside her.

By and by from the black mud at the river's bottom a water sprite arose. It rose quickly, it leaped high into the air and with its long fingers clutched at Ilmarinen. Then, indeed, would the hero have met his death had not the eagle saved him. She seized the fearful sprite by the head; with her iron talons she twisted the creature's neck and forced it to hide again in the slimy, pitch-like ooze in the bed of the murky stream.

Suddenly from amid the darkness the Great Pike came swimming. No small fish was he, for his back was seven times longer than the longest boat, his teeth were like great spears set round the entrance to a cavern, and his eyes glowed like two flaming fires on the summit of a mountain. Fiercely he dashed through the water, high into the air he leaped, thinking to seize and swallow Ilmarinen.

But now the eagle rushed to the rescue. No small eagle was she, for her beak was six times longer than the longest boat oar, her talons were like the sharpened scythes of the mowers in the meadows of Hero Land, and her eyes glittered like two great suns glaring down from the top of the sky. Terrible indeed was the fight that followed. Dashing swiftly upward the fish sought to seize the eagle with his spear-like teeth; he caught the tip of her right wing, he drew it into the water and with might and main strove to pull the giant bird into the depths. But the eagle, with one foot gripping the rock, struck fiercely at her foe; with her iron beak she tore the scales from the fish's back, she forced him to retreat into the murky deep.

Not long, however, was the fight delayed, for soon the furious fish rose again and, swift as lightning, leaped upward to the combat. The bird of iron, her wings all glowing as with fire, was ready for him. She struck with her scythe-like talons; she seized

him midway behind his gills; with a mighty effort she drew him
from the water and bore him, struggling, helpless, dying, to the
topmost branch of a wide-spreading oak. There she sat, scream-
ing with joy and anon tearing her prey and feasting upon it. She
ripped the scales from the Great Pike's glistening sides; she tore
the fins away; she devoured the long breast and the jointed tail;
she sundered the head from the mighty shoulders, cleaving the
gills with her iron beak.

And under the tree stood Ilmarinen, helpless, imploring,
angrily remonstrating, "O faithless bird! O wicked eagle! Why
do you devour the fish that you were created to capture? What
shall I say to the pitiless mother at Pohyola when I return
empty-handed? What proof shall I offer that the Great Pike has
indeed been taken?"

The eagle screamed until the sky seemed rent in twain by the
shrill echoes of her voice. Then she threw the fish's head from
her—it fell at Ilmarinen's feet. She flapped her fiery wings until
the sun glowed hot above her; she leaped from her perch; she
soared upward, higher and higher, above the treetops, above the
desolate mountains. Into the land of clouds she soared. The
thunder rolled; the lightning flashed; the rainbow-bridge,
Jumala's bridge of many colors, was shivered and broken. Not
for a moment did the bird of iron pause, nor did she rest in her
flight until she reached the distant moon. There, folding her
fiery pinions, she alighted, content to make her home on that
changeable orb. And there, on clear summer nights, you may
often see her pecking at the stars and scarring the sky with her
scythe-like talons.

Ilmarinen, wondering at the might of his own invention, lifted
the head of the Great Pike from the ground. With much labor
he laid it across his shoulders and adjusted it upon his sturdy
back. Then, with hope in his heart and courage in his feet, he
turned his face once more towards distant Pohyola and the
Frozen Land.

XXV. THE BRIDEGROOM'S TRIUMPH

The short summer was ended and the days were growing cold. The song of the cuckoo was hushed, and the wild geese in the inlets were huddling together and preparing for flight. The cranberries had disappeared from the marshes. The meadows were purple and golden, but fast putting on their accustomed robes of dreary brown.

In the long, low dwelling by the sea the fires had been rekindled, for the air was crisp with frost and the wind of the North was blowing strong. Upon her couch the Mistress was reclining, grim and gray, toothless and unlovely, as of yore. Beside the hearth sat Wainamoinen, the prince of minstrels, sad of face, but resigned and wisely contented. And at her loom the Maid of Beauty plied her daily task, weaving fine blankets for winter wear, and sighing as she looked out from her narrow window and out upon the lonely sea and the lonelier land.

"Will he ever come?" she murmured, half aloud though speaking to herself; and her mother, Dame Louhi, from her couch echoed her words, "Will he ever come?"

Then suddenly up spoke a little child who was sitting on the floor—a little child too young to walk, too small to know the meaning of his words:

"I see an eagle coming to our house. He is a great eagle, a beautiful eagle. With one wing he fans the air, with the other he flaps the sea. He is coming nearer and nearer; he is hovering above our dwelling. Now he rests upon our roof. He is whetting his beak. He is looking down at our doves. Soon he will fly right into our house. He will seize the best one of all our birdlings—the rosiest, the whitest, the sweetest-voiced, the shapeliest. He will fly away with her; he will carry her far, far away into his own country, there to live with him forever."

"What does the child mean?" queried the Mistress, rising half-way from her couch beside the fire. "Surely, never have I heard an infant speak in this way."

"He speaks in riddles," answered Wainamoinen, "yet he speaks wisdom and truth. No doubt we shall understand him soon."

"True! true!" croaked Sakko, the earth woman, from her snug corner beyond the hearth. "See you not that dark cloud hovering in the sky? It is the wing of the mighty eagle. See you not the shadow that has fallen on our threshold? It is the shadow of the eagle's noble form. He is peering in. He is looking for the birdling that is his own!"

The Minstrel rose from his seat and went quickly to the door. He threw it wide open and looked out. The Mistress also rose, slowly, painfully, her stiffened joints creaking. The Maid of Beauty rose from her loom, joyful because her task was finished. All three looked out through the narrow door. Before them was the bare ground, sloping gently towards the shore and the smooth gray surface of the little inlet; above them was the cloud-flecked sky, cold and cheerless, without sign of bird or other living creature.

The child on the floor laughed.

They looked a second time, and from the meadow pathway they saw the hero coming, even Ilmarinen the Smith, the mightiest of all wizards. Gaunt and tall he was, and pale and wan from long toil and endless wanderings. His garments were soiled and torn, his feet were bare and scarred with wounds, his head was uncovered. But his step was firm as the step of a conqueror, and his eyes glowed brightly with joy as the eyes of one who has been victorious in battle.

And on his shoulders he carried the monstrous head of the Pike.

"Welcome, welcome, friend and brother!" cried Wainamoinen,

rushing out eagerly, boisterously, to meet him. "Long indeed have we waited for you."

"Welcome, welcome, hero of the later day!" muttered Sakko, small of stature, weak of body, wisest of earth women. "Bravely have you proved yourself a hero, thrice bravely have you shown your wizard power."

And Louhi, the gray Mistress, also cheerily cried, "Welcome, welcome! You have won the prize, Ilmarinen; your courage has been tested, your wisdom has been tried, and now you shall be rewarded. The duckling that I have cherished shall be yours, to sit on your knee, to nestle dove-like in your arms, to be the queen of your household, the mistress of your kitchen."

But where was the Maid of Beauty? She was not with those who stood at the door to welcome the conquering hero. Her seat at the fireside was empty; her place at the loom was vacant. She was hiding in her own room, her body all a-tremble, her face bathed in tears.

Proudly and joyfully then did the hero enter the low-roofed dwelling.

"O Jumala!" he murmured. "O giver of good gifts, grant thy blessing to this house! Bless all that live beneath this roof!"

"All hail, all hail!" cried the Mistress earnestly, but with voice cracked and broken. "Welcome to the great large man who deigns to enter this lowly cottage, this poor little house of wood, this humble hut so unworthy of the presence of one so noble!"

Then she called to her waiting-maiden, and bade her hasten to bring a light, that all might see the hero and be glad.

"Kindle the fattest knot of pine and fetch it hither blazing," she said. "Fetch it quickly that we may see the hero's eyes whether they are blue or grayish, whether they are green or brownish."

The waiting-maiden ran quickly to obey. She lighted a pine-knot that was always ready, and brought it blazing to her mistress.

"Ah! no, no!" shouted the aged wise one, grim and gray in the flickering light. "See how the ugly torch flares and sputters, and how the black smoke rises in clouds above it. The hero's face will be smutted, his eyes will be filled with soot. Take the cheap thing away and bring us better torches, torches made of white wax, cleanly and beautiful."

The maiden obeyed. She brought torches of the purest wax, white and clear, and held them before the Mistress, before the waiting hero.

"Now I see his eyes!" cried the wise one. "They are neither blue nor whitish. They are not green, they are not gray; but they are brownish like the sea-foam in the shadow of a rock, brownish like a bulrush in the early days of winter."

Then Ilmarinen took the head of the Great Pike from his shoulders and set it upon the floor by the side of the hearth. And all that were in the house admired its size and its wonderful shape and the mighty teeth that were set in the mighty jaws. But most of all, they wondered at the manner in which the bones were laid, this way and that, and knit firmly into a framework both neat and strong.

"It will serve you as a throne, O mother of my Maid of Beauty!" said Ilmarinen. "I will dress it, and polish the bones, and make of it a great chair wherein you can sit on winter evenings, feeling yourself the queen of all that is around you."

Then, while food was brought to him and the people of the household both high and low sat round him listening, he told the story of his adventure by the shore of Tuonela's river.

XXVI. THE WEDDING FEAST

Who shall find tongue to tell of the wonderful feast at Ilmarinen's wedding? Who shall invent words to describe its vastness, its grandeur, its joy?

Dame Louhi, the wise, the cunning Mistress, planned it. She it was who provided the food and the drink; she it was who directed the cooks, the butchers, the brewers, the bakers, the serving maidens; and she it was who invited the guests.

First, she built in Pohyola a house so roomy and large that even minstrels blushed to tell its dimensions, and story-tellers feared to speak the truth. It was so long that when a dog barked at one end the sound of his voice could not be heard at the other. The roof was so high that when a cock crowed on the ridge-pole the hens on the ground below could not hear him. In this house the fires were kindled, the tables were set up, and the feast was prepared. Here, back and forth upon the planking, the aged Mistress walked, pondering, planning, instructing, commanding.

"We must have roast meat and plenty of it," she said. "So, bring hither the great bull of Carelia and let him be slaughtered. No finer beef was ever fattened; no nobler beast was ever butchered."

The great bull was quickly brought—a ship's rope around his horns, a hundred strong men tugging at the rope. A stupendous ox he was, larger by far than any that grows in our degenerate times. Six fathoms long were his horns; and his back was a highway where squirrels frisked and birds built their nests as in the branches of a tree.

Think you he yielded much meat for the feast, much food for the hungry? Of roasts and steaks there were certainly a hundred barrels; of sausages in large round links they made a hundred fathoms. Seven boat loads of blood flowed from the great beef's veins. Six strong sledges could scarcely hold the fat that was rendered from him.

"Surely now we have meat in plenty," then said the Mistress; "but what shall we do for pleasant drinks to give joy to our guests? How shall we brew enough ale for the multitude that will come to the wedding feast?"

Forthwith she ordered all the tubs in Pohyola to be half filled with water, fresh water from the springs and rivers. Then into each she poured new barley and added flowers of hops in greatest plenty, stirring all with a magic paddle. Quickly the ale began its working, it filled the tubs, the white foam rose like mountains and poured itself in bubbles over the ground.

"Surely the guests shall not go thirsty," said the Mistress, well contented with her labor. And she called the serving-men to store the ale safely away in rock-walled cellars till the time for the wedding feast.

Thus did Dame Louhi, the wise one, provide everything needed for eating or drinking. All the kettles were singing, all the stewpans were hissing on the glowing coals. The pots were full of porridge. In the ovens loaves of bread in great plenty were baking for the banquet. All day, all night, the fires were glowing; all day, all night, the bakers, the brewers, the kitchen maids were running hither and thither, each busily working, each busily preparing his part of the wonderful feast.

Then the Mistress, the wise but loveless one, sent out her messengers to invite the guests.

"Invite all the folk of Pohyola," she said; "forget not one. Invite the people of Hero Land to come in boats, in sledges, by sea, by land. Ask Wainamoinen, the prince of minstrels, to come with his sweet songs. Call the blind, the lame, the poor and wretched. Lead the blind ones kindly with your hands, bring the lame ones in sledges or on your backs, fetch the children, fetch the old and feeble, let not one be slighted or forgotten."

And the messengers departed, carrying the invitations north ward, southward, eastward, westward. In four directions they went, yes in eight directions they hastened, telling all the world how the hero, Ilmarinen, was to be wedded on a certain day to the Maid of Beauty, whom all the world adored.

The day came, the morning dawned. Bright was the sun above Pohyola's chilly shores. The sea was calm, the air was mild, the meadows were golden. Dame Louhi, wisest of women, rose early to put her house in order. First, she busied herself in-doors, then out she hastened. She put her hand to her ear and listened. Far out on the sea she heard the sound of oars splashing, she heard the rippling of the waves as they were cut by the prows of many vessels, she heard the voices of a multitude approaching. On land she heard the clatter of reindeers' hoofs, the galloping of horses, the rattle of sledges and the grating of their birchwood runners upon the sand.

"What do I hear? What do I see?" cried she. "Is this a hostile army coming to attack me? Or is it only the billows breaking on the beach, or the wind whistling and moaning among the pines?"

She looked again, and again she listened. Her face was less grim, her voice was less harsh; never did she appear so handsome.

"Oh, no, no!" she muttered. "I thought I heard the North Wind blowing, a pine tree falling in the forest, the billows roaring and the breakers beating. But it is not so. The air is mild, the sea is calm, no storm is near. That which I hear is not the wind, it is not a hostile army. It is the multitude of guests assembling, the hosts of friends coming to rejoice with us because it is Ilmarinen's wedding day."

"How shall we know the bridegroom when we see him? How can we distinguish him in the great crowd of friends and neighbors?" asked a little waiting-maiden.

"You shall know him as you know an oak among the willows, as you know the moon among the tiny stars," answered the Mistress. "The steed which he drives is as black as a raven. His magic sledge is glowing bright and golden as the sun. Six yellow birds sit on his shafts sweetly singing, and of bluebirds there are seven perched gayly on the dashboard. You cannot fail to distinguish the noble hero."

Even while she spoke there was a clatter in the roadway, a humming and a bustling and a tramping of many feet. The bridegroom had arrived with all his friends around him. Swiftly he drove his bright-hued sledge into the courtyard, and quickly he alighted while the bluebirds sang and the cuckoos called lustily to the swallows beneath the eaves. The young men shouted, the old men laughed, and the very air was bubbling with joy.

"Hostler, hasten!" called the Mistress. "Take the bridegroom's horse, and loose him gently from the shafts. Remove the copper-plated harness, the silver breast-band, the reins of silver. Lead the noble steed to the spring and let him drink his fill of the gushing water. Then put him in the hindmost stable, in the stall reserved for heroes' horses. Tether him to the ring of iron that is set in the polished post of birchwood. Set three trays of food before him, the first filled with oats, the second with soft hay, the third with finest chaff. And when you have curried him and smoothed his shining hair, cover him with a soft blanket and leave him alone, locking the stable door behind you."

"I will do everything as you have bidden me," answered the serving-man, and he led the steed gently from the courtyard.

"Now, my boys," said the Mistress, "you little lads of Pohyola! Conduct the bridegroom to the house and show him the doorway. Take off his hat gently, gently. Remove his gloves also. Let us see if the door is wide enough for him to pass through; let us see if it is high enough to admit so great a hero."

Without delay the waiting-lads took their appointed places, four at the right hand and four at the left, six in front of him and six behind, and thus they marched lightly and orderly into the dwelling.

"Now let all give thanks to Jumala, the gracious," said the Mistress, and her unlovely face grew pleasanter for the moment. "Give thanks to Jumala, for the hero has passed through the door in safety, he has entered the house of the bride."

And the bridegroom responded, "Give thanks to Jumala, and may his blessing rest upon this house and all that abide beneath its roof."

The table was ready, the feast was spread, the guests were waiting. The lads, with much ado, led the bridegroom to his place—the highest seat at the end of the room. He sat down by the side of the blushing bride, the Maid of Beauty, while all the guests clapped their hands and shouted for joy.

Then, as one accustomed to entertaining a multitude, the wise old Mistress feasted her guests in the noblest fashion. Busy, very busy, were the little waiting-maidens, serving food to all the people. Of roast beef and savory sausages there was great plenty. Broiled salmon, pork, the meat of lambkins were served to each guest's liking. The whitest of bread and the yellowest of butter, cream cakes, nuts, and apples—who could ask for more than these? And there was the ale, the foaming white ale which the Mistress herself had brewed—it was handed round in great tankards so that each of the heroes present might drink his fill. When it came to the Minstrel, old Wainamoinen, he rose and sang a new song:

> "O ale, sweet ale!
> Let no one fail
> To sing of thee
> And merry be.
>
> "O hero, strong!
> List to my song,
> Be glad, be gay
> On your wedding day."

Then, changing his theme and the subject of his song he tuned his voice to a higher key.

> "What would our Creator do
> If to-day he sang to you?
> He would sing the sea to honey,
> Sing the stones to precious money,
> Sing the sand to foaming ale,
> Sing the rocks to rain and hail,
> And the mountains sing to lakes,
> And the hilltops sing to cakes.

"As a minstrel and magician,
  He would bless this land's condition;
  He would fill the fields with cattle,
  Make our treasure boxes rattle;
  He would fill the mines with metal,
  Fill each pot and fill each kettle;
  He would fill the lanes with flowers,
  Bless each day, bless all the hours.

"As a minstrel and a singer
  He would with this household linger,
  Give the bride a ring of gold,
  A dress of silk, and wealth untold;
  And to the bridegroom, he would give
  More skill than to all smiths that live.
  Let us therefore crave his blessing,
  All our prayers to him addressing."

Thus did the people feast, and thus did the mighty Minstrel sing on Ilmarinen's happy wedding day. All day, all the long night, the guests sat at the table, eating and making merry and listening to the songs and pleasant speeches that were made in honor of the bride, the bridegroom, and the noble hostess.

Much good advice was given to her who had lately been the Maid of Beauty but was now the Bride of Beauty: how she should keep her husband's house in order; how she should obey and serve him; how she should love and cherish her mother-in-law and all the members of her family. Much sage counsel also did the hero, Ilmarinen, receive: how he should always be very gentle to the dove that he had captured; how he should not forget to praise her industry in the kitchen, at the loom, in the hay field; how he should never upbraid her in hissing tones, or beat her with a slave whip; but how he should stand like a wall before her to protect and defend when others were unkind.

XXVII. THE HOME COMING

Long were the speeches, lengthy were the songs, and many were the stories to which the people listened and the patient bride and bridegroom hearkened. Then, as the day was breaking, all was ended. The guests rose and made ready to depart. The last good-byes were spoken, the last words of counsel were delivered.

The hero's steed was led from the stable, it was harnessed to the magic sledge while the cuckoos called loudly and the bluebirds sang sweetly as before.

"Farewell, farewell, to all my friends and kindred," then murmured the Bride of Beauty. "I must now go far, far away from the home I love so dearly. I must leave my mother's dwelling, leave the farmyard, fields, and meadows where as a maiden I was happy. Farewell, dear house; farewell, my mountain-ash tree; farewell, roads and pathways; farewell, sweet hills and forests. Who now will answer the cuckoos when they call? Who now will welcome the bluebirds in the springtime? Who will milk my pet reindeer? Who will care for my lambs? Farewell, farewell to all! Farewell, farewell!"

Then Ilmarinen, noble hero, lifted her into the sledge; he tucked the robes of fur about her; he wrapped her feet in soft, warm blankets. The serving-man handed him the reins and the whip. One word to the steed, and they were away; the low-roofed dwelling, the village, the friends at Pohyola, all were quickly left behind. And the happy triumphant Ilmarinen, shouted back his farewells.

"Good-bye, good-bye, to all the people! Good-bye to the seashore and the creeks and inlets! Good-bye to the house with smoke-browned rafters! Good-bye to the grasses in the meadows, to the lonely marshes, to the willow bushes, and the lone pine woods where my smithy stands! Good-bye to all! Good-bye, good-bye!"

Onward, with gliding feet, the swift steed flew. The magic sledge scarcely touched the ground, its birchwood runners seemed to skim through the air, so rapid was its motion. Across the broad meadows, over the hills, through dark ravines, along the sandy shore the hero pursued his course, never pausing, never doubting. The whip-lash whistled in the air, the copper rings on the horse's harness made merry music.

All day, all night, yes, through a second day and then a third, the joyful journey continued. With one hand the hero guided the horse, with one arm he supported his bride. The North Wind gently drove him along, the South Wind beckoned him forward. At length, just as the sun was setting, he saw his own fair dwelling nestling among the trees of Wainola. The smoke was rising from the roof-hole, Dame Lokka was preparing the evening meal, the good sister, Anniki, was watching at the door.

"Welcome, welcome, bridegroom and brother! Long have we watched for you, long have we waited!" shouted the glad maid of the morning.

"O Ilmarinen, my son, my joy!" cried the mother and matron. "Welcome home with thy birdling, thy fair one!"

Then quickly all the village people came running to greet their neighbor Ilmarinen and his beautiful young bride. They led the noble pair into the house, the men and women singing joyously, the children dancing before them. A feast was soon provided—meats the tenderest and most delicious, loaves of the whitest flour, yellow cakes both light and sweet, lumps of fresh butter just from the churn, broiled salmon smoking hot. All these they brought in great abundance, heaped up on Dame Lokka's pretty dishes. And the villagers shouted:

"Welcome, Bride of Beauty, to this Land of Heroes! Welcome

to this lovely village! Hail to the hero, our friend and neighbor! Hail to all within this dwelling! Blessed be this homecoming. Blessed be the bridal pair, and may their lives be long and their love lasting!"

Thus did Ilmarinen win his bride and thus did he bring her in triumph to his home in Wainola.

XXVIII. THE SLAVE BOY

Happy, happy Ilmarinen! With her who had been the Maid of Beauty as queen of his household, naught but good fortune was his. Wherever he went, whatever he did, he was sure to prosper. His smithy was full of rare and beautiful things, the work of his own skilful hands. His barns were full of grain, barley, and wheat, hay and soft straw for his horses. His farmyard was full of lowing cattle, broad-horned milk cows, fat beeves, and sleek-coated yearlings. And his house was full of joy, the abode of peace, the home of plenty.

Now among the servants of the hero was a young slave whose name was Kullervo. A worthless fellow he was, ill-favored, ill-natured, selfish, and unkind. When any work was given him to do he was sure to spoil it; he could not be trusted, he seemed to be unfit for any duty. Ilmarinen had bought him for a small price: two old cracked kettles, three broken hooks, four dull-edged scythes, and five toothless rakes.

"It is a good price for him, more than he is worth," said all his neighbors, for they knew that the slave would serve him ill. "Never will he earn the food that is given him, never will his master have any joy from his labor."

Ilmarinen smiled and said nothing. He gave the boy an axe and bade him cut an armload of kindlings for the fire; but the worthless fellow began chopping the beams of the house. He sent him into the garden to pull up weeds; but the worthless fellow destroyed the useful plants and flowers and left the weeds untouched. He sent him to pick berries in the marshes; but the worthless fellow picked only the green fruit and trampled upon the ripe.

"The new slave is good for nothing," said Dame Lokka, Ilmarinen's busy mother.

"No, no!" answered his wife, the mistress of his household. "Every man has his place in the world, and surely there is something for this poor fellow to do."

And so, one day when Ilmarinen was far away, she said to the mother, "I have a mind to send Kullervo out with the cattle. Surely he can drive them to the hill pastures and the marshes, he can watch them while they graze, he can keep them from wandering in the woods and thickets."

"Do as you like," answered Dame Lokka. "A herdsman's task requires neither skill nor wearying labor, and perhaps the slave will find his proper place among the cattle in the quiet pastures."

Forthwith the wife and mistress called to the old cook, the kitchen wench, and said, "The new slave, Kullervo, is to go with the cattle to-day. Make haste and put up a luncheon for him— something that will stay his hunger in the middle of the day, for he will be far from home and the noon sun is hot in the lonely hill pastures."

"Yes, my mistress," answered the cook, "I will fill a basket for him with food good enough and wholesome enough for any such slave as he. I will bake a fresh, hot cake for him and have it ready when he starts with the herd."

So to her task she went, chuckling and growling, for she hated Kullervo and not without reason. First, she rolled out the dough and then she baked the cake. The upper half was of wheaten flour, the lower half was of coarse oatmeal, and in the centre was a round black sandstone cunningly concealed.

"He will enjoy that when he comes to it," laughed the wicked wench, holding her sides and grinning with mirth.

When the cake was baked very hard and dry she took it from the oven and rolled it in butter, laying a slice of raw bacon around it. The she put it in a small basket and covered it with green oak leaves.

"He must needs have strong teeth to eat it," she muttered, "but it is good enough for him."

Soon Kullervo came to get his luncheon. The cattle were waiting to be driven to the pasture, the milk cows were lowing impatiently, the yearlings were browsing beside the hedges.

"Here's your luncheon, you worthless fellow," said the old cook. "It is fresh and hot, and far too good for such as you; keep the green leaves over it till you're ready to eat, for the flies are many and very bad to-day."

The slave took the basket. Although ill-favored, his face was not wholly bad, for his father had been a freeman and a hero. His coat was of coarsest cloth, much patched; his trousers were of reindeer skin; his stockings were of blue-dyed wool; his shoes were heavy and serviceable. No beard was yet on his chin or sun-browned cheeks; his eyes were blue with shades of savagery lurking in their depths; his uncombed hair was yellow, long, and frowzy.

With the basket on his arm he opened the farmyard gate and shouted to the cattle. The broad-horned oxen crowded them-selves out into the road and walked briskly but sedately down the well-worn pathway towards their accustomed pasture, the mild-eyed milk cows followed, and the calves and yearlings hur-ried impatiently to the front.

The wife and mistress, she who had been the Maid of Beauty, was sitting in her chamber counting the days that must pass before her husband's return. She heard the tinkling of the bells and the hoarse discordant mooing of the beasts. She heard the shouts of the slave boy and the trampling of the younger cattle. She rose quickly and hurried to the door, waving her hand to Kullervo and calling to him in shrill, commanding tones:

"Have a care that you do your work well to-day, young man. Drive the milkers to the high meadows where the grass is green and sweet. Drive the oxen and the yearlings to the woodlands; let them browse among the bushes and lie down in shady places. See that you guard them all to keep them safe from wily wolves and lurking bears. Watch them well, and when the day is almost done, bring them home. Woe be to you if you leave one of them behind. Bring them home and drive the milkers into the pad-dock; then call loudly, and I will come down with the milkmaids to milk them. Do you hear, Kullervo?"

The slave boy growled a surly answer, and went slouching behind the herd, shouting to the laggers and casting stones at the browsing oxen.

He drove the milk cows to the meadow pastures where the grass was tall and green, but the oxen and the younger cattle he allowed to wander as they would in the open fields or the marshy thickets. Then, at length, when all were peacefully feeding, he sat down upon a grassy hummock and looked around him, sad, lonely, vindictive. The autumn sun beamed hot upon his head, and the fresh sea breeze fanned his face and played in his yellow hair. The grasshoppers chirped at his feet and the crows scolded him harshly from the treetops. Kullervo looked and listened, but he saw nothing beautiful, he heard nothing musical. His heart was filled with dismal thoughts, and he loudly bewailed his wretched fate.

"Ah, me! ah, me! Wheresoever I go I am still a miserable slave and hard tasks are set for me to do. While others are happy and free I am forced to trudge unwillingly among briars and thorns, over hills and through marshes, watching the tails of hateful cattle. O Jumala, giver of good! Let the sun shine gently upon me, a wretched slave boy; but make it scorch and blister my master and my master's household. Turn their boasting into grief and their success into dire misfortune. So hear me, O Jumala, friend of the friendless!"

The noon hour came, the sun began its downward course. In the farmhouse the Smith's mother, Dame Lokka, was sitting in sweet content. On her right sat Anniki, the maid of the morning, and on her left was Ilmarinen's wife and mistress whom he had won in the far-off North Land. Joy beamed in every face and pulsed in every heart.

The table was spread and the mid-day meal was served—white bread fresh from the bake-oven, choice butter and yellow cream from the dairy, tid-bits of beef and smoked salmon. How good was everything!

"Praise be to Jumala for all these blessings!" said Dame Lokka, fervently.

"Praise be to Jumala!" echoed both the daughters.

Meanwhile the slave, Kullervo, was still sitting on his lonely

THE SLAVE BOY

Then, at length, when all were peacefully feeding, he sat down upon a grassy
hummock and looked around him, sad, lonely, vindictive.

hummock, keeping watch over the cattle and nursing his evil thoughts. The crows among the pines cawed loudly; the grasshoppers at his feet chirped mockingly.

"Wake up, sad slave boy! The day is past the noon," croaked an old crow.

And a thrush in the thicket of bushes sang, "O orphan boy, the luncheon hour has come! Take the fine cake from the basket where the old cook so kindly placed it. Eat it. Feast upon it and forget your sorrow."

Kullervo was hungry, for his breakfast had been light. He picked the oak leaves from the basket and took the round, buttered cake in his hands. It was heavy, and he eyed it closely. He turned it over and examined the under side.

"It looks good, it smells sweet," he said. "But the handsomest of people are sometimes rotten at heart, and the handsomest of cakes are sometimes unfit to be eaten."

He took his hunting knife from the sheath that hung at his belt. It was but half a knife, the edge nicked deeply, the point broken off. But its temper was good, for it had been forged by a master smith in the days when men did honest work.

Kullervo cut through the upper crust of the cake, he cut through the wheaten layer at the top; but when the knife struck the stone in the centre it broke short off at the hilt and only the handle remained in his grasp. The slave looked at it, and as the blade fell to the ground he burst out weeping.

"Oh, sorrow upon sorrow!" he moaned. "This knife was my only friend. I had no one to love but this iron, so true, so ready to help. It was once my father's knife, and well it served him in the chase and in the fight. And now it is broken by this cake of stone which Ilmarinen's women have given me for food."

He picked up the broken blade and tried to fit it in the handle. It was vain; both blade and handle were useless. With a cry of despair he flung them far from him; with a cry of wrath he threw the stone-filled cake still farther, and it fell with a thud among the bushes. Then up flew a pair of ravens, one lighting upon a blasted pine and one taking shelter in a grove of oaks.

"Caw! caw!" cried the one in the pine. "What can ail the wretched slave boy?"

"He is angry," answered the other. "His mistress has treated him badly. She has given him a stone for bread."

"It is thus that the rich feed the poor," said the one in the pine. "But what will the slave do about it?"

"If he is wise he will pay them well for their cruel jest," cawed the one in the oak. "He will seek revenge, he will have it. Caw! caw! caw!"

Kullervo leaped up and stood upon the hummock. He stretched out his arms and shook his clenched fists in the face of the sky.

"Hear me, Jumala!" he cried. "O Jumala, friend of the friendless, help me. I will have revenge. I will pay those women well for the sorrow they have made me feel. The slave will whip the master, and the master shall serve the slave."

All the savagery that had been lurking in his blue eyes burst forth, as lightning bursts from the drifting clouds. He ran to the woody thicket and broke off a long branch of hemlock to serve him as a whip. Slashing it this way and that, he rushed hither and thither collecting his herd. With great ado he drove the lazy milkers far into the savage woods. He gathered the yearlings together and, after much shouting and cursing, chased them into the tangled thickets where the wild beasts had their lairs.

Out of the shady places wolves leaped up, howling, snarling, snapping their teeth. The bears were roused from their lurking holes and came forth growling, their tongues lolling out. The gentle milk cows, the timid yearlings, even the stolid oxen, were overcome with fear. They ran together in groups, trembling and helpless. Instantly the wild beasts leaped upon them with bared claws and gnashing teeth. If any escaped the wolves, they were seized by the bears; if any fled from the bears, they were devoured by the wolves. The whole herd perished.

From a safe seat in the crotch of a pine the slave boy looked on and watched the slaughter; and he laughed a wild, discordant, triumphant laugh. Then, clapping his hands together and knocking his knees against the trunk of the tree, he began to sing. He sang a wild, strange song of enchantment—a song he had learned from a witch woman in the land of mists and shadows. And as he sang, behold, a wonderful thing occurred: all the wolves so lately feasting were changed into sleek, fat yearlings, and all the bears so lately gorging themselves became fine milk cows with mild, soft eyes and pendent udders.

The slave boy descended from the tree, still singing, still shouting, still working the magic spell. The beasts with one accord looked up to him as their master. One after another, they marched slowly and orderly out of the marshes and out of the woods, the false milk cows going foremost calmly chewing their cuds, and the false yearlings gambolling behind. The sun was now well down towards the western hills, and the evening milking time was nigh at hand.

Homeward, over the hills and along the well-known pathways, the slave boy drove his herd. With noiseless steps he ran among the beasts, breathing words of magic, words of cunning in their ears.

"Spare not the mistress when she comes out to milk you," he whispered to one.

"Seize the maidens when they come with pails to milk you," he said to others.

"Seek the old cook in the kitchen and remind her of her cake," he muttered to still another.

"Be bold, be fierce, be very hungry," he counselled them all.

The sun was still above the hills when he drove the herd into the farmyard. He put the milkers inside the paddock, the yearlings following after. Then he closed the gate without locking it and climbed up on the fence. From his belt he unloosed his herdsman's whistle, a whistle carved from an ox's horn; he put it to his lips and blew it loudly, shrilly. It was the signal by which the mistress and her milkmaids would know that the cows had been brought home and were ready for the milking.

Five times—yes, six—Kullervo blew a long, piercing blast which might have been heard half-way across the sea. Then, as the last echoes died, he leaped nimbly to the ground and ran out of the farmyard. Half crouching, he slunk away behind hedges and bushes until his ungainly form was lost to sight among the evening shadows. Never more would his feet cross the threshold of Ilmarinen's dwelling.

XXIX. A DREADFUL VENGEANCE

B eside the door of Ilmarinen's dwelling the women of the household were assembled. Dame Lokka, best and busiest of matrons, was planning the evening meal. Sister Anniki, maid of the morning, was assorting the week's washing and toying with the ribbons in her hair. And she who had been the Maid of Beauty—she who was now the wife and helpmate of the master Smith—was busy at the churn. Suddenly the sound of the slave boy's whistle—the herdsman's whistle—aroused and startled them. The sound filled the air with its shrill but welcome music, and was echoed sharply from the hills and the forest beyond. Again it was heard, and again and again, each time more distinct, more persistent, less musical.

"Praise Jumala!" cried the wife and helpmate. "There is the herdsman's horn. The cows are at home and it is milking time."

"The slave boy has tended the cows well, I hope," said Dame Lokka. "If he has not lost any of them he shall have a good supper to-night."

"But why does he blow so loudly?" said Anniki, holding her head. "The sound is deafening. My ears are surely split and my head will burst from the unearthly noise."

"Never mind, sister," said the wife and helpmate, gently, soothingly. "That was the last blast and we shall not hear another. Does your head ache? You shall have the first cup of milk that is taken from Brown Bossy to-night. I myself will milk her, and I will give it to you, warm and frothing and fit for a queen. Surely that will heal your ear-drums, surely that will ease your throbbing head."

Then she called cheerily to her milkmaids: "Come, girls, the cows are in the paddock and it is milking time! Fetch the new pails and fetch also my milking stool. Let us get at our task before the daylight fades."

The milkmaids came—three young serving-girls, rosy-faced, red-lipped, and ruddy with health. Methinks I see them even now, tripping lightly from the doorway, each with a sweet-smelling cedar-wood pail, and the foremost with a three-legged stool for the mistress.

Along the garden walk, between rows of blue and yellow flowers, they pass joyously. In their blue gowns and white aprons, their long braided hair falling far down their backs—how handsome they are! The wife and helpmate goes before, queenly as when men called her the Maid of Beauty. Anniki, the sister, comes after, thirsty and impatient for the cup of fresh and frothing milk. They walk across the farmyard; they open the great gate into the paddock; they enter and look around them.

"Ha! how sleek the milkers are to-night!" says the wife and helpmate. "Their hides shine as though they had been rubbed down with lynx-skin brushes and smoothed with lamb's wool dipped in oil."

"And how full they are!" says Anniki, the sister. "They have eaten so much they can hardly breathe. Surely the slave boy knows where to find the best pastures for the herd."

"Yes, and see how large their udders are!" says one of the milkmaids. "Methinks our pails are too small to contain such quantities of milk. The whole milk-house will be flooded."

"But look!" suddenly cries the second milkmaid. "What ails the yearlings? They stare at us so and their eyes glow like balls of fire."

"Oh, I am afraid! I am afraid!" whispers the third milkmaid, shrinking back into the shadows.

The brave mistress laughs at her fears. "It is only the light of the setting sun shining in their eyes," she says. "Surely no harm can come from these gentle creatures."

But sister Anniki shivers with cold and draws nearer, her cheeks pale and her limbs trembling.

"Bring hither my stool," says the wife and helpmate, "and give me the new pail of polished cedar. Here is Brown Bossy, patiently waiting to give a cup of milk to Anniki. I will milk her first, and do each of you girls choose a cow. The yearlings will not disturb you."

She places her stool by the side of the great brown beast; she takes the new milk-pail in her hands; she sits down; she bends forward to begin the milking.

Suddenly a great shout, a whoop, a scream is heard far down the road. It is not the shouting of a lone traveller; it is not the whooping of a home-coming ploughboy; it is not the scream- ing of a frightened woman. The milkmaids hear it and are overcome with terror. Sister Anniki turns to flee through the open gateway.

But the wife and mistress stamps her foot with anger. "How silly!" she cries. "It is only the cry of an owl or the call of a lone wolf in the darkening woods. Get to your milking!"

Her own hand trembles as she reaches for the teat. Quickly the dreadful sound is repeated, deafening the ears, freezing the blood of both mistress and maidens. It is the savage whoop of the slave Kullervo, bidding the beasts perform the dreadful business which he alone has planned. Instantly the broad-horned, mild-eyed creature which has played the part of Brown Bossy becomes a huge bear, grim and terrible; instantly all the milkers are turned to growling beasts; instantly the bright-eyed yearlings resume their proper forms and become fierce wolves snapping and snarling and eager for blood. Oh, the savage uproar! Oh, the terror, brief but indescribable!

The milkmaids with their white aprons and braided hair van-ish like snow-flakes in a turbulent flood of waters. The wife and helpmate, she who erstwhile was the Maid of Beauty, is swept away in the storm, is swallowed up, and naught but a blood-stained lock of hair remains to tell of her fate. And Anniki, maid of the morning, flees shrieking through the gateway, is seized by cruel jaws, is devoured—no magic skill of hers availing to avert her doom.

Ah, me! that it should be my task to tell of this strange tragedy so brief but terrible! No minstrel's song can depict that scene so fraught with woe, so horrible to contemplate.

The maddened, hungry wolves ran out of the paddock, out of

the farmyard; the hideous bears rushed after them. They ran hither and thither devouring every living thing. Like a destroying flood they invaded the farmhouse, breaking down the doors, overturning the tables and benches, filling every room with their horrid presence. In the kitchen they found the old cook, the wench who had caused this unheard-of disaster. She was praying to Jumala, but Jumala did not save her. In her own chamber Dame Lokka, the best loved of matrons, fell before the pitiless tide. Not one of the household escaped the jaws of the furious beasts. Women and men, children, birds and fowls, dogs and horses, all perished. Even the gardens and the fields were overrun and trampled into worthlessness. The once prosperous home of Ilmarinen became in a single night an uninhabited waste.

Ah! if only the master, Ilmarinen, had been there! But what could even he have done in that storm so fierce, so irresistible, so overwhelming?

XXX. THE GOLDEN MAIDEN

Far away in northern inlets Ilmarinen and his friend the Minstrel were catching salmon for the winter's store. The days were growing shorter and the nights were getting cold. Ice was beginning to form in the sheltered creeks and coves and frost lay white on the shaded slopes of the hills.

Fishes were scarce and shy and the fishermen were disheartened. For five days—yes, for six toilsome days—they had sailed hither and thither, casting first on the landward side and then on the seaward, and still the boat's hold was far from being filled.

"I wish I were at home," sighed the master Smith.

"There is no place so sweet as one's own fireside," responded the Minstrel.

"I long to see the faces of those whom I love," said the Smith. "I am impatient to hear their voices."

"Sweeter than the chirping of song-birds—yes, sweeter than the warbling of meadow larks—is the merry prattling of one's own home folk," returned the Minstrel.

They drew in the net. Not a salmon did it contain. Naught but seaweed did they get.

"Oh, I am sick of this business," complained Ilmarinen. "I am sick of fishing, sick of sailing on these barren waters, sick of life itself."

"Take heart, brother, take heart," answered the Minstrel cheerily. "To-morrow we shall have better luck; we shall make a great catch, and soon we shall sail back to Wainola with a full cargo and great plenty of salmon."

159

But on the morrow their bad luck continued. Their net was broken, they lost their best whalebone hook, their boat was grounded in the shallows, and half the day was wasted.

Suddenly from the shore they heard some ravens calling among the storm-beaten pines. They listened to the voices of the ill-omened birds.

"See those fishermen," said one. "See how they toil in these empty waters."

"Caw! caw! caw!" answered its mate. "They are foolish. They know not what is going on at home."

"If they were wiser they would spread sail and hasten back to Wainola," croaked a third.

"Hasten back to Wainola!" echoed the cold, gray cliffs and the ragged rocks on the shore.

"Back to Wainola!" came a voice from the waveless waters.

"To Wainola!" shouted Ilmarinen, as he seized the ropes and hurriedly hoisted the sail.

"Wainola! Wainola!" sang the ancient Minstrel as he wielded the long rudder and deftly turned the vessel before the wind.

All night, all day, the willing little ship speeded southward, cutting through the waves with lightning swiftness, throwing the foam to the right and the left, leaving a track of boiling waters behind it. And the word that was oftenest on the lips of Smith and Minstrel was "Home! home! home!"

Three days they sailed, and then—ah, then! Who shall depict that home-coming? Who shall describe the dismay, the grief, the heart-breaking of the hero, Ilmarinen?

As the boat neared the shore he shouted a great sky-shaking shout as was his custom when arriving home from a long voyage. But no answering cry of welcome came to his ears. He saw no faces of loved ones waiting at the landing-place to greet him. Quickly, he leaped ashore. He paused not a moment, but hastened along the silent pathways towards the grove that sheltered his roomy farmhouse. But ere he reached it his eyes detected many a sign of the fearful scenes that had been enacted there. The hedges had been torn down, the flower-beds had been trampled and destroyed, the bordering fields were laid waste. The farmhouse itself had been ransacked from kitchen to attic chamber, and not one article of ornament or use had been left untouched or unbroken.

Frantically the hero ran from one spot to another loudly calling to his mother, to his sister, the maid of the morning, to his wife, the best beloved, the beautiful. But no voice answered him save the echoes of his own words. The floor of the farmhouse was reddened with blood; on every side were the marks of cruel teeth, the imprint of sharp and pitiless claws. In the farmyard, he found the milking stool and the pails, all battered and scarred and broken; and there, too, he found a long lock of blood-covered hair which he knew too well had once belonged to the Maid of Beauty, the mistress of his household and his life. Then despair took hold of him and hope was dead. He looked no farther, but sat down upon the ground and gave expression to his overwhelming grief.

Thus, all day and for many days, Ilmarinen mourned and wept. Through sleepless nights he bewailed his great misfortune, and through all the hated mornings he lamented the loss of his wife, his mother, his sister, his loved household. In his smithy the fire no longer burned, the anvil no longer echoed his song. His hammer was idle and his forge was cold. The beauty of life had departed and he longed to die—to meet the shades of his loved ones in the land of Tuonela.

For two, four—yes, six—long and dreary months he mourned, and his strength waned and he grew weak from sorrow. He ate little, slept little, talked not at all, mingled never with his friends and neighbors. Often, in the still hours of midnight, he fancied that he heard the voice of his dear one calling him by name. Often in fitful dreams he reached his hand out in the darkness thinking to touch hers, but grasping nothing, seizing only empty air.

At length, in his madness, he said to himself: "With gold and magic and smithing skill I will shape a body like hers—beautiful beyond compare—and then perhaps she will return from Tuonela and dwell therein as she did in her former body of flesh and blood."

And so, from the rocks by the seaside he gathered flakes of gold, scales of gold, nuggets of gold, until he had filled a basket almost as large as himself. Then from the forest he cut and brought together many logs of willow and white maple and mountain ash, and of these he made charcoal for his smithy. With much care he prepared his furnace, and in the midst of it he set a magic caldron, large and round and deep. He heaped the wood around it, he threw on coal, he kindled the fire; and all the while he sang runes and songs of wizardry and power which no lesser man would have dared to recite.

Then he called loudly to his slaves and working men: "Now, my faithful ones, start the bellows to blowing. Make it roar like a storm at sea, like a whirlwind in a mountain valley. Blow, blow, and cease not until I command you."

The men obeyed. With their bare hands they laid hold of the long lever, they put their naked shoulders against it and worked steadily with might and main. And Ilmarinen stood by his magic caldron, throwing into it great handfuls of gold, smaller handfuls of silver, cakes of fine sugar from the red mountain-maple, honey and honeycomb, daisies, buttercups, wild flowers of every hue, and a hundred strange and potent articles the names of which I have not the courage to pronounce.

For a brief hour the workmen toiled and paused not. Then one said, "I am tired," and slunk away in the darkness; and the second said, "I am faint with the heat," and let his hands fall from the bellows; and the third said, "The work is too hard for one man alone to perform," and he, too, abandoned his post. The bellows ceased blowing, the fire was fast dying down.

"Blow, my men, blow!" cried Ilmarinen, and then, lifting his eyes, he saw that he was alone in the smithy.

Angry and half-despairing, he seized the lever of the bellows in his own hands, he put his own naked shoulder to the work, and again the flames leaped up, the fire glowed, the caldron quaked and trembled in the terrible heat. For hours and hours he toiled, till the sweat poured in torrents from his brow, and his hands were blistered and his fingers cramped with grasping the long, unyielding lever of iron. At length he paused from his labor and looked down into the furnace. He lifted the lid from the caldron and sang a wild, weird song, every word of which was a word of enchantment. And what do you think arose from the mixture in the vessel, from the gray clouds of vapor which filled it?

It was not that which the Smith had hoped to see, for the ill-working serving-men had broken the spells that he was weaving. It was not a golden war-steed with shoes of silver. It was not a monstrous eagle with beak of hardest iron. It was only a young lamb, small and feeble, with fleece of mingled gold and silver.

Ilmarinen looked at the tiny beast and felt no pleasure. A child might have liked it as a plaything, but a hero delights not in useless toys.

"I did not call for you, my lambkin," he said, disappointed and sorrowing. "You are gentle, you are harmless, but my magic spells should have wrought something far better and more beautiful. I desire a golden maiden and no other form will please me."

So saying, he thrust the lamb back into the boiling caldron, forcing it down to the very bottom. Then he threw in more gold, and with each handful of the yellow metal he muttered a new rune of magic words and magic import. The fire burned fitfully beneath and around the caldron. Tongues of blue flame encircled it, sheets of white flame enveloped it, a sound like the humming of bees issued from its broad mouth.

Ilmarinen threw fresh coal into the furnace and heaped it high above the draught hole. He worked the bellows, steadily, gently, persistently. The fire roared, the flames danced, the heat became intense. For hours the hero labored without cessation; for hours he muttered spells of enchantment, suffering nothing to break in upon his thoughts or distract from the mystic power of his words. When he at last, had reached the end, had recited all the proper runes and sayings, he stopped blowing the bellows, and with great caution stooped down and looked into the caldron.

The flames died suddenly away, and out of the vessel there sprang a wonderful image—the image of a beautiful maiden. In face and form she was indeed lovely—lovelier than any other woman, save one, that Ilmarinen had ever seen. Her head was of silver and her hair was golden. Her eyes sparkled like precious stones and were blue as the summer sky, yet she saw nothing. Her ears were dainty and blushing like pink rose leaves, yet she heard nothing. Her lips were tender and sweet and red like twin cranberries meeting beneath her faultless nose, yet she tasted not, smelled nothing. Her mouth served not for speaking

nor yet for eating or smiling. Her fingers were long and taper-
ing and her hands small and shapely, yet she felt nothing. Her
feet were well-formed and comely, yet they would not support
her, she could not stand.

"O my loved one! O my lost one! O thou who wert once the Maid
of Beauty, come and dwell in this golden body!" cried the enraptured Smith. "Come, and once more be the joy of my poor life!"

He lifted the Golden Maiden and placed her in the cushioned
seat wherein his lost wife had often reposed. He put his arm
around her waist, but she did not return his caress. He kissed
her cherry red lips, but they were cold, cold, cold. He spoke
many endearing words in her ear, but she gave him no answer.
He took her hands between his own, but there was no throbbing
of life in them.

"She is cold, so cold!" he muttered. "She is like ice, like snow
in midwinter!"

Then he laid her on a silken couch, put soft pillows beneath
her head, and covered her with warm blankets and quilted cov-
erlets. And as he did so he prayed unceasingly to the dear dead
one whom he had loved so much:

"O thou who wert once the Maid of Beauty, come and dwell
in this body of gold! Come and give life to this precious maiden;
fill her veins with blood, give warmth to her body, sight to her
eyes, hearing to her ears!"

All night long he sat beside the couch, holding the maiden's
hands and breathing his own warm breath into her face. All
night long he moaned and wept and called the name of his lost
wife whom the beasts had devoured. At length the new day
dawned and the sunlight streamed into the room and fell upon
the couch. The Golden Maiden was as cold as before, her face
was white with frost, her body was frozen to the blankets.

"Ah, me! there is no hope!" said the Smith, despairing utterly;
and he lifted the image from its resting place. "Never will the
dead come to life again, never will my loved one return to me.
Henceforth I shall walk alone upon the earth."

He took the Golden Maiden gently in his arms, he smoothed
the drapery about her, and carried her to his old friend, the
Minstrel.

"O Wainamoinen, tried and true!" he cried. "Here I bring you a present—a maiden of great worth, golden and beautiful. See her fair face, her comely form, her feet so small and shapely."

The Minstrel, wise and steadfast, looked at the image closely, admiringly. Then he said, "She is indeed a pretty maiden, and the likeness is perfect. But wherefore do you bring her to me?"

"Dear brother, friend, companion," answered the Smith, "I bring her to you because I love you, because I would make you happy. Years ago we both wooed the same Maid of Beauty. I won her because I was young; you lost her because you were old. I know what must have been your sorrow and disappointment. Now, when there can be no more joy for me, I bring you this Golden Maiden to be your solace and delight. She has the form and features of the Maid of Beauty, and I doubt not she will please you. She will sit on your knee and nestle dovelike in your arms—and she is worth her weight in gold."

"I want no golden maiden!" cried the Minstrel half angrily, sternly. "For what is gold without sense, without soul? I have heard of young fools who wedded silly maidens, brainless women, soulless ladies, just for gold. But think you that one in my position would stoop to such folly?"

"I know that you are wise, my brother," said the Smith, "and you are the master of all magic. Perhaps you might endow this Golden Maiden with sense, with warm blood, with a noble soul."

"Jumala alone has that power," answered Wainamoinen, "and to Jumala let us give all praise. Carry this image back to your smithy, thrust the Golden Maiden into your furnace, and then you may forge from her all sorts of objects, beautiful, useful, precious. For never will your Maid of Beauty return from Tuonela to dwell in a body so base and worthless."

Sorrowfully, regretfully, Ilmarinen obeyed. Back to his smithy he carried the golden image; he thrust it into his furnace; he watched it melt and disappear in the terrible heat. Then he turned himself about and walked out silently into the darkness. And for many a sad day the people of Wainola sought him in vain and then mourned him as dead.

XXXI. THE FAMINE

Sad were the days and joyless were the months in the Land of Heroes. The sky was cloudless and gray and the ground was parched and dry for long lack of rain. In the fields the crops failed and the cattle died. In the forest there was no game for the huntsmen. In the sea the fishes had fled to other waters, leaving the fishermen to toil in vain. In Wainola the children were crying for food and the men and women were sitting on their doorsteps, silent, with stony faces, hopeless, helpless, despairing.

Then one day a little boat came creeping into the harbor with but one man on board. Many of the people saw the lone sailor as he moored his vessel to the shore, but none had the courage to go and meet him. He walked slowly up the deserted pathway to the village, looking at the barren fields and the fruitless trees, the empty barns and the gloomy houses, the many signs of poverty and distress. His eyes wandered onward to the ruined farmhouse, and past it to the smokeless smithy which had once been the joy and the pride of the hero, Ilmarinen.

"Ah, me! Can this be Wainola, the village once so happy and prosperous?" he said to himself. "Can this be the smithy, can this be the home which echoed to the merry sounds of love and peace?"

Then from out of the shadows an old man, feeble and tottering, came to meet him. It was Wainamoinen, pale with fasting, gaunt with hunger, but brave and steadfast as in former days.

"Hail, stranger!" said the Minstrel. "Welcome to Wainola and to the best that its people can offer!"

"Hail, friend and brother!" answered the stranger heartily and with gentleness. He lifted the cap which had concealed his forehead, he loosed the broad scarf that had been well drawn up about his chin and cheeks. His ruddy face was wrinkled with sorrow although for the moment it was wreathed in smiles.

The Minstrel old and feeble uttered a cry of joy. "O Ilmarinen! Ilmarinen! Have you returned? We had mourned you as dead! We had given you up as lost!" And the next moment each was locked in the other's arms.

"Now, tell me, my young brother, where have you been since you departed from Wainola and the Land of Heroes? Word came to us that you had perished, that you had gone to dwell in Tuonela; and when this great blight of famine and sorrow came upon the land, we were fain to believe that it was indeed so. Why did you leave us? Where have you been?"

"I went away from Wainola because of my sorrow," answered Ilmarinen sadly. "I went to the far North Land, to Pohyola's shores, because the voice of my dear lost Maid of Beauty seemed to call me thither. For twelve months—yes, for two long, sorrowing years—I sought her in that land. But Tuoni holds her captive in his castle beside the river of silence. She cannot come to me, but I can go to her. I am even now seeking the road to Tuonela."

"You need not go far to find it," said the Minstrel. "Look around you and see your neighbors starving, dying—hear your neighbors' children moaning, crying. The road to Tuonela is here, and many are the feet that are travelling in it. But tell me, was it thus in Pohyola? Have they a famine there also?"

"A famine! Far from it," answered Ilmarinen. "Never was there a more prosperous people than those of Pohyola. They plough, they sow, they reap in great abundance. Of grain and fruit there is no end, and no man nor woman, child nor dog, knows the meaning of hunger."

"How strange that a land of mists and fogs, a land so dreary and forbidding, should be so blessed with plenty!" said the Minstrel. "Is it by some power of magic that this is so? Why is it that you, the prince of wizards, cannot find some way to bless and save our own kinsmen, our own people?"

"Do you remember the Sampo?" said the Smith. "Do you remember the magic mill which I made for Dame Louhi many years ago? That mill is still grinding in Pohyola, its lid of many colors turns and turns and turns forever. Safely locked in a stony cavern, still it grinds wealth and food and clothing without end. The soil draws richness from it, the fields of grain thrive upon its grindings, the fruit trees send their roots downward and suck up the wealth which it pours out."

"The Sampo, the Sampo!" said the Minstrel, feebly as in a dream. "If only we might bring it to our own country, how quickly we could save our people!"

"It was I that forged the wonderful mill, I, the prince of smiths and wizards," said Ilmarinen with a far-off look in his eyes. "Never can another be made that is like it."

"And if you forged it, why is it not your own?" queried Wainamoinen, wise though feeble.

"I forged it for another," answered Ilmarinen. "I made it for wise old Louhi, the Mistress of Pohyola; and the reward which she ought to have given me, I obtained by other means. Neither gold nor silver nor aught else have I ever received for my labor."

"Then surely you have a valid claim upon the Sampo," said Wainamoinen. "O my friend and brother, we must hasten to Pohyola and seize that mill of plenty, that we may bring it to our own sweet land. We must save our starving people."

"Nay, nay, it cannot be," returned the Smith. "The mill is securely stored away in a stony cavern beneath a hill of copper. Nine heavy doors shut it in, and nine locks of strongest metal make each door fast and safe. No man nor men can seize the mighty Sampo."

But the Minstrel persisted. All that night he held the Smith's strong hand and talked of naught but the Sampo and how, by it, they might save the lives of their famishing friends and neighbors. At length Ilmarinen ceased objecting. "You are wise, my elder brother," he said, "much wiser than I. The task is a mighty one, but for the sake of our people and our country I will not shrink from it. None but women say, 'I cannot,' none but cowards say, 'I dare not.'"

XXXII. THE WEEPING SHIP

Hour after hour the two heroes sat together and talked of their great project and the desire of their hearts. Nor could they readily agree by what road they should journey to Pohyola, whether by sea or whether by land.

"Twice have I sailed thither in a ship," said the Minstrel.

"Twice have I made the journey in a sledge," returned the Smith.

"It is nearest by water," said the Minstrel.

"It is safest by land," said the Smith.

"It is pleasantest to go thither by ship."

"It is surest to ride thither along the shore."

"Well, let this be as it may," at length said Wainamoinen. "We shall not quarrel. If the land way pleases you, I say no more; but it is beset with perils, and we must be well armed. As you know, it is not the habit of minstrels to carry weapons, and I have neither spear nor club. So get you to your smithy, kindle the fire in your furnace so long idle and cold, and forge me a keen-edged sword with which to fight wild men and savage beasts."

The Smith obeyed. Once more the flames leaped up within his furnace, once more the black smoke poured from the roof-hole, and once more the song of the anvil rang out cheerily in the morning air. Into the fire the mighty wizard threw first a bar of purest iron, then upon this he scattered a handful of gold, all that remained of the Golden Maiden. He blew the bellows with might and main till the whole smithy trembled and groaned and the flames leaped up to lick the sky. Then he drew out the half-melted mass and held it upon the anvil while he beat and turned it, and beat and turned it, until he had shaped it into a wonderful weapon the like of which no man had seen before.

"Ha! this is indeed a sword well suited to a hero," he said when it was finished.

He held it up and looked admiringly at its well-shaped blade and jewelled handle. Pictures rare and beautiful adorned its sides. The hilt was shaped like a prancing horse, the knob was the image of a mewing cat.

He looked long and lovingly at the blade and then handed it to Wainamoinen. "Take it, friend and brother," he said. "It is worthy of you. Its name is Faultless. With it you can cleave the hardest rocks; with it you can vanquish all your foes; with it you can carve for yourself great honor and fame."

Soon came the time for starting, and the courage of both began to waver. "We must have horses," said the Minstrel. "The way is long, the paths are rough, the journey cannot be made on foot. Let us seek out steeds for ourselves."

So into the fields they went, wondering whether any of Ilmarinen's steeds had escaped the wolves and the hungry bears and the starving days of the drought. Long they sought, and at last they found among the bushes in the great marsh a wild colt, scarcely grown, and a gaunt, long-legged, yellow-maned steed which had once been the pride of Ilmarinen's stable. With much labor they caught these beasts and bridled them, and upon their backs they threw rough blankets to serve in place of saddles.

They mounted and rode through the woods, the Minstrel going first with his great sword drawn. They rode along the pathway which each had travelled once before, the pathway which followed the windings of the coast; for this they judged was the safest way. They rode slowly, for their horses were neither swift nor strong, and their eyes and ears were alert for every strange sight or unexpected sound.

Suddenly, as they were skirting the shore of a small secluded inlet, they heard what seemed to be the moaning of some one in great distress. They stopped and listened.

"What can it be?" asked the Smith.

"I know not," answered the Minstrel. "It may be some child

who has lost his way and is weeping by the shore. It may be some she-bear moaning for her dead cubs. It may be only a dove cooing among the branches of her nesting-tree. Let us ride along the beach and learn what we may."

So they rode onward, close to the water-side, listening and looking and drawing nearer and nearer to the place from whence the strange sounds issued. Presently, in a little cove, they saw not a child nor a mother bear nor even a dove, but a fine large boat with red hull and scarlet prow, and with oars and rowlocks and everything needed for a lengthy voyage. As the wavelets rippled against the sides of the pretty vessel and caused its keel to grate upon the sandy beach, it gave forth groans and lamentations like the cries of some living creature suffering from sorrow or pain.

"O little red vessel, why do you weep?" cried Wainamoinen. "Why do you complain so loudly, so grievously?"

"I weep for the great deep sea," answered the boat. "I am unhappy because I am tied to the shore. I long to be free, to speed over the water, to glide upon the waves."

"Where is your master, and why do you lie here idle?" asked Ilmarinen.

"I am waiting for my master," said the boat. "The wizard who sang my boards together bade me wait here for the hero who is to guide me across the sea. But he does not come, he does not come!" and with that it began again to cry and lament in tones of impatience and grief.

"Do not fret yourself, O boat with rowlocks!" said Wainamoinen. "Your master will surely come soon to claim you. Then you shall ride proudly upon the waves, you shall sail to unknown shores, you shall mix in the battle struggle and return home laden with plunder. Only be patient and wait."

"I have waited long already," answered the boat. "I have waited till my rowlocks are rusty and my deck boards are rotting. Worms are gnawing through my beams; toads are leaping in my hold; birds are nesting on my mast; all my sails and ropes are mildewed. I would rather be a mountain pine tree, or an oak in the valley with squirrels leaping among my branches."

"Have patience, O boat!" said Wainamoinen. "Lament no more, for your master has surely come."

Then the heroes leaped from their horses, turning them loose to wander free among the sand-hills. They put their shoulders to the little vessel and pushed it into deeper water. They climbed quickly on board of it, singing as it floated slowly from the shore:

> "Little boat so snug, so strong,
> Listen to our earnest song.
> You are fair to gaze upon,
> Are you as safe to sail upon?"

The boat answered:

> "Two men may on me safely sail.
> Two men I surely will not fail;
> A hundred men with oars might row me;
> A thousand men could not o'erthrow me."

While the Smith sat at the helm and guided the vessel out through the narrow inlet, the Minstrel stood up beneath the flapping sail and sang songs of magic, songs which he had well-nigh forgotten. He sang of the earth and the sea, of the sun and the stars, of love and battle, and of the great mysteries of life and death. Then, while with his sword he kept time to the rhythm of his song, he began a soft carol, sweet and low and very persuasive. And, behold! as he sang, one side of the boat was filled with strong young men, handsome youths, with long hair and downy cheeks and hands all hardened by labor.

He changed his theme, and the other side of the boat was filled with maidens—pretty girls, their hair in puffs and curls, with belts of copper round their waists and rings of gold upon their fingers. And as the Minstrel continued to sing, the boat grew broader, longer, roomier, and became a gallant ship. On each side were seats for fifty rowers, and in each of the fifty rowlocks a long and supple oar lay resting.

No sooner was the vessel outside of the inlet than it paused and refused to go farther. It stood in its place, rocking on the waves of the open sea. The Minstrel sat himself down in the prow and bade the young men begin their rowing.

"Wield the oars with strength, my heroes," he cried. "Row

hard, row hard, and drive our good ship o'er this wide expanse of water, speed it through this treeless region."

The fifty youths obeyed. They leaned forward, they dipped their oars in the waves, they strained every muscle till the rowlocks groaned and cracked. But all in vain: the ship stood still.

Then in anger the Minstrel bade them drop their oars and change seats with the maidens, who had been idly looking on.

"Wield the oars with love, girls, wield them with all your power. Row hard, row hard, and speed our good ship on its way. Make it float lightly, joyously, swiftly over the curling waves."

The maidens obeyed. They grasped the oars with their slender fingers, they strained with their arms, their faces blushed scarlet red. But all in vain: the ship stood still.

Thereupon the hero Ilmarinen went toward the prow and seated himself upon one of the benches. He took the oar in his labor-hardened hands, he dipped its blade in the singing water and began rowing. Instantly the ship sprang forward like a wild bird beginning its flight. Instantly the prow of copper began to sing and the waves parted to make a path for the speeding vessel. Instantly the fifty maidens and the fifty stalwart youths, with joyous hearts, renewed their rowing.

The hero Ilmarinen shouted to the ship, to the sea, to the hundred rowers; and the ship, the sea, and the rowers answered him in tones of gladness. The oars bent and groaned, the rowlocks creaked, the seats shook and trembled. The dashing spray fell in showers to the right and the left. The slender mast croaked to the wind like a raven croaking to its mate. And Wainamoinen stood at the helm and wisely steered the fair red vessel on its pathless way.

By his hut on that bleak headland which juts farthest into the great icy sea a poor fisherman was sitting. He was mending his net and weeping because the fishes were so few. Suddenly a sound, seemingly far, far away but drawing nearer, touched his ears and caused him to start up. What was it? Was it a sea-gull breasting the morning gale and crying to its mate in the shelter of the ragged cliffs? Or was it some beast of the shore wandering along the desolate beach and howling from hunger and loneliness?

Very small was the fisherman's body, but his head was large and his arms were long. Very awkward were his fingers and dull of feeling, but his hearing was keen and his sight even keener.

He leaped quickly to his feet and gazed northward. Nothing there did he behold but the endless sea, the white-capped waves, and the cheerless, chilly sky. He turned and looked southward. At first he saw nothing there; then suddenly on the horizon a rainbow appeared with a single gray cloud beyond it.

Was it indeed a rainbow? Was it a gray cloud? Ah, no! It was a red ship speeding onward, and the rainbow was the spray that she dashed from her cleaving prow.

The vessel drew nearer, she was in plain sight, she loomed up large upon the waters. The fisherman could see the oars rising and falling, he could see the rowers sitting upon the benches. Then he heard clearly the shouting of the young men and the singing of the maidens, and above all the clear, commanding tones of the master.

With wild gestures he ran far out upon the beach, shouting loudly over the water:

"Who are you, O sailormen? What ship is this with crimson prow that ploughs the sea so swiftly?"

Three times he shouted and made inquiry, and then from the rowers came the answer:

"Who are you, lone fisherman? Why do you dwell on this bleak promontory far from your fellow-men?"

"My name is Ahti," answered the long-armed one. "I dwell here because it is my home and I have no other. I am strong, I am wise. Even though you tell me nothing I know your steersman: he is Wainamoinen, the great Minstrel. I know your master oarsman: he is Ilmarinen, the prince of wizards."

By this time the ship was close inshore, but still speeding on its way. Then the rowers rested on their oars, and it was easy to understand all that was being said whether on the ship or on the shore.

"Where are you going, O heroes?" asked the fisherman. "Why do you sail so swiftly through these barren waters?"

"We are sailing to the North Country," answered the Minstrel. "We are going to the Frozen Land, to the shores of

Pohyola, where we shall ask Dame Louhi to share the Sampo with us."

"And what if she will not do so?" asked Ahti, running along the shore to keep abreast of the ship.

"Then we shall seize the mill of plenty and carry away its lid of many colors," said Ilmarinen.

"O take me with you! take me with you!" shouted the fisher-man, waving his long arms and leaping into the sea.

A sturdy swimmer he was, like the seals, his only neighbors; and the water held no terrors for him, buffet him as it might. Bravely he launched out toward the speeding vessel, and quickly he came abreast of her fast-receding stern. The Minstrel reached over, he seized the man's long arms and drew him aboard. Then the hundred rowers took to their oars again and the ship bounded forward into the vast and trackless sea of the North.

XXXIII. THE KANTELE

With eyes that never failed and arms that never tired the Minstrel stood by the helm and guided the vessel around the jutting headland and straight forward into the great white sea. On the benches the rowers sat, wielding their oars with strength and deftness and singing and shouting for gladness. On the deck the long-armed Ahti danced nimbly and joyously, forgetful of his fishing, forgetful of his hunger.

For one long day and through the moonlit night the ship sped onward across the open sea. On the next day it skirted the low, marshy shores of the Frozen Land. On the third day it sailed through narrow straits between small islands, approaching by stealth the longed-for haven of Pohyola. And now the rowers were silent, the maidens had ceased their singing, the young men refrained from shouting, even the nimble Ahti left off his dancing and sat quietly at the feet of Ilmarinen.

Suddenly, in a deep channel, the vessel's bottom grated upon something, and the ship shivered and stood still. It remained fast in its place and no effort of the rowers could move it. The nimble Ahti seized a long pole and thrust it into the water, trying with all his great strength to push the ship along. What was it that had thus so suddenly stopped the flight of the gallant vessel?

"O thou lively Ahti," then cried the Minstrel, "lean far over the gunwales and look below. See what it is that keeps us moveless. Is it some rock, or is it the snaggy trunk of some forest tree lying deep beneath the waves?"

The long-armed hero obeyed. Holding fast with one hand to the vessel's edge, he let himself down into the water. He looked under the ship's hull, he peered closely at her keel, and then he leaped quickly back among the rowers.

"It is not a rock," he shouted, "neither is it a tree! It is a fish, a mighty pike that has stopped the vessel. Never have I seen so large a fish. It lies in the water silent, motionless, asleep, like a senseless mountain. The ship is wedged against its back fin—a fin as large as the sail upon our mast. If the fish should sink, it will drag our vessel down into the depths; if it should rise, it will tumble us all headlong into the sea."

"Too much talk will never save us," said Wainamoinen. "Never yet was pike slain by idle words. Draw your sword and wield it valiantly with your long, ungainly arms. Sever in twain the fish on which we are grounded."

"Surely I will do so," answered Ahti. "I will carve him into a thousand pieces."

He drew his fish-knife from his belt, he reached downward with his long arms, he slashed furiously this way and that; but nothing did he cut save the yielding water.

Up leaped Ilmarinen from his seat among the rowers. He seized the boaster by the hair and thrust him back among the benches. "Easy it is to brag," he said, "but to do is quite another story."

Then with his sword of truest metal he reached down—deep down beneath the ship's round hull. With all his strength he struck at the fish, thinking to cleave it in twain. But the scales of the monster were like iron plates lapping one upon another. The sword was shivered in pieces, it fell from the hero's hand, and the pike still slept unharmed in the quiet water.

"This is no boy's work!" cried Wainamoinen. "A man is needed—a man's sense, a man's strength, a man's skill. Stand aside, and see what a real man can do."

Then, drawing the sword—the keen-edged sword, Faultless, which the Smith had forged for him—he leaped into the sea, he dived deep down to the fish's resting-place. With one tremendous stroke he severed the mighty pike in twain, with another he hewed off its head. The monstrous body sank to the bottom, but the Minstrel dragged the head up to the surface, and with Ahti's help he hoisted the mighty jaws into the vessel.

"Now, row! Row all together!" shouted Ilmarinen.

Instantly the hundred oars were dipped into the waves, all the rowers pulled together and the ship began again to move steadily, proudly through the water. Wainamoinen stood at the helm. With masterly skill he piloted the vessel through narrow ways, he guided it along deep, winding channels, and finally steered it to the mainland, where it rested in a safe, well-sheltered haven close by the village of Pohyola.

All leaped out upon the sands, glad that the long voyage was ended. A fire was built and the young men and maidens clustered round it. The head of the pike was brought, and all examined its huge scales, its staring eyes, its sharp-pointed teeth.

"It is long since we tasted food," said the Minstrel. "Let the fairest of the maidens cook this fish. Let them broil it for our breakfast. Never shall we enter Pohyola while hunger pinches us, while famine robs us of strength."

Forthwith the maidens began the cooking. Ten of the most beautiful were chosen to perform the work. The young men hastened to gather sticks on the shore to feed the fire, to make hot coals for the broiling. Wainamoinen drew his knife blade from its sheath and with skilful strokes divided the head into a hundred pieces—yes, into more than a hundred he cleaved it, that each of the crew might have abundance. The flames roared, the red coals glowed upon the sand, the juicy morsels sizzled loudly and gave forth savory odors very pleasant indeed to the nostrils.

Soon the breakfast was prepared and all sat down upon the sand to eat the delicious morsels which the maidens had cooked. Sharp were their appetites, and when they had finished, nothing was left of the mighty head save its bones and its dagger-like teeth which lay scattered on the beach.

"What a pity that these should be wasted!" said the Minstrel, picking up a fragment of the jawbone—a fragment with the teeth still fast within their sockets. "Surely, if Ilmarinen had them in his smithy he might shape them into something useful, beautiful, wonderful."

"Nay, nay!" answered Ilmarinen. "Nothing can be made from such useless things. The skilfulest smith can never fashion fish-bones into anything of value."

"It may be so," said Wainamoinen thoughtfully, "and yet, perhaps I, who am not a smith, may make something from them that will give joy to men and women."

Thereupon, with his sharp-edged knife he set to work to fashion from the fish-bones a thing to give forth music. Of a piece of cedar he made the framework; of the pike's jawbone he made the bridge; of the pike's sharp teeth he made the pegs to hold the harp strings. Then out into the fields he went, searching in the thickets and among the briars. Soon he found five horsehairs which the wild steeds of Pohyola had lost while pasturing there—five horse-hairs, long and strong and resonant. "These will serve right well for harp strings," he said.

He hung the horsehairs in their places, he stretched them tight, he gave to each its proper length and tension. "Ha! ha!" he laughed. "Who now will say that nothing can be made of fish-bones? Here is something that will breathe forth music sweeter than a minstrel's song. It will delight the young, the old, the rich, the poor—all sorts of people—with its rare and matchless melodies. Call it the *kantele,* call it the harp of the North, and let minstrels never fail to play upon it."

The news of his invention spread quickly. The youths, the maidens came crowding round him. From the fields and the fishermen's boats the men came running. From the huts and the washing pools the women came dancing. Half-grown boys and little girls pushed shyly forward—all curious to gaze on the wonderful kantele, all anxious to hear its sweet music. And Wainamoinen passed it from hand to hand, saying, "Look at it, let your fingers play upon it, let its melodies rejoice your hearts."

Wistfully the little girls, the maidens, the older women, all held the harp in their hands and with their tender fingers swept the harp strings. Boldly, confidently, the half-grown boys, the young men, the old fishermen, all grasped the wonderful instrument and tried to play upon it. But the tones which they drew from it were harsh, unpleasant, unmusical.

"It is not thus the kantele is played," said Wainamoinen. "Not one of you can draw cheerful music from it, and yet the melodies are there; they lie hidden in the strings of horsehair, in the jawbone of the pike."

"I can play it," said the nimble Ahti. "With my long arms I can call forth the melodies that now lie slumbering within it. Let me try what I can do."

Wainamoinen put the harp of fish-bone in his gnarly hands; he rested it upon his knees; very eagerly the little fellow swept the harp strings with the tips of his long fingers. But the sound which came forth was not music—it was a noise, discordant, grating, painful to the ears.

"It is always thus," said the Minstrel, growing impatient at last. "The poorest doers are the biggest boasters. The music of the kantele lies still beneath its bridge, beneath the jawbone of the pike. Not one of you has the skill to coax it forth from its lurking-place. Let us all go now to the village, to the roomy dwelling of Dame Louhi. Perhaps the Mistress of the land, the old, the grim, the gray, the Wise Woman of the North, will be able to touch the harp strings aright—perhaps she will know how to play the kantele and bring sweet melodies from its heart."

And all the young men shouted, "To Dame Louhi's dwelling! Let us see what the Wise Woman can do. Yes, lead us to Dame Louhi's dwelling."

XXXIV. THE TRIUMPH OF MUSIC

Old Dame Louhi, unlovely and unloved, sat in the doorway of her dwelling. She looked out and saw that which made her wrinkled, uncanny face beam with joy. Her toothless mouth expanded into the mockery of a smile. Her small, greedy eyes twinkled beneath her shaggy eyebrows. Her long, crooked fingers trembled nervously, they seemed to be grasping at something invisible.

She was pleased because where once were naught but vast brown meadows she now saw fields of ripening grain. Where once were miry marsh lands she saw green pastures with hundreds of sleek cattle grazing thereon. Where once were sandy barrens and wind-swept hills she saw fruitful orchards and blooming gardens. And in the village, instead of wretched huts she saw neat cottages and well-filled barns, the homes of contentment and plenty. Who can wonder that her face was wreathed with smiles while her heart was overflowing with joy?[1]

"My mill of fortune has done all this," she muttered to herself. "This fair, sweet country shall now no longer be called the Frozen Land. It shall everywhere be known as the Land of Plenty, the home of the Sampo."

She turned her head and listened. A faint, musical sound, far away, came to her ears. It was the sound made by the magic mill, grinding, grinding forever in the cave beneath the hill of copper. She could hear its pictured cover turning, turning—pouring out

---

[1] See Note G, at the end of this volume.

wealth for all the people. She could hear the grains of gold dropping, dropping—the precious royal sap feeding the rootlets of the corn, filling the apple blossoms with nectar, and pervading the rich warm soil itself.

Suddenly she was startled by hearing another sound—a strange, unusual noise, a clamor as of the voices of many people all trying to speak at once, all trying to make themselves heard. The sound grew louder every moment. It became a confused uproar; it drew rapidly nearer. What could it be?

The Mistress, looking eagerly, soon saw whence the clamor came. A great crowd of excited people appeared coming up from the seashore. The road between the gardens was filled with half-grown boys, chattering little girls, shouting young men, singing maidens, hard-working women from the farms, and old men from the fishing boats; and all were using their voices vigorously, excitedly, as though some wonderful thing was happening.

The Mistress was alarmed. "Surely the world has gone mad!" she cried in dismay. "Who are these people, and what do they mean by their strange actions?"

The rabble came nearer. Dame Louhi could distinguish some of the faces. She was sure that the children and some of the old men and old women were her own subjects—she had seen them every day of their lives, but never in so jolly a mood as now. But who were those noisy young men and maidens, dressed in foreign garb, who formed the greater portion of the noisy company? And who were the two heroes who led them—one white-bearded and tall, the other sad-eyed and pale but with the limbs of a giant? Ah! Dame Louhi knew them only too well.

"Hail to you, heroes!" she said, as they paused beside her dwelling and silence fell upon the company. "Your faces are familiar to me and your names I have not forgotten. If you come in peace, I welcome you to this land of plenty."

"We come in peace," answered the Minstrel, wise and truthful. "We have heard strange stories in our country concerning the magic Sampo and the great changes it has wrought in Pohyola. Now our eyes see that which our hearts could not believe and we would fain rejoice with you and be glad because of your good fortune."

"Good fortune comes to those who labor for it and who most deserve it," said Dame Louhi coldly. "But tell me, what fresh news do you bring from the Land of Heroes?"

"There is no news but of famine and sorrow," answered the Minstrel. "The children are crying for food, and men and women perish because of the poverty of the land. Therefore we have come to ask you to share the Sampo with us. It has made you rich and happy, now give us a small portion of it that it may bless our suffering people also."

The face of the Mistress grew ashy-white with anger. "The Sampo is but a little thing," she said, "and never will I share it with another. Can two hungry men share a sparrow? Can three divide a tiny squirrel? You may hear the Sampo whirring, you may hear its pictured cover grinding in the cavern where I placed it—but it whirs for me alone, it grinds out wealth and plenty for my people and for no other."

"Surely you are unwise and selfish," then said the Minstrel, "and foolish it would be to waste words in argument. Since you will not share the Sampo with us I warn you that you shall lose the whole of it. We will take it out of the cavern where it is grinding and we will carry it far away to our own country to give comfort and joy to our neighbors and food and clothing to our loved ones."

When Dame Louhi heard this she rose up quickly and stood, furious, in her doorway. She clenched her bony fists and shook them high above her head, calling upon all her people, all her armed men, all her servants, to come quickly in their might and drive the robbers from the shores of Pohyola. Loud was her voice, stern were her commands, and there was no one who did not hear her. Instantly a hundred swordsmen were at her side, a thousand spearsmen answered her call. They stood ready to smite and to slay, to drive the intruders into the sea.

But Wainamoinen, old and fearless, stood in his place unflinching and firm as a rock in the midst of a storm. He held the kantele in his hands and began to play upon it, softly, gently. Instantly every voice was hushed and every arm was stayed. He raised his fingers nimbly and moved them swiftly over the harp strings. One sweet note followed another, pleasures indescribable issued from the harp of fish-bone, while the Minstrel sang his rarest, richest songs—songs so melodious that every heart was entranced, bewitched, overcome with joy.

Forthwith all the creatures of the woods and fields came near to listen. The squirrels came leaping from branch to branch. Soft-furred ermines, minks, otters, and seals laid themselves down in the grass before him. Sharp-eyed lynxes looked out from the foliage of the thickets and drank in the wonderful music. Herds of reindeer came racing over the meadows. In the marshes the savage wolves awoke and stretched themselves, and then with one accord rushed out and ran with speed to the spot where the kantele was playing. There they squatted down in orderly rows, their ears pricked up, listening and rejoicing. Even the lazy bears came ambling from their lurking-places; they climbed upon the rocks and into the trees and sat there in solemn silence, drinking in the bewitching sounds.

The birds of the air also came on silent wings from the four corners of the sky. They flew backwards and forwards, soared in circles, and paused with outstretched pinions, looking down to enjoy the wondrous melodies. The eagle left her fledglings in her lofty eyry and came to listen to the hero's playing. Wild ducks from the deep inlets of the northern sea and snow-white swans from the marshes of Pohyola came in flocks to hearken to his singing. Sparrows and wrens and all the tiny birds of the fields and woods assembled by thousands; they perched on the Minstrel's head and shoulders, they filled the branches of the trees, they hovered in the air, forgetful of everything save the sweet notes that issued from the kantele.

The fairies of the rainbow and the mists also came, some riding on the yellow sunbeams and some resting on the crimson borders of the clouds. The slender daughters of the air, who weave the golden fabrics of each man's life, paused in their work to listen, and as they paused their shuttle fell from their hands and the precious thread of their spinning was broken.

Nor did the creatures of the sea fail to hear the all-entrancing melodies. Little fishes and large fishes came in shoals and lifted up their heads along the beach to rejoice and wonder. The slender pike, the graceful salmon, nimble herrings, all kinds of finny creatures, came crowding to the shore to listen to the songs of

Wainamoinen. White whales from the icy seas, savage sharks, and squirming eels swam side by side and trembled with emotion. And the Old Man of the Sea, even the king of the boundless deep, came, and sitting upon a throne of water-lilies listened with joy to the ravishing melodies that issued from the kantele. The water nymphs, also, cousins of the reeds that grow in the still waters between the hills, they heard the sweet music and were enraptured by it. They left off playing with their silken tresses, they dropped their combs and their silver brushes and lifted their comely heads to enjoy the Minstrel's wondrous songs. And their mother, the Wave Mistress, terror of seafaring men, raised herself from the billows and listened. Then with speed she betook herself shoreward, hiding her awful head among the rushes, and there she lay until the music soothed her to deepest slumber.

For one whole day—yes, for two long, dreamy days—the Minstrel played thus upon the harp strings, upon the inimitable kantele, and as he played he sang the songs of truth and beauty which he had learned from the Wisdom Keeper, from the earth, the sea, and the sky. And all the creatures, all the people, were spellbound and motionless because of the great joy and comfort and wonder that had come upon them.

At length he changed his theme and sang of the grandeur and glory of life, of things mighty and things lowly, and of the great hereafter beyond the silent river. And from the kantele he drew forth such marvellous melodies that not one among all his hearers could refrain from weeping. The heroes wept, old men and matrons, swaggering youths and timid maidens, half-grown boys and lovely little girls, all wept, for their hearts were melted. Tears welled up even in the eyes of the beasts and the birds and fell like rain upon the leaves and the grass and the gray sand by the shore.

Meanwhile, as he played, the Minstrel himself was moved to weeping. Down his cheeks the water-drops went coursing, they ran down his beard and down his heaving breast. Round as cranberries and large as the heads of swallows his tears fell, chasing each other to the ground. They rolled like hailstones down upon his feet, they flowed in streams till they reached the margin of the sea, and there they fell tinkling and splashing into the sparkling water, down to the black ooze at the bottom.

"Who will bring my tears back to me?" asked Wainamoinen, his voice trembling while his long fingers still played upon the harp strings. "A dress of softest feathers shall be given to that one who gathers my tears from beneath the crystal waves."

The raven heard him and flew down, snapping with his sharp beak and trying to gather up the tears. But not one could he recover from the sparkling water.

The blue duck also heard him and with swift strokes swam to the spot where the tears had fallen. She dived deep down into the water and there she found the tear-drops lying on the black ooze at the bottom. Hastily with her spoon-like beak she gathered them up, she carried them to Wainamoinen and laid them on the grass before him. Lo! every tear-drop was a pearl of wondrous beauty—a pearl of priceless value, fit to adorn a queen or deck the crown of the mightiest king.

"O brave blue duck, friend and helper!" said the Minstrel. "You have done well and you shall be rewarded quickly." And so saying, he gave her a dress of feathers—a dress of wondrous beauty, well-fitting and soft and suited to one who lives in northern climates by icy seas. And all this while the music never ceased, the kantele kept pouring out its sweetest, rarest treasures, while Wainamoinen sang new songs to charm the listening multitude.

At length, however, the people could hold out no longer. Their strength forsook them and they sank, one by one, upon the ground, all overcome with weariness. They closed their eyes and gave themselves up to slumber. Children and young people and men and women, all lay drowsing. The hundred brave swordsmen and the thousand spearsmen of Pohyola were soundly sleeping. Even old Dame Louhi yawned and closed her eyes and sank back upon her couch overcome with slumber, forgetful of the Sampo, forgetful of everything. Of all the multitude none remained awake save the heroes and the young men and maidens that had plied the oars on board of the crimson ship.

Softly, more softly, the strains of music issued from the kantele; sweetly, more sweetly, the tones of the wonderful singer vibrated in the air. Then suddenly both stopped and silence reigned.

XXXV. THE FLIGHT

Quietly, very quietly, the Minstrel rose and looked around upon the sleepers. With finger-tips upon his lips he beckoned to the hero Ilmarinen and to the young heroes who stood beside him.

"Be cautious, be brave," he whispered, "and soon we shall win the Sampo. Speak no word, make no sound to break the magic spell, but follow me and do my bidding."

Then with great care he opened the wallet of reindeer leather that he carried always beneath his belt. He looked within and picked out, one by one, a handful of sleep-needles, long and slender and exceedingly sharp. Silent as the moon among the clouds he moved on tiptoes cautiously between the rows of slumbering people. With his magic needles he crossed the eye-lashes of the sleepers, pinning their eyelids close together and thus holding them so that they might not waken.

"Sleep! sleep!" he murmured softly. "Sleep till the daylight fades in Pohyola. Sleep, and waken not till the golden sun rises bright in the Land of Heroes. Sleep, and let no dreams disturb you."

He waved his arms above them, silently bidding them farewell, and left them there where they had fallen. The unlovely Mistress, the swordsmen and the spearsmen, the old men and the married women, the young men and the half-grown girls, and the little children—he left them all sweetly slumbering, forgetful, senseless, harmless.

"Now for the Sampo!" he whispered, and with noiseless foot-steps he hastened away toward the hill of copper. Behind him followed the heroes and the young men and the maidens with curling hair, and not one dared utter a word or in any way disturb the wonderful silence that prevailed.

As they drew near to the hill, however, they could hear the magic Sampo grinding, grinding in its darksome prison; they could hear the lid of many colors turning, turning, and pouring out wealth without cessation. But at the entrance to the cavern the great doors were shut—nine huge and heavy doors, and each door was made secure by nine locks of hardest metal.

The Minstrel paused, he could go no farther; the heroes stood waiting around him. Gently he began to sing, softly he chanted a song so sweet, so strong, that it had power to move the rocks and even persuade the mighty hills and the restless sea. And as he sang, the copper mountain began to tremble and the doors of the cavern were shaken. Thereupon the hero Ilmarinen and the young men that were with him hastened to pour oil upon the rusty metal. With reindeer fat they smeared the locks, and they greased the hinges with butter, lest they should creak and make a rattling.

Then Wainamoinen, still singing, touched the locks with his wizard fingers and the bolts slid back; he pushed gently against the yielding metal and the nine mighty doors opened silently and without a sound.

The heroes pressed forward to the entrance, eager to see what the cave contained; and lo! as they looked within, they saw the Sampo with its lid of many colors standing in its place in the middle of the strongly built prison. Very beautiful was the magic mill, its resplendent sides embossed with gold and lined with silver; gorgeously beautiful was its rainbow cover, full of pictures of men and beasts and trees and flowers. The wheels of the mill were whirring softly, its levers were moving in their places; it was grinding out riches for Pohyola.

"Who now will carry this Sampo out of its prison-house?" asked the Minstrel.

"I will carry it out," answered Ahti, the nimble, long-armed fisherman. "I am a man of strength, a son of heroes. Stand back and see how quickly I shall remove it to our waiting ship. See, I have only to touch it with the toe of my boot and the deed is done."

He pushed against the Sampo; he twined his long arms about it and lifted with all his might; he braced himself with his knees and strained till the blood rushed from his mouth and nose. But the Sampo stood in its place unmoved, grinding and turning without cessation.

"Foolish boaster!" cried Wainamoinen. "A big mouth has never yet moved mountains. Great talkers are always little doers."

Then he began to play softly upon the kantele; and as he played, the Sampo began to rock to and fro, it turned itself around as though breaking away from the chains which held it. At a sign from the Minstrel the young heroes, with Ilmarinen as their captain, seized hold of it and carried it forth from the hill of copper. Silently, without rustling a leaf or snapping a twig, they bore it across the fields and the meadows and placed it on board of their waiting vessel. There they lashed it with ropes to the strong deck beams. They bound it securely so that it could not be moved.

"Now let every one work valiantly at his oar," said Ilmarinen, "and let the red sail be hoisted on the mast."

Instantly the benches were filled with rowers; all the young men and also the fifty fair maidens bent to their work; the water boiled with the strokes of a hundred long oars.

"Speed thee, O crimson vessel," said Wainamoinen. "Hasten from the hostile shores of Pohyola. And O, thou North Wind, come and urge the ship along. Blow and give assistance to the oarsmen. Give lightness to the rudder, give skill to the helmsman, and swiftly bear us over this vast expanse of water."

Merrily and hopefully, then, the rowers rowed; the Minstrel steered, and the strong North Wind pushed against the well-stretched sail. And away and away, onward and onward, the vessel flew over the lonely sea. From morning until mid-day, and from mid-day until evening, it ploughed its way through the surging waves; the land faded from sight, and the heroes, looking forward, could see naught but one vast field of tossing waters. "We are lost! We shall never find the Land of Heroes," they murmured.

"Have courage! be brave!" said Wainamoinen. "Beyond this sea lies our own sweet country, the home of heroes."

Then Ahti, the nimble boaster, spoke up and said, "Why should we still speak in whispers, fearing to be heard? The shores of Pohyola are far away, the Mistress sleeps, there is no one to listen. Let us be jolly and glad, and even a little noisy, rejoicing over our victory."

"Nay, nay, we are not yet out of danger," said the Minstrel.

"But the time is passing," answered the long-armed one; "daylight is fading and darkness is approaching. Let us at least have a little song to cheer our drooping spirits."

"Nay, nay," repeated the steadfast Minstrel. "We must not sing upon these waters; singing would turn the ship from its right course, songs would hinder the rowers. The night and darkness would find us bewildered, and we should indeed be lost on a shoreless sea. Nay, nay, keep silent, and sing no songs till we sight the shores of our own fair land."

So the rowers rowed in silence, and the steersman steered and spoke not, and the hearts of all were hopeful. All night long they rowed and sailed and felt no weariness. The second day passed, and still no land was seen. The third day came, it was mid-day, when a long white shore and the lofty headland of Wainola appeared lying far away between the sea and the sky.

"O master! Why may we not sing?" cried Ahti, always restless and in the way. "Before us is the Land of Heroes, and we have won the glorious Sampo. Let us sing and be glad."

"Nay, nay," again said Wainamoinen. "It is too early to rejoice. When we hear our own home doors creaking behind us, then will be the time to sing and rejoice. When we see the fire burning on our own hearth-stones, then we may be glad because of victory."

"Well, then," answered the long-armed, thoughtless one, "I, at least, feel like rejoicing this very hour. If no one else will sing, I will. I will give you a song of my own composing."

He stood in the stern beside the Minstrel. He turned his face toward the prow and pursed up his mouth to sing. His voice was hoarse, his tones were discordant, there was no music in his song. He opened his mouth till his beard wagged and his long chin trembled. He waved his arms and shouted—he shouted so loudly that the sound was heard far across the water. In many villages it was heard, alarming all the people and filling their hearts with terror.

By the long white shore a blue crane was wading, looking down to count his toes in the clear sea-water. Suddenly he heard the noise of Ahti's singing—a noise most strange, most unlike any other that had ever broken the silence of the sea. The crane, alarmed, spread his wings and leaped upward. He screamed in terror and flew rapidly up, up to the sheltering sky. He flew rapidly and paused not till he had reached the distant shores of Pohyola. There below him he saw the fields and the meadows and the old familiar places where he and his mate had often-times nested and reared their young. Then, to his great wonder, he saw all the people lying asleep on the ground and the mighty Mistress slumbering in their midst, her eyelids pinned together with magic needles.

This sight gave new alarm to the blue crane. His terror was too great to be described. He screamed, not once only, but ten times, loudly, harshly, terrifically. The noise awoke Dame Louhi the Mistress; it awoke all her slumbering people. They shook the sleep-needles from their eyes and looked around, dazed, bewildered, wondering what had happened to them. The armed men formed themselves in battle array, waiting for commands; the old men and the married women hastened to their homes, ashamed of their weakness; the children, too, sought their own firesides, for night was approaching.

Up rose Dame Louhi, angry and apprehensive. She saw that the Minstrel and his heroes had disappeared, and anxious fore-bodings filled her heart. She ran to her treasure-room; her chests of gold and silver had not been disturbed. She hastened to the barnyard; all her favorite cattle were there, not one was missing. She looked into the barns; they had not been plun-dered, not an ear of corn had been taken.

"But the Sampo, the Sampo!" she cried. "It was the Sampo that the robbers demanded. Have they carried it away?"

Then came an old serving-man with trembling limbs and with tears in his eyes, who knelt in the dust before her and begged her mercy.

"Yes," he said, "they have carried away the Sampo and its pic-tured lid. While we were all drowned in slumber they broke into the cavern beneath the copper mountain, they drew back the bolts and opened the mighty doors. Then they lifted the Sampo from its place and bore it away, but whither I cannot tell."

"They must have carried it to their red-prowed ship," said

another old man, "for the haven where it was moored is empty and no crimson sail is anywhere in sight."

Dame Louhi, grim and old and haggard, fell into the greatest fury. She stormed, she screamed, she wept, she prayed. "O Maiden of the Air," she cried, "O queen and ruler of the mists and stormclouds! Send me help I pray thee. Cover the sea with dense fogs and clouds of vapor. Send down the winds and let the tempest rage round those wicked robbers. O Maiden, sink them all beneath the billows, but save the Sampo. Let it not fall into the raging sea, but hold it in thy large hands and bring it safe back to Pohyola's lovely shore."

The Maiden of the Air heard her and was pleased with her prayer. She called to her servants, the mists, the clouds, and the winds, to wreak vengeance upon the heroes, to drive their ship far out of its course and sink it in the bottomless sea.

Forthwith thick clouds obscured the sky and dense fogs covered the waters like a cloak of darkness. The winds rose in fury and a mighty storm swept down from above. All the winds, save the North Wind alone, assailed the heroes' gallant vessel. The mast was splintered just above the sail-yard, the red sail itself was blown away, the rudder was unmanageable, all the oars were made useless, so terrible were the winds and the tossing waves.

Like a withered leaf of autumn the ship was driven hither and thither through the mists and fearful darkness. The young men hid their faces, and the golden-haired maidens cowered beneath the benches. The nimble Ahti, cause of all this trouble, lay prone upon the deck speechless with fright. Even the hero Ilmarinen crouched himself down in the narrow hold and bewailed their great misfortune.

"Never before have I seen such a storm as this," he moaned. "My hair is soaked with salt-water and my beard trembles with the shaking of the ship. My very heart thumps wildly as I hear the noise of the mighty tempest. O winds, have pity! O waves, deal gently with us all!"

The Minstrel, alone of all on board, stood up fearless and calm and steadfast as though no danger threatened.

"This is no place for weeping," he said. "You cannot save yourselves by howling. Groaning will not preserve you from evil, nor will grunting dispel misfortune."

He raised his hands high above his head and called upon all the powers of air and sky and sea to befriend the heroes in their dire distress.

"O sea, so vast, so grand, remember that we are small and weak, and deal gently with us! O waves, do not play too roughly with us, do not fill our ship with water, do not break her ribs or hull beams. O winds, rise up higher and play with the clouds in heaven. Drive away the mists that blind us, but blow gently upon our crimson vessel, and waft, oh! waft it safely southward to the shores of Hero Land."

And the lively Ahti, still sprawling prone upon the high deck, lifted up his voice also and prayed to his god, the great bird of the mountains:

"O thou mighty eagle, come down from thy eyry on the heaven-high cliffs, and help us. Bring with thee a magic feather—yes, two or three—that they may put a charm upon this ship and protect it from disaster."

But still the storm raged; the waves dashed furiously against the vessel; the winds howled and fought and gave no heed to Wainamoinen's prayer; the fog still hung darkly upon the waters or drifted in mist-like clouds before the wind; the eagle of Ahti screamed in vain.

Thus all day the red ship drifted helpless upon the raging sea; for two long days the tempest prevailed and the heroes were in despair. But on the third day the Minstrel's prayer was answered. The storm ceased, the fog was lifted, and the sun shone out, bright and clear in the midst of the sky. The heroes sprang up and shouted for joy; they had forgotten their fears.

"To your oars, my brave men, to your oars!" shouted Ilmarinen, and every man bent willingly to his task.

The maidens also regained their courage. The color returned to their cheeks; their eyes, so long tear-wet, now sparkled with joy; with songs of gladness they woke the echoes of the sea, and cheered the laboring oarsmen.

"It is well to rejoice and be merry," said the steadfast Minstrel, "but we are still upon the uncertain sea, we are still far away from our own safe home land."

XXXVI. THE PURSUIT

Already great changes were taking place in Pohyola. The frost spirit, peeping over the mountains, saw that the hill of copper had been robbed of its treasure, that the prison-house of the Sampo was empty. He listened; he could no longer hear the whirring of the wheels or the busy clacking of the pictured cover. So he stretched his long, cold fingers over the land, and everything that he touched was frozen and blasted. He breathed in the air, and chilling mists hovered over the hills and descended upon the fields and gardens. The reign of plenty in Pohyola was ended.

Dame Louhi, old and grim and undaunted, called loudly to her serving-men, her warriors, and her sailors. As a mother hen summons her chickens around her at the approach of a danger, so did she marshal her swordsmen, her spearsmen, and her stout-hearted oarsmen.

"Make ready now our great warship," she said. "We must pursue the hated robbers; we must overcome and destroy them and bring the precious Sampo back to our own shores. Lose not a moment, be courageous, be skilful, be strong—and hasten, hasten, hasten."

They sprang forward by tens and by hundreds, every one eager and impatient to obey her commands. They pushed the mighty warship out into the deep water. They hoisted her mast and spread her broad sail upon the sail-yards. The rowers sat down in their places and each seized his long oar. The warriors shouted and all the crew joined in singing the war-song of Pohyola. And the Mistress herself stood at the helm and with gaunt hands wielded the great rudder and steered the vessel out to sea. The friendly North Wind filled the sail, the rowers bent to their oars, and the famous voyage was begun.

Like a monstrous sea-bird skimming over the waves, or like a white cloud scudding low upon the billows, so did the swift war-ship speed onward over the vast and measureless sea. With lips drawn tightly over her toothless mouth, Dame Louhi stood at her post, silent and determined, and but one thought filled the minds and hearts of her courageous crew—the thought to serve her and obey her.

Meanwhile the heroes on their storm-battered red ship were sailing hopefully homeward, thanking Jumala for their escape from the fog and the storm. The Sampo was still safely secured with strong ropes to the bow beams of their brave vessel; its wheels were whirring; its levers were at work; it was grinding out great streams of salt to feed the hungry sea.

"To-morrow we shall turn it over," said Ilmarinen; "and then it will pour out gold and silver enough for every hero in Wainola. To-morrow—but who knows what may happen to-morrow?"

The Minstrel, with steady hand and hopeful heart, sat at the stern, guiding the vessel straight through the pathless waters. "Ah! who knows what may happen to-morrow?" he echoed, as he gazed with expectant eyes toward the dim, distant horizon.

"Ahti," he cried, "climb up on the broken mast and look around at the sea and the sky. Tell us whether the horizon is clear or whether clouds are rising in the air to vex us. Look before us, look behind us, and then tell us what you see."

Quickly the long-armed one obeyed. He climbed the mast to its splintered top, and there he stood, balanced on one foot, unmoved and unafraid, as though on solid ground. Eastward he looked and westward, and naught did he see but the trackless waters and the unscarred sky. He looked toward the south, and a smile of pleasure overspread his face.

"Far away, I see the lofty headland and the long, white shore of your own dear country, O heroes!" he said. "It is the same shore from which the storm drove us three days ago; but the distance is great."

Then he looked toward the north and with his sharp eyes eagerly scanned the horizon.

"Away, away in the northwest I see a little cloud," he said. "It is a white cloud, and a small one, and it sits low down upon the water."

"Nonsense!" said Wainamoinen, losing patience. "No sailor ever saw a white cloud in the northwest sitting low upon the water. Look again!"

Ahti obeyed. "I see it more plainly now," he said. "It is not a cloud but an island—a small island looming up on the horizon. And I see dark specks hovering over it—they must be falcons or nesting ravens flying among the birch trees."

"Nonsense!" a second time cried Wainamoinen. "Give your eyes a moment's rest and then look again."

The long-armed one shaded his brows with his broad palm and looked long and eagerly. Then he leaped nimbly down upon the deck as though content to see no more.

"It is a warship from Pohyola," he said, trembling and much disturbed. "It is a great ship with a hundred oarsmen and a thousand armed warriors. It is pursuing us, it is gaining upon us. Look now, and all of you can see it plainly."

Loudly then did the Minstrel call to the heroes. "Row, now, with all speed, my brave men! Rush the ship forward! Let us not be overtaken."

"Row, row, and let no man falter!" shouted Ilmarinen, himself wielding the foremost oar.

Loudly did the rowlocks ring with the quick, even pressure of the oars. The red ship swayed from side to side as its sharp prow cut its way through the billows. Behind it the water boiled as beneath a mighty cataract. On the right and on the left the spray was dashed as the rain in a furious hurricane. But, swiftly as the heroes rowed, their vessel moved not half so swiftly as the warship of Pohyola.

"We are lost!" moaned the young men, desperately bending to their oars. And the fifty maidens hid their faces in their bosoms and echoed the hopeless cry, "We are lost!" Even the hero Ilmarinen, the mighty wizard, could see no way of escape from their pitiless pursuers, and he, too, losing all his courage, began to bewail their luckless fate. But Wainamoinen, steadfast even in misfortune, spoke up cheeringly and with encouraging words.

"There is yet one way by which we may escape," he said. "There is still one trick of magic that I have reserved for a time like this. I will try it."

From beneath his belt he drew his tinder-box of silver. He opened it skilfully with his left thumb and finger. From its right-hand corner he took a bit of soft pitch, black and pliable, and from its left-hand corner a piece of tinder no larger than a pea. Then with care he enclosed the tinder within the pitch and cast it over his left shoulder far out into the sea.

"O wonderful tinder and pitch," he said, "do marvellous things now, and shield us from the wrath of Pohyola's mighty Mistress. Raise up a barrier between her ship and ours—a barrier past which she cannot sail. Work quickly, work powerfully, and help us soon to arrive safe in Wainola's sheltered harbor!"

And now the great warship was but a little way behind. The heroes looking back could see a host of armed men standing beneath the wind-filled sail. They could see the hundred long oars rising and falling as though moved by a single hand. They could see the Mistress herself, even Dame Louhi, sitting in the high seat at the stern and shouting her commands to the crew. Her face was grim with determination, her eyes shone green with the joy of expected triumph, the sound of her harsh voice rose high above the din of clashing oars and dashing waves and the shouts and cries of pursuers and pursued.

XXXVII. THE FATE OF THE SAMPO

Like a cruel eagle in pursuit of a young falcon the mighty war-ship of Pohyola sped onward, relentless, pitiless, triumphant. At every sweep of the hundred oars she seemed to leap from the waves, to spring forward like a wild beast pouncing upon its prey. The swordsmen shouted, the spearsmen poised their weapons, they waited only for Dame Louhi's command.

"In another moment!" she shouted; "but have a care not to harm the Sampo."

Then suddenly a wonderful thing took place. Right in the ship's pathway a huge iceberg rose dripping from the sea, a mighty, impassable barrier blocking the way like a massive wall of iron. High above the masthead of the speeding vessel, the white cliff towered—it towered even to the clouds and the blue sky beyond. The magic spell of the Minstrel's small bit of tinder had done its work.

In an instant there was a dreadful crash, a sound of breaking timbers, of grinding ice, of shouts and groans and despairing cries. The warship was wedged firmly in a rift of the great ice cliff. The mast was broken short off and fell splashing into the sea. Every rib of the strong vessel was shattered, the rowlocks were broken, the oars were lost in the turbulent waves, the deck boards were loosened and carried away.

Then it was that the Mistress, the mighty Wise Woman of the North, showed her great power. With one foot in the sea and the other firmly placed in the rift of the icy barrier, she quickly changed her form into that of a monstrous gyrfalcon, the fiercest, the most untiring of birds of prey. Of the sides of the ship she formed herself wings, wide-spreading and powerful. Of the long rudder she fashioned a tail, flat and broad, with quill-like feathers overlapping each other as do the boards on the roof of a house. Of the ship's dragon-headed prow she made herself a beak of copper, sharp, relentless, cruel. Of the two massive war shields that hung at the ship's bows she made herself a pair of round eyes, keen as the eyes of a panther, restless, untiring. And lastly, of ten sharp scythes in the ship's hold she formed talons for herself, fierce, curved fingers, ending in needle-like claws, with which to fight her battles.

With a voice like that of a tempest she screamed to her warriors who were clinging to the remains of the wreck: "Make yourselves very small! Make yourselves very small and do as I bid you!"

They obeyed her, and beneath her wings she hid her hundred swordsmen, while upon her tail she placed her thousand spearsmen.

With a screech that thrilled the sea to its very bottom and made the great iceberg tremble and totter, the mighty bird extended her wings and soared aloft. Up, up, she flew, surmounting the icy barrier that had risen in her path, undismayed, triumphant. Like a dark storm-cloud in the depth of winter, obscuring the sky and overshadowing the earth, she hovered midway between the blue heavens and the boundless sea, eagerly looking for the prey which had wellnigh escaped her.

Meanwhile the heroes, rejoicing because of their deliverance, were rapidly nearing their wished-for haven of safety. The headland of Wainola and the long, white shore so dear to them rose plain and clear above the horizon; soon their perilous voyage would be ended. Joy beamed in every countenance and hope cheered every heart.

Suddenly the sun was obscured and an ink-black shadow fell upon the deck of the red ship—it fell upon the Sampo where it was bound with ropes to the bow beams. The rowers paused in their rowing and looked up, amazed, confounded. Even Wainamoinen, so brave, so steadfast, turned pale as he gazed aloft and saw the peril that menaced them. The next moment the fierce gyrfalcon, the transformed Louhi, swooped down and perched herself upon the splintered mast. With one horrid foot she grasped the sail-yard, while with the other she reached down and sought to seize the Sampo.

Surely then did the hero Minstrel feel that his doom was at hand. He let go of the long oar, the rudder with which he had steered the vessel, and as it fell splashing into the sea, he lifted his eyes and prayed:

"O Jumala, good and kind, help me in this my time of peril. Cast a robe of fire round me. Shield my head, my arms, my body, and let no stroke of weapon harm me. Help us all with strength and wisdom."

With a hasty effort he drew his enchanted sword, the sword, Faultless, the last piece of workmanship wrought in Ilmarinen's smithy. He raised it to strike the mighty bird upon the sail-yard. But first he spoke to her, humbly, pleadingly, as an earnest peace-maker:

"Hail! hail! O Mistress of Pohyola! Will you not now divide the Sampo with me, each taking half of the precious treasure? Much better it will be for us to share it like friends than to fight for it and then lose it."

Fearfully screamed the fierce gyrfalcon, the transformed Wise Woman, as she answered, "No, I will not divide the Sampo with you. The mill of plenty is mine, and no part of it will I share with strangers and robbers."

Having said this she gaped horribly with her beak of copper, and again reached far out with her sharpened talons, trying to grasp the coveted Sampo. Failing in this, she screamed a second time, and from her wings the swordsmen leaped down. She screamed again and a host of spearsmen dropped upon the red ship's deck. Dreadful was the confusion that followed, and sad would have been the fate of the heroes had not Wainamoinen, with unheard-of swiftness, let fall his sword of magic. He struck with all his might the extended talons, the crooked fingers, the horrid feet of the relentless gyrfalcon. The sharp edge of the weapon fell squarely upon the scythe-like, grasping claws; it sheared them off close by the ankle joints; it shattered them every one, save only the smallest, the crookedest, the indescribable little finger of Dame Louhi.

Loudly, most horribly did she shriek, not more from pain than from intensest anger and despair. And now on the fated red ship of the heroes an awful struggle began—a struggle the bloodiest and the woefullest that sea or sky ever looked upon or minstrel's song ever painted in words. Swords flashed, spears crashed, men shouted. The screams of frightened maidens, the moans of the wounded and the dying, the victorious cries of the warriors, and the despairing lamentations of the heroes—all these sounds were mingled in one awful chorus. But above every other sound the hoarse cries of the dauntless Mistress were heard, making the earth shudder and causing the deep sea to quake.

One by one the heroes fell; and by fives and tens the low-browed warriors of Pohyola were thrust overboard to perish in the waves.

Towering above both friends and foes, mighty in strength and endurance, the master Smith moved to and fro performing many deeds of courage. But the weavers of his fate had decided against him; it was not for him to prevail. Covered with wounds, the blood flowing from his arms, his head, his heart, he felt his end approaching. "O thou who wert once the Maid of Beauty!" he cried, looking upward. "O thou matchless one among women! I see thee in the mist-filled air, I hear thy voice calling from the rainbow arch. I come! I come! I come to meet thee!"

Overwhelmed in the fight, his arms unnerved, his strength departed, he fell toppling into the sea. As a giant pine, when rent by the storm, falls crashing from the mountain top and is swallowed in the bottomless gorge below, so fell the hero. The pitying waves closed over him; he was with his loved ones in the halls of rest.

Bravely, too, did the ever-ready Ahti struggle to defend the Sampo, wielding his long arms valorously, until his strength failing he also was hurled into the hungry deep. And Wainamoinen, immovable as the lofty headland of his own sweet country, stood steadfast at his post, directing and cheering his comrades and overwhelming with terror the foes who dared approach him.

Suddenly, in the midst of the mêlée, the mighty bird of prey, even the transformed Mistress of Pohyola, leaped down from her lofty perch, and sweeping across the vessel's bows sought to carry away the Sampo. With her maimed and useless feet she struck it, and with her one crooked, indescribable finger she grasped it. But the ropes with which the heroes had bound it confused her—she could not break them. She therefore seized the pictured cover with her monstrous beak, she pulled it from its place, and, twisting it until it broke into three jagged pieces, she cast it into the sea. Angry and despairing, she flapped her rude wings against the sides of the mill, smashing the wheels and levers and breaking the wonderful framework into a thousand pieces.

Dismayed by the ruin she had caused, the fierce gyrfalcon, the determined Wise One, ceased her destroying work and looked around her. Slowly, as in pain, she spread her wings and rose from the crimson deck all strewn with fragments; but, as she leaped high into the air, she seized with her one indescribable finger a single small, three-cornered piece of the precious Sampo; with the strength of despair she clutched it within her crooked claw.

"Alas! this is all that I can recover for my poor country, my ruined people!" she screamed. "O my Pohyola! O my dear land, once so prosperous! May Jumala give me strength to carry this small, precious gift to you!"

Feebly, she soared upward, she turned her flaming eyes toward Pohyola, and with laboring wings made her way slowly across the sea.

By now the red ship had floated far, and the few remaining heroes shouted as, looking upward, they saw the friendly headland looming right above them. The next moment the vessel's keel was grating upon the sand; its long prow was jutting quite over the safe, inviting beach. The fighting had ceased with the breaking of the Sampo. With the flight of the baffled Mistress all animosity was ended.

Like one awaking from a swoon, the Minstrel looked around him. Where were the heroes who had survived the great struggle? Where were the frightened maidens? Where were the Pohyolan warriors whom the sea had not claimed? Not one remained; all had leaped ashore and fled. The Minstrel stood alone on the red, disordered deck.

The fragments of the Sampo had been scattered in many places. Some of the wheels had rolled into the sea; they had sunk to the bottom, there to be covered with tangled weeds and the slimy ooze of the unseen depths. The levers and the lighter parts of the framework were still floating upon the water, tossed hither and thither by the waves and the wind. The fragments of the pictured cover had already been carried far away, were sailing like little ships across the vast expanse of the sea.

"Alas, alas! that the grandest treasure in the world should thus be scattered and lost!" cried the Minstrel.

He leaped quickly overboard into the shallow water and with anxious haste began to gather up the few remaining pieces that were still floating around the vessel. With much labor and care he picked them up, laying them one by one for safe keeping in the folds of his long cloak. But alas! all these pieces were small, and he searched in vain for any trace of the precious pictured cover.

At length, when not another vestige could be found, the Minstrel with tired limbs went up to the misty summit of the headland, carrying the fragments with him. Very old and feeble he was, but steadfast and brave as in former days. He stood alone upon the lofty shore, gazing far out over the illimitable sea. He stood there alone, his head erect, his white beard streaming in the wind, and his hands uplifted toward the heavens.

"O Jumala!" he prayed, "O Jumala, thou giver of blessings, grant that these small fragments of the mill of fortune may take root and flourish and in time bring great joy and many comforts to the dear people of this pleasant land."

Then taking the pieces reverently in his hands, he planted them one by one in the ground, covering them deep in the rich soil of Wainola's headland. And even while he stood there and watched, his prayer was answered. For the small broken fragments of the Sampo took root and grew up quickly, producing great crops of rye and barley, and luscious fruits of all kinds, and other foods in great abundance. Thus were the famishing people fed and made glad, prosperity smiled upon all, and the Land of Heroes again became the land of plenty and of peace.

As the Minstrel still stood on the lofty headland and looked into the far distance, his eyes became very bright and his vision wonderfully clear. He saw all the other fragments of the Sampo and its pictured cover, and he watched each one as it was carried east, west, or south and left upon some strange, unheard-of shore. Some of the pieces floated far, far to the summer islands where the sun shines hot every day in the year. And on the shores where they were drifted, wonderful trees sprang up, bearing delicious fruits and gorgeous flowers, such as the people of northern climes had never seen nor dreamed about. The fragments that were carried to the eastern seas spread their influence and took root in many lands. Like the Sampo itself, they poured out wealth in many forms and in endless profusion. And from them sprang numberless beautiful and priceless objects—pearls and precious stones, gold and silver, fine silks, strong castles, and kingly palaces.

As for the pictured cover, it was borne far, very far, to the utmost bounds of the western sea. Broken though it was, and battered and torn into strips and fragments, it, too, performed most marvellous things. For in the places wherein it rested and took root, noble men and women sprang up, scholars and statesmen and skilful workers in all kinds of metals, and these were destined to rule the world.

The heavier fragments which had sunk beneath the waves and were buried, invisible, in the black ooze and among the tangled seaweed, they also took root and spread out many branches toward every corner of the earth. And from them sprang the wealth of the seas, the joy of all fishermen, the triumph of sailors, white-sailed merchant-ships and mighty vessels of war.

And the tiny, rough-cornered piece, which with her last strength the baffled Mistress had carried with her only finger back to her home land—what became of that? Small and without beauty it was, and there was little that it could do; but from it sprang such scant comforts and pleasures as the people of the Frozen Land have enjoyed until this day—warm underground huts, fishes for food, soft furs for clothing, and the reindeer for all kinds of uses.

With great wonder and thankfulness Wainamoinen saw these

marvellous transformations—these changes by which the Sampo enriched and blessed not only his own land, but many an undiscovered and far-distant shore. His heart throbbed with joy immeasurable, and his fingers began to play on the strings of his kantele. Sweet was the music that he called forth, sweeter than any that mortal man has ever heard since that day; and as he played he sang again the old, old songs of the world's beginning, the old, old songs with which he had already charmed not only men and women, but all living things. And when he had ceased singing and the sound of the kantele was heard no more, he again raised his hands and called earnestly to the mighty, the invisible Jumala:

"O thou great and good Creator, look down and hear our last petition. Grant that we may live in joy and comfort, and when our span of life is ended, let us die in peace and hope, loved by all who know us, and worthy to be honored through the ages."

So, also, prays the weaver of tales, whose story is now ended.

NOTES

NOTE A.—A very long time ago, among the ancestors of the people known as Finns, there were professional minstrels called *runolainen*, whose business it was to preserve the memory of the national songs, folk-lore tales, and old sagas of the race. They went from place to place, among the lowly as well as the great, singing their songs and playing the *kantele*, a primitive sort of harp from which they drew entrancing music. Through them a vast store of legends, wonder tales, songs, proverbs, tales of magic, etc., survived from generation to generation solely in the memories of the people. It was not until about a century ago that any systematic effort was made to give this legendary lore a permanent form by putting it into writing. The first person to attempt this was the Finnish poet Zakris Topelius, who put together and published a small volume of traditions and folk tales. An interest in the subject being awakened, Dr. Elias Lönnrot undertook the task of collecting and putting into permanent form all that was best in the legendary literature of his countrymen. Many years were occupied in this work. He travelled to every part of Finland, lived with people of every condition, and listened to their recitals of stories and songs which they had learned from the lips of their ancestors. These he committed to writing, and from them he constructed a single poem which he called "Kalevala." This poem is remarkable for its great length and its tiresome, monotonous metre—qualities which discourage English readers from attempting its acquaintance. From the folk-lore tales of the *runolainen* and from portions of this long poem, the present weaver of tales has constructed the story of "The Sampo," with such variations and connecting links as seemed most necessary to fit it to the tastes and requirements of modern readers.

NOTE B, *page 2.*—The Frozen Land may have been identical with modern Lapland. In any case, it was situated in the far-distant North and was known in the original tale as Pohyola, or Sariola. Hero Land, or the Land of Heroes, was the ancient home of the Finns. It was known sometimes as Kalevala, sometimes as Wainola, but of its exact location there is no certain knowledge.

NOTE C, *page* 5.—"Sampo"—compare this with Aladdin's lamp, with the philosopher's stone of the mediæval alchemists, with Solomon's carpet, etc.

NOTE D, *page* 19.—This story of the origin of iron is derived from the ninth rune of the poem "Kalevala." It is here related with numerous variations.

NOTE E, *page* 72.—The Minstrel's journey to Tuonela is briefly related in the sixteenth rune of the "Kalevala." The story-teller has not attempted to follow the poetical account closely. Compare the visit of Odysseus to the Land of Shades ("Odyssey," bk. XI); also see Virgil's "Æneid," bk. VI, and the "Elder Edda" for similar narratives.

NOTE F, *page* 124.—The story of the tests of courage to which Ilmarinen was required to submit is related in the nineteenth rune of "Kalevala." Some points of similarity are found in the story of Jason and Medea.

NOTE G, *page* 181.—Old Persian books tell us that at an early period the climate of some distant northern countries was so mild that they enjoyed nine months of summer with only three months of winter. Finally, sudden changes occurred which completely reversed this order of the seasons. Can we believe that in the present story we have a faint reminiscence of that very ancient time?

A CATALOG OF SELECTED
DOVER BOOKS
IN ALL FIELDS OF INTEREST

A CATALOG OF SELECTED DOVER
BOOKS IN ALL FIELDS OF INTEREST

CONCERNING THE SPIRITUAL IN ART, Wassily Kandinsky. Pioneering work by father of abstract art. Thoughts on color theory, nature of art. Analysis of earlier masters. 12 illustrations. 80pp. of text. 5⅜ x 8½.   0-486-23411-8

CELTIC ART: The Methods of Construction, George Bain. Simple geometric techniques for making Celtic interlacements, spirals, Kells-type initials, animals, humans, etc. Over 500 illustrations. 160pp. 9 x 12. (Available in U.S. only.)   0-486-22923-8

AN ATLAS OF ANATOMY FOR ARTISTS, Fritz Schider. Most thorough reference work on art anatomy in the world. Hundreds of illustrations, including selections from works by Vesalius, Leonardo, Goya, Ingres, Michelangelo, others. 593 illustrations. 192pp. 7⅛ x 10¼.   0-486-20241-0

CELTIC HAND STROKE-BY-STROKE (Irish Half-Uncial from "The Book of Kells"): An Arthur Baker Calligraphy Manual, Arthur Baker. Complete guide to creating each letter of the alphabet in distinctive Celtic manner. Covers hand position, strokes, pens, inks, paper, more. Illustrated. 48pp. 8¼ x 11.   0-486-24336-2

EASY ORIGAMI, John Montroll. Charming collection of 32 projects (hat, cup, pelican, piano, swan, many more) specially designed for the novice origami hobbyist. Clearly illustrated easy-to-follow instructions insure that even beginning papercrafters will achieve successful results. 48pp. 8¼ x 11.   0-486-27298-2

BLOOMINGDALE'S ILLUSTRATED 1886 CATALOG: Fashions, Dry Goods and Housewares, Bloomingdale Brothers. Famed merchants' extremely rare catalog depicting about 1,700 products: clothing, housewares, firearms, dry goods, jewelry, more. Invaluable for dating, identifying vintage items. Also, copyright-free graphics for artists, designers. Co-published with Henry Ford Museum & Greenfield Village. 160pp. 8¼ x 11.   0-486-25780-0

THE ART OF WORLDLY WISDOM, Baltasar Gracian. "Think with the few and speak with the many," "Friends are a second existence," and "Be able to forget" are among this 1637 volume's 300 pithy maxims. A perfect source of mental and spiritual refreshment, it can be opened at random and appreciated either in brief or at length. 128pp. 5⅜ x 8½.   0-486-44034-6

JOHNSON'S DICTIONARY: A Modern Selection, Samuel Johnson (E. L. McAdam and George Milne, eds.). This modern version reduces the original 1755 edition's 2,300 pages of definitions and literary examples to a more manageable length, retaining the verbal pleasure and historical curiosity of the original. 480pp. 5³⁄₁₆ x 8¼.   0-486-44089-3

ADVENTURES OF HUCKLEBERRY FINN, Mark Twain, Illustrated by E. W. Kemble. A work of eternal richness and complexity, a source of ongoing critical debate, and a literary landmark, Twain's 1885 masterpiece about a barefoot boy's journey of self-discovery has enthralled readers around the world. This handsome clothbound reproduction of the first edition features all 174 of the original black-and-white illustrations. 368pp. 5⅜ x 8½.   0-486-44322-1

PSYCHOLOGY OF MUSIC, Carl E. Seashore. Classic work discusses music as a medium from psychological viewpoint. Clear treatment of physical acoustics, auditory apparatus, sound perception, development of musical skills, nature of musical feeling, host of other topics. 88 figures. 408pp. 5⅜ x 8½.   0-486-21851-1

LIFE IN ANCIENT EGYPT, Adolf Erman. Fullest, most thorough, detailed older account with much not in more recent books, domestic life, religion, magic, medicine, commerce, much more. Many illustrations reproduce tomb paintings, carvings, hieroglyphs, etc. 597pp. 5⅜ x 8½.   0-486-22632-8

SUNDIALS, Their Theory and Construction, Albert Waugh. Far and away the best, most thorough coverage of ideas, mathematics concerned, types, construction, adjusting anywhere. Simple, nontechnical treatment allows even children to build several of these dials. Over 100 illustrations. 230pp. 5⅜ x 8½.   0-486-22947-5

THEORETICAL HYDRODYNAMICS, L. M. Milne-Thomson. Classic exposition of the mathematical theory of fluid motion, applicable to both hydrodynamics and aerodynamics. Over 600 exercises. 768pp. 6⅛ x 9¼.   0-486-68970-0

OLD-TIME VIGNETTES IN FULL COLOR, Carol Belanger Grafton (ed.). Over 390 charming, often sentimental illustrations, selected from archives of Victorian graphics—pretty women posing, children playing, food, flowers, kittens and puppies, smiling cherubs, birds and butterflies, much more. All copyright-free. 48pp. 9¼ x 12¼.
0-486-27269-9

PERSPECTIVE FOR ARTISTS, Rex Vicat Cole. Depth, perspective of sky and sea, shadows, much more, not usually covered. 391 diagrams, 81 reproductions of drawings and paintings. 279pp. 5⅜ x 8½.   0-486-22487-2

DRAWING THE LIVING FIGURE, Joseph Sheppard. Innovative approach to artistic anatomy focuses on specifics of surface anatomy, rather than muscles and bones. Over 170 drawings of live models in front, back and side views, and in widely varying poses. Accompanying diagrams. 177 illustrations. Introduction. Index. 144pp. 8⅜ x 11¼.   0-486-26723-7

GOTHIC AND OLD ENGLISH ALPHABETS: 100 Complete Fonts, Dan X. Solo. Add power, elegance to posters, signs, other graphics with 100 stunning copyright-free alphabets: Blackstone, Dolbey, Germania, 97 more—including many lower-case, numerals, punctuation marks. 104pp. 8⅛ x 11.   0-486-24695-7

THE BOOK OF WOOD CARVING, Charles Marshall Sayers. Finest book for beginners discusses fundamentals and offers 34 designs. "Absolutely first rate . . . well thought out and well executed."—E. J. Tangerman. 118pp. 7¾ x 10⅝.   0-486-23654-4

ILLUSTRATED CATALOG OF CIVIL WAR MILITARY GOODS: Union Army Weapons, Insignia, Uniform Accessories, and Other Equipment, Schuyler, Hartley, and Graham. Rare, profusely illustrated 1846 catalog includes Union Army uniform and dress regulations, arms and ammunition, coats, insignia, flags, swords, rifles, etc. 226 illustrations. 160pp. 9 x 12.   0-486-24939-5

WOMEN'S FASHIONS OF THE EARLY 1900s: An Unabridged Republication of "New York Fashions, 1909," National Cloak & Suit Co. Rare catalog of mail-order fashions documents women's and children's clothing styles shortly after the turn of the century. Captions offer full descriptions, prices. Invaluable resource for fashion, costume historians. Approximately 725 illustrations. 128pp. 8⅜ x 11¼.
0-486-27276-1

THE MALLEUS MALEFICARUM OF KRAMER AND SPRENGER, translated by Montague Summers. Full text of most important witchhunter's "bible," used by both Catholics and Protestants. 278pp. 6⅝ x 10. 0-486-22802-9

SPANISH STORIES/CUENTOS ESPAÑOLES: A Dual-Language Book, Angel Flores (ed.). Unique format offers 13 great stories in Spanish by Cervantes, Borges, others. Faithful English translations on facing pages. 352pp. 5⅜ x 8½.
0-486-25399-6

GARDEN CITY, LONG ISLAND, IN EARLY PHOTOGRAPHS, 1869–1919, Mildred H. Smith. Handsome treasury of 118 vintage pictures, accompanied by carefully researched captions, document the Garden City Hotel fire (1899), the Vanderbilt Cup Race (1908), the first airmail flight departing from the Nassau Boulevard Aerodrome (1911), and much more. 96pp. 8⅞ x 11¾. 0-486-40669-5

OLD QUEENS, N.Y., IN EARLY PHOTOGRAPHS, Vincent F. Seyfried and William Asadorian. Over 160 rare photographs of Maspeth, Jamaica, Jackson Heights, and other areas. Vintage views of DeWitt Clinton mansion, 1939 World's Fair and more. Captions. 192pp. 8⅞ x 11. 0-486-26358-4

CAPTURED BY THE INDIANS: 15 Firsthand Accounts, 1750-1870, Frederick Drimmer. Astounding true historical accounts of grisly torture, bloody conflicts, relentless pursuits, miraculous escapes and more, by people who lived to tell the tale. 384pp. 5⅜ x 8½. 0-486-24901-8

THE WORLD'S GREAT SPEECHES (Fourth Enlarged Edition), Lewis Copeland, Lawrence W. Lamm, and Stephen J. McKenna. Nearly 300 speeches provide public speakers with a wealth of updated quotes and inspiration–from Pericles' funeral oration and William Jennings Bryan's "Cross of Gold Speech" to Malcolm X's powerful words on the Black Revolution and Earl of Spenser's tribute to his sister, Diana, Princess of Wales. 944pp. 5⅜ x 8⅜. 0-486-40903-1

THE BOOK OF THE SWORD, Sir Richard F. Burton. Great Victorian scholar/adventurer's eloquent, erudite history of the "queen of weapons"–from prehistory to early Roman Empire. Evolution and development of early swords, variations (sabre, broadsword, cutlass, scimitar, etc.), much more. 336pp. 6⅛ x 9¼.
0-486-25434-8

AUTOBIOGRAPHY: The Story of My Experiments with Truth, Mohandas K. Gandhi. Boyhood, legal studies, purification, the growth of the Satyagraha (nonviolent protest) movement. Critical, inspiring work of the man responsible for the freedom of India. 480pp. 5⅜ x 8½. (Available in U.S. only.) 0-486-24593-4

CELTIC MYTHS AND LEGENDS, T. W. Rolleston. Masterful retelling of Irish and Welsh stories and tales. Cuchulain, King Arthur, Deirdre, the Grail, many more. First paperback edition. 58 full-page illustrations. 512pp. 5⅜ x 8½. 0-486-26507-2

THE PRINCIPLES OF PSYCHOLOGY, William James. Famous long course complete, unabridged. Stream of thought, time perception, memory, experimental methods; great work decades ahead of its time. 94 figures. 1,391pp. 5⅜ x 8½. 2-vol. set.
Vol. I: 0-486-20381-6   Vol. II: 0-486-20382-4

THE WORLD AS WILL AND REPRESENTATION, Arthur Schopenhauer. Definitive English translation of Schopenhauer's life work, correcting more than 1,000 errors, omissions in earlier translations. Translated by E. F. J. Payne. Total of 1,269pp. 5⅜ x 8½. 2-vol. set.   Vol. 1: 0-486-21761-2   Vol. 2: 0-486-21762-0

CATALOG OF DOVER BOOKS

LIGHT AND SHADE: A Classic Approach to Three-Dimensional Drawing, Mrs. Mary P. Merrifield. Handy reference clearly demonstrates principles of light and shade by revealing effects of common daylight, sunshine, and candle or artificial light on geometrical solids. 13 plates. 64pp. 5⅜ x 8½. 0-486-44143-1

ASTROLOGY AND ASTRONOMY: A Pictorial Archive of Signs and Symbols, Ernst and Johanna Lehner. Treasure trove of stories, lore, and myth, accompanied by more than 300 rare illustrations of planets, the Milky Way, signs of the zodiac, comets, meteors, and other astronomical phenomena. 192pp. 8⅜ x 11. 0-486-43981-X

JEWELRY MAKING: Techniques for Metal, Tim McCreight. Easy-to-follow instructions and carefully executed illustrations describe tools and techniques, use of gems and enamels, wire inlay, casting, and other topics. 72 line illustrations and diagrams. 176pp. 8¼ x 10⅞. 0-486-44043-5

MAKING BIRDHOUSES: Easy and Advanced Projects, Gladstone Califf. Easy-to-follow instructions include diagrams for everything from a one-room house for bluebirds to a forty-two-room structure for purple martins. 56 plates; 4 figures. 80pp. 8¾ x 6⅜. 0-486-44183-0

LITTLE BOOK OF LOG CABINS: How to Build and Furnish Them, William S. Wicks. Handy how-to manual, with instructions and illustrations for building cabins in the Adirondack style, fireplaces, stairways, furniture, beamed ceilings, and more. 102 line drawings. 96pp. 8¾ x 6⅜. 0-486-44259-4

THE SEASONS OF AMERICA PAST, Eric Sloane. From "sugaring time" and strawberry picking to Indian summer and fall harvest, a whole year's activities described in charming prose and enhanced with 79 of the author's own illustrations. 160pp. 8¼ x 11. 0-486-44220-9

THE METROPOLIS OF TOMORROW, Hugh Ferriss. Generous, prophetic vision of the metropolis of the future, as perceived in 1929. Powerful illustrations of towering structures, wide avenues, and rooftop parks–all features in many of today's modern cities. 59 illustrations. 144pp. 8¼ x 11. 0-486-43727-2

THE PATH TO ROME, Hilaire Belloc. This 1902 memoir abounds in lively vignettes from a vanished time, recounting a pilgrimage on foot across the Alps and Apennines in order to "see all Europe which the Christian Faith has saved." 77 of the author's original line drawings complement his sparkling prose. 272pp. 5⅜ x 8½. 0-486-44001-X

THE HISTORY OF RASSELAS: Prince of Abissinia, Samuel Johnson. Distinguished English writer attacks eighteenth-century optimism and man's unrealistic estimates of what life has to offer. 112pp. 5⅜ x 8½. 0-486-44094-X

A VOYAGE TO ARCTURUS, David Lindsay. A brilliant flight of pure fancy, where wild creatures crowd the fantastic landscape and demented torturers dominate victims with their bizarre mental powers. 272pp. 5⅜ x 8½. 0-486-44198-9

Paperbound unless otherwise indicated. Available at your book dealer, online at **www.doverpublications.com**, or by writing to Dept. GI, Dover Publications, Inc., 31 East 2nd Street, Mineola, NY 11501. For current price information or for free catalogs (please indicate field of interest), write to Dover Publications or log on to **www.doverpublications.com** and see every Dover book in print. Dover publishes more than 500 books each year on science, elementary and advanced mathematics, biology, music, art, literary history, social sciences, and other areas.